ASHFORD CREEK MYSTERY

BOOK 1-3

ELLA ANDREW

www.ellaandrew.com

First edition November 2025

Backspace Press

Houston, Texas

Cover design by BACKSPACE PRESS

ISBN 979-8-9932530-7-7 (Paperback)

Printed in the United States of America

DEATH AT THE TEACUP INN

PROLOGUE

SATURDAY MORNING - ONE
WEEK BEFORE THE MURDER

*E*liza Prescott stood in the doorway of Bookmark &
Brew, her bookstore and café, breathing in the
particular satisfaction that came from perfectly shelved books
and fresh-ground coffee. At forty-two, she'd found her
rhythm in Ashford Creek—a rhythm that moved between
book deliveries, weekend tourists, and the comfortable
predictability of small-town life.

"Come on, Bruno," she called to the German Shepherd mix
sprawled across the shop's welcome mat. "Time to open."

Bruno, two years into his retirement from the K-9 unit,
lifted his graying muzzle with the dignity of a dog who knew
his worth. He'd been her partner during her eight years as a
detective in Portland, and when early retirement had
beckoned—him due to age, her due to a case that had carved
too deep—they'd moved to Ashford Creek together.

The bell above her door chimed as Mrs. Henderson
entered, punctual as sunrise.

"Eliza, dear! Please tell me the new Louise Penny arrived."

"Yesterday afternoon," Eliza said, producing the book from behind the counter. "I saved you the first copy."

"This is why you're my favorite person in town." Mrs. Henderson clutched the book like treasure. "Don't tell my husband I said that."

As Mrs. Henderson left, Eliza flipped her shop sign to OPEN and surveyed Main Street through the window. Ashford Creek was postcard perfect this morning—flower boxes overflowing with petunias, the old-fashioned lampposts the town council had fought to preserve, and the comforting bustle of Saturday morning routines.

Across the street, the Teacup Inn was already glowing with warm light. Millie Hart waved from the inn's doorway. Eliza waved back, making a mental note to grab lunch there. Millie's lemon scones were legendary, and Saturday was always test batch day for new recipes.

"Eliza! Eliza!" Young Jamie Morrison burst through her door, nearly tripping over Bruno, who side-stepped with practiced ease. "Did you see? Did you see?"

"Breathe, Jamie. What am I supposed to have seen?"

"The newspaper! You're in it!" He thrust the Ashford Creek Gazette at her.

Eliza unfolded it to find her photo on page three under the headline: "Local Bookstore Owner Solves Mystery of Missing Church Funds." The article recounted how she'd noticed discrepancies in the church restoration fundraiser receipts and quietly helped Sheriff Wade trace the theft to the contractor's creative accounting.

"Mom says you're better than the TV detectives," Jamie announced. "'Cause you're real and you have Bruno."

Bruno's tail thumped approval.

"I just noticed something odd," Eliza said, uncomfortable

with the attention. "Sheriff Wade did the real work."

"That's not what he says," a voice said from the doorway.

Wade Colton stood there, tall and solid as an oak, carrying two cups from the inn. "Brought you coffee—that Colombian Geisha blend from the inn. I know you don't carry it here. Millie says it's too expensive for anyone but tourists."

"Bribing me with Millie's special blend?"

"Is it working?" He set the cup on her counter. "I actually came to warn you. Tilda Crane is on the warpath about that article. Says if you can solve the church fund issue, you should investigate who's been spreading 'malicious rumors' about her recipe stealing."

Eliza groaned. Tilda Crane had been the town's self-appointed social arbiter for twenty years, wielding gossip and grudges like weapons. She'd tried to shut down Bookmark & Brew when Eliza first arrived, claiming the town didn't need "outsider businesses."

"She's just upset because the article mentions her nephew was one of the suspects," Eliza said.

"Among other things. She's called a town meeting for next Thursday. Says she has 'revelations that will shake Ashford Creek to its foundations.'"

"How dramatic."

"It's Tilda." Wade sipped his own tea. "Just watch yourself. She doesn't like being upstaged, and solving that theft case put you in the spotlight."

After Wade left, Eliza settled into her morning routine—updating the mystery section, preparing the book club discussion questions, and greeting the steady stream of Saturday customers. It was comfortable, predictable, safe. Everything she'd wanted when she'd left Portland.

Around noon, she closed the shop for lunch and walked to

the Teacup Inn with Bruno. The place was packed, as always on Saturdays. She found her usual table by the window and wasn't surprised when Millie appeared immediately with a plate of scones.

"New recipe," Millie said proudly. "Honey lavender with lemon glaze. Tell me what you think."

Eliza bit into one and closed her eyes. "Perfect. As always."

"Flatterer." Millie beamed. "Oh, Charlie's home from culinary school for the week. He's helping in the Kitchen. Owen's teaching him proper knife skills."

Eliza glanced toward the Kitchen where she could see Owen Kraft, the inn's cook, demonstrating something to Millie's nervous nephew. Owen moved with military precision, every gesture controlled and efficient. He'd appeared in town three years ago, quiet about his past, excellent at his job. Eliza recognized the bearing of someone carrying secrets—it took one to know one.

"Ms. Prescott?" A smooth voice interrupted her thoughts.

A woman stood beside her table—elegant, forties, with the kind of careful composure that suggested practice. "I'm Marina Blackwood. I'm researching Victorian architecture for a book. I heard you're something of a local historian?"

"Hardly. I've only been here two years."

"But you pay attention." Marina's smile didn't reach her eyes. "I can tell. You're a watcher, like me."

Something about the woman set off Eliza's old instincts— the ones from her detective days. But before she could respond, a crash came from across the room.

Tilda Crane had knocked over someone's tea in her dramatic entrance. She stood in the doorway like an actress awaiting applause, her silver hair perfect, her expression thunderous.

"Millie Hart!" she called out. "I demand to know why this establishment is serving MY grandmother's lemon scones without attribution!"

The inn fell silent.

Millie emerged from behind the counter, color high in her cheeks. "Tilda, we've been through this. The recipe was my grandmother's."

"Lies!" Tilda's voice could have etched glass. "And after Thursday's meeting, everyone will know the truth about this inn, about your family, and about everyone else in this town who's been harboring secrets."

She swept her gaze across the room, pausing on Eliza. "Including our newest resident who thinks she's so clever. I know why you really left Portland, Ms. Prescott. Thursday will be very educational for everyone."

She turned and left, leaving arctic silence in her wake.

Eliza felt Bruno press against her leg, a comforting weight. The cozy bubble of her new life suddenly felt very fragile.

"Don't let her rattle you," Millie said quietly. "She threatens everyone."

But as Eliza walked back to her bookstore, she couldn't shake the feeling that something was about to shatter in Ashford Creek. The comfortable rhythm she'd found was about to be broken.

She had no idea how right she was.

One week later, Tilda Crane would be dead, and Eliza would be pulled into a mystery that would reveal just how many secrets lurked beneath the town's picturesque surface.

But for now, it was still Saturday, the sun was shining, and the biggest mystery in Eliza's life was which book to recommend to Mrs. Henderson next.

It was the last truly peaceful day she would have for quite some time.

CHAPTER 1

STORM BREWING

The morning started with Tilda Crane's voice cutting through Main Street like a rusty saw through wet wood.

"Incompetent! Every last one of you!"

Eliza Prescott looked up from arranging the new arrivals in her bookstore window, her hands pausing on a pristine copy of the latest Ruth Ware. Through the rain-spotted glass, she could see Tilda standing outside City Hall, waving a manila folder at Mayor Doyle like it was a weapon. Which, knowing Tilda, it probably was.

The bookstore was Eliza's sanctuary, all dark wood shelves and warm lighting, with comfortable reading chairs tucked into corners and the permanent scent of paper and lavender candles. She'd opened Bookmark & Brew two years ago, after leaving Portland, and had carefully cultivated it into exactly the kind of place she'd always wanted to escape into. The mystery section took up the entire north wall, organized not just alphabetically but by subgenre—cozy mysteries at eye level where they sold best, nordic noir brooding on the upper shelves, classic British mysteries in their own special section with burgundy bookends she'd found at an estate sale.

Bruno lifted his head from his bed behind the counter—a custom cushion in police dog blue, a retirement gift from the Portland K-9 unit. His ears swiveled toward the window, tracking the commotion outside, before he gave a questioning whine.

"Just Tilda being Tilda," Eliza told him, returning to her display. She'd gotten in a shipment of the latest Margaret Atwood, and she wanted them prominently featured before the afternoon rush. Though 'rush' was perhaps too strong a word for the gentle flow of customers that kept her business comfortable but never overwhelming.

The morning light through the rain-spotted window cast everything in shades of gray, reminding Eliza of Portland mornings. But Portland had never felt like this—charged with the particular tension that came from too many people knowing too much about each other. She'd been here two years now, long enough to understand that Ashford Creek's postcard prettiness was like fondant on a cake—sweet on the surface, but underneath, the layers held surprises.

The town had been founded in 1842 by textile mill owners who'd wanted to create their own version of paradise. They'd built the Victorian houses that still lined Main Street, established the library that still used its original card catalog system, and created the traditions that governed social life like unwritten laws. The Harvest Festival, the Spring Antique Fair, the Christmas Carol Walk—all orchestrated with the precision of military campaigns and the politics of royal courts.

Tilda Crane had inserted herself into every one of these traditions like a splinter under the skin—painful, persistent, and surprisingly difficult to remove. She'd moved here twenty-five years ago from Boston, newly widowed with old money and new ambitions. Within five years, she'd become the unofficial arbiter of everything from the proper way to arrange flowers for the church altar to who deserved to have their business featured in the tourist brochures.

Eliza had watched it all with an outsider's eye, cataloging the dynamics the way she'd once cataloged evidence. The Henderson sisters, who'd run their antique shop for forty years, always deferred to Tilda in public but rolled their eyes behind her back. Tom Garrett at the pharmacy had a nervous tic that only appeared when Tilda entered his store. Even Mayor Doyle, elected by a landslide three times running, seemed to shrink when Tilda appeared at town meetings with her manila folders and her knowing smile.

She placed the last book and stepped back to admire the arrangement when she noticed something odd. Across the street, people were gathering in small clusters, heads bent together, casting nervous glances toward City Hall. Tom Garrett from the pharmacy stood with Dr. Pemberton, both men looking unusually grave. The Henderson sisters had actually stopped walking their matching Pomeranians to watch Tilda's performance.

Bruno padded over to stand beside her, his solid presence reassuring as always. Two years into retirement, he still moved with the controlled grace of a working dog, seventy pounds of trained muscle and instinct. His muzzle had gone silver, and he was a bit stiff on cold mornings, but his eyes remained sharp, always watching, always evaluating.

"Something's different today, isn't it, boy?" Eliza murmured, scratching behind his ears in the spot that made his back leg twitch.

The bell above her door chimed with its familiar brass song. Millie Hart bustled in, her signature pink scarf fluttering behind her like a distress signal. Millie usually moved with the measured calm of someone who'd run a successful inn for thirty years, but today her steps were quick, agitated.

"Did you hear?" Millie said without preamble, not even pausing to pet Bruno, which was unusual enough to make Eliza truly pay attention. "Tilda's on the warpath again."

"I can see that." Eliza nodded toward the window where Tilda was now jabbing her finger at Patsy Doyle, the mayor's wife. Even from here, Eliza could see Patsy's face flushing red. "What's she upset about now?"

"Everything. Absolutely everything." Millie's hands fluttered like nervous birds. "The antique fair judging, the gazebo renovation, the new parking meters, my lemon scone recipe —" She ticked off on her fingers, each point making her more agitated. "She claims she has 'proof' of some scandal that will 'rain down like judgment' if the mayor doesn't bend to her demands."

Eliza shelved another book, using the familiar motion to study Millie. In two years, she'd never seen the innkeeper this rattled. "She says that every month."

"She came into the inn this morning before dawn—before dawn, Eliza!—demanded to use the private parlor for some kind of meeting today. Said she'd be 'unveiling the truth about this town's dirty secrets today.'"

"Today's Thursday—the town council meeting," Eliza mused, her detective instincts stirring despite her best efforts to keep them dormant.

"Exactly. And she reserved the parlor for right before it." Millie twisted her scarf between her fingers, a gesture Eliza recognized as genuine distress. "Eliza, she looked at me and said, 'Some of us have been keeping secrets about our recipes, haven't we, Millie?' She knows about grandmother's formula."

Eliza's hands stilled on the book she was holding—a vintage Agatha Christie worth more than most people guessed. "Your grandmother's recipe has been in your family for seventy years."

"And it's in my safety deposit box at the bank. The only copy." Millie's voice dropped to a whisper, though they were alone in the shop. "But Tilda had this smile. You know the one —like a cat that's already eaten the canary and is just waiting for you to notice the feathers."

"She's bluffing," Eliza said firmly, though something cold was settling in her stomach. "That recipe is what makes the inn special. She couldn't have—"

"But what if she photographed it somehow? Or bribed someone at the bank? You know how she is." Millie's voice cracked slightly. "And I'm not the only one she's threatening. Charlie's terrified she'll expose his scholarship issues. Owen thinks she knows about his record. Even that new woman who's been hanging around—Marina something—Tilda pulled her aside yesterday and whispered something that made her go white as bone."

The door chimed again with more force than necessary. Charlie Harris, Millie's nineteen-year-old nephew, stumbled in looking like he'd seen a ghost. His culinary school uniform was rumpled, flour dusting his sleeve and caught in his black hair. There was a smudge of what looked like chocolate on his jaw, and his eyes had the wild look of someone running on no sleep and too much coffee.

"Aunt Millie, she's coming to the inn. Right now. She says she wants the 'special treatment' for her tea." His voice cracked on the last word, breaking like he was thirteen instead of nineteen. "She had that look."

"What look?" Eliza asked, though she suspected she knew.

"Like a cat that's cornered a whole family of mice," Charlie said miserably. "She knows about the admission essay. I know she does. She kept making comments about 'creative writing' and 'fiction versus truth' when she saw me at the grocery store yesterday."

Millie squared her shoulders, visibly pulling herself together. "Well, we'll give her our finest service, as always. Kill her with kindness, that's what grandmother always said."

Eliza winced at the unfortunate turn of phrase. "I'll come with you. I need a break from inventory anyway, and Bruno's been eyeing the door for the past hour."

Bruno's tail thumped agreement, already moving toward the door with the eagerness of a dog who knew the inn meant potential treats.

Eliza grabbed her raincoat from the hook by the door—a practical navy that had served her well in Portland and was proving equally useful in Ashford Creek's temperamental spring weather. She flipped the shop sign to "Back at Three" and locked the door, though crime in Ashford Creek usually extended no further than teenagers sneaking beer and the occasional tourist shoplifting postcards.

They crossed Main Street together as the morning mist began to thicken into proper rain. The cobblestones—the town council's pride and the road department's nightmare—gleamed like oil in the wet. The Teacup Inn glowed warmly at the corner, its Victorian gingerbread trim and leaded glass windows making it look like something from a fairy tale.

The inn had been built in 1892 by a railroad magnate's widow who'd wanted to create "a place of refinement and grace in the wilderness." What had been wilderness then was now downtown Ashford Creek, but the inn maintained its air of genteel hospitality. The painted exterior was a symphony of cream, sage green, and dusty rose, colors Millie had agonized over for months before the last restoration. Even in the gray morning, it looked inviting.

The chalkboard under the awning—Millie's one concession to modern marketing—read in Charlie's artistic script: Rainy Day Special - Lemon scones with our signature glaze, clotted cream, and exceptional service.

"I should change that," Millie muttered. "Take out the 'signature' part before she sees it."

"Don't you dare," Eliza said. "That's letting her win."

Inside, the inn was already half-full despite the early hour. The antique fair had brought tourists, their voices creating a pleasant hum against the clink of china and silver. But the locals had gathered in worried clusters, and Eliza could feel the undercurrent of tension like electricity before a storm.

The interior was everything the exterior promised—warm wood paneling, William Morris wallpaper in the front parlor, Turkish rugs worn soft by generations of feet. The tea room opened to the right, round tables dressed in crisp white linens with small vases of fresh flowers at each center. Today's flowers were yellow roses from Millie's own garden, their cheerful color at odds with the mood.

Eliza recognized the usual suspects: the Hendersons whispering over their Earl Grey at their customary table by the bay window, Dr. Pemberton hiding behind his newspaper in the corner like a turtle in his shell, and in the far corner, the mysterious Marina—a sleek woman in her forties who'd appeared in town two weeks ago claiming to be researching Victorian architecture but who seemed more interested in the townspeople than the buildings.

Marina sat alone, as always, drinking tea with precise, measured sips. She wore black today—elegant slacks and a cashmere sweater that looked expensive. Her dark hair was pulled into a neat chignon, and she had the kind of posture that suggested ballet lessons or military training. Maybe both.

Owen Kraft moved between the kitchen and dining room with practiced efficiency, his military bearing evident in every economical movement. He navigated the tight spaces between tables without ever brushing against a chair or customer, each plate balanced perfectly, each cup set down without a sound. The burn scar on his left hand caught the light as he set down a tray at the Henderson's table. He'd been Millie's cook for three years now, ever since his dishonorable discharge—though Millie was the only one who'd hired him despite the whispers about what had happened at Fort Bragg.

"Ladies," he said to the Hendersons with a slight nod, his voice carrying just enough warmth to be polite but not enough to invite conversation.

"She's here," Charlie whispered urgently, and sure enough, Tilda Crane swept through the door like she owned the place.

At sixty-three, Tilda had the kind of sharp, preserved beauty that came from expensive face creams and sheer spite. Her silver hair was pulled into a perfect chignon that had probably taken an hour to achieve but was meant to look effortless. Her tweed suit—Chanel, if Eliza's eye was correct—was impeccable despite the rain. She carried herself like visiting royalty forced to mingle with peasants, her posture so rigid it could have been used as a architectural level.

She paused in the doorway, letting everyone notice her

arrival, her pale blue eyes scanning the room like a predator cataloging prey.

"Millie," she announced, loud enough for everyone to hear. "I'll take my usual table. And do bring out your best china—the Spode, not that department store nonsense you use for tourists. I'm expecting someone special at eleven." She glanced at her Cartier watch with theatrical precision. "That gives you ninety minutes to impress me. I'm sure you'll want to, given what's at stake."

Patsy Doyle, who'd followed Tilda in, her face still flushed from their confrontation outside, bristled visibly. "Tilda, you can't keep threatening—"

"Can't I?" Tilda's smile was arctic, her voice carrying the kind of cultured menace that had been perfected in finishing schools. "Your husband seems to think that gazebo can stay half-painted through the antique fair. I have photographs that suggest his renovation budget went somewhere far more... personal. That weekend in Burlington, perhaps? The charges at the jewelry store? Shall I continue?"

Patsy's face flushed red, then drained white. Her mouth opened and closed like a landed fish.

"Your table is ready, Mrs. Crane," Millie said smoothly, though Eliza could see her hands trembling slightly. "Charlie will show you up to the private parlor."

"The private parlor?" Dr. Pemberton looked up from his paper, his reading glasses sliding down his nose. "Bit grand for morning tea, isn't it?"

Tilda's eyes glittered with malicious pleasure. "I prefer privacy for certain conversations. One never knows who might be listening." Her gaze swept the room, pausing meaningfully on each face. "Isn't that right, Marina?"

The elegant stranger in the corner stiffened slightly, her

teacup pausing halfway to her lips, but she continued sipping without responding. Only someone watching closely—as Eliza was—would have noticed the slight tremor in her hand.

"Charlie," Tilda commanded, her voice cracking like a whip. "My tea. Earl Grey, properly steeped—four minutes, not a second more or less. And I'll have one of your aunt's special lemon scones. The ones with the signature glaze that everyone raves about." Her emphasis on 'signature' made Millie flinch. "I'm quite particular about my glazes, you know. I've been experimenting with my own. In fact, I brought a sample for comparison."

She produced a small glass jar from her handbag with the flourish of a magician revealing a rabbit. The jar was crystal, old-fashioned, with a silver lid that caught the light. Inside, white crystals glinted like crushed diamonds. "My special sugar blend. Adds just a hint of almond essence to comple-ment the lemon. I insist you try it on my scone. Call it... a peace offering."

Charlie took the jar with shaking hands, holding it like it might explode. "Yes, Mrs. Crane."

"And Charlie?" Tilda's voice turned silky, dangerous. "Do make sure you use it. I'll know if you don't. I always know."

As Tilda climbed the stairs to the private parlor, her heels clicking against the wood in a rhythm that sounded like a countdown, conversation exploded in her wake.

"That woman is pure poison," someone muttered from a corner table.

"Someone should do something about her," another voice added, low and bitter.

"Did you hear what she said about the Mayor? And that jewelry store business?"

"Burlington? But that's where his mother lives..."

"Ladies," Millie called out, her innkeeper's voice cutting through the gossip. "We sip. We do not spar. Not with porcelain in hand."

Eliza slid into the window seat, her favorite spot where she could observe both the tea room and the street outside. Bruno flopped under the table with a deep sigh, his body creating a warm weight against her feet, paws crossed like a gentleman. The rain had picked up, drumming against the glass in an irregular rhythm that made her think of codes and secrets.

She watched the room's dynamics with her detective's eye, a habit she couldn't quite shake even after two years of civilian life. Owen had returned to the Kitchen but kept glancing toward the stairs. Marina had pulled out a small notebook and was writing something in quick, sharp strokes. The Hendersons huddled closer together, their Pomeranians picking up on the tension and whining softly.

Millie arrived with a tray, her movements less graceful than usual. "Your usual—English Breakfast with milk, no sugar," she said, setting down the cup with a slight rattle. "And lemon scones. On the house. I need friendly faces today."

"What's this about Marina?" Eliza asked quietly, glancing at the woman in question.

"She showed up two weeks ago, said she was writing a book about Victorian architecture. But yesterday, Tilda cornered her in the post office. I couldn't hear what was said, but Marina left looking shaken." Millie lowered her voice further, leaning in close enough that Eliza could smell her lavender hand cream. "And here's the strange thing—I could swear I've seen Marina before, years ago. Maybe at one of the summer festivals? But she insists this is her first time in Ashford Creek."

Before Eliza could respond, a crash came from the Kitchen, followed by raised voices. The sound of metal hitting the floor, then angry words.

"I won't do it!" Charlie's voice, high and strained, carrying clearly through the service door.

"You will, or you'll find another job." Owen's deeper rumble, authoritative but with an edge of something else—fear?

Millie hurried toward the Kitchen, her scarf fluttering behind her. Eliza followed, Bruno padding silently beside her, his ears pricked forward in alert mode.

They found Charlie holding a tray with Tilda's tea service, his face pale as parchment. The Spode china—white with delicate blue flowers—rattled slightly from the tremor in his hands. Owen stood blocking his path to the stairs, solid as a wall, arms crossed over his broad chest.

"She wants her special sugar on the scone," Charlie said, his voice barely above a whisper. "But something seems off about it. It smells wrong."

Owen took the jar, unscrewed the lid with quick, efficient movements, and sniffed. His expression darkened, the scar on his hand standing out white against his skin. "Bitter almonds," he said quietly, immediately sealing the jar and setting it down carefully. "That's not sugar blend.

"What do you mean?" Millie asked, though her face suggested she already suspected.

Owen's jaw tightened, a muscle jumping in his cheek. "In the service, we were trained to recognize certain... substances. Chemical weapons, poisons. This smells like—" He stopped himself, glancing at Charlie. "We shouldn't use this."

"But she'll raise hell if we don't," Charlie protested, his voice climbing. "You know she will. She'll tell everyone about

—" He caught himself, glancing at Eliza with the guilty look of someone who'd almost revealed a secret.

"About what?" Eliza asked gently, using her interview voice—the one that had gotten countless witnesses to open up.

CHAPTER 2

DEATH IN THE PARLOR

*C*harlie's shoulders slumped in defeat. "I... I had help with my culinary school admission essay. Not cheating exactly, but... a service that 'polished' it. Made it sound better than anything I could write. Tilda found out somehow. She's been holding it over me for weeks, threatening to tell the school board."

"And you?" Eliza looked at Owen, who'd gone still as stone.

Owen's expression was granite. "My business is my own." But his hand had moved unconsciously to his side, where Eliza recognized the tell-tale adjustment of someone used to carrying a weapon.

We'll use regular sugar," Millie decided, her voice firm with the authority of three decades of hospitality. "She won't know the difference." "She will," Charlie said miserably. "She always knows. She's like a bloodhound for deception."

A bell tinkled from upstairs—the private parlor's service bell, an antique pull-cord system Millie had preserved. It rang again, more insistent, imperious demand in every chime.

"I'll take it up," Owen said, reaching for the tray.

"No," Charlie straightened, squaring his thin shoulders. "It's my job. I'll face her." He took the tray and headed for the stairs. At the last second, despite Millie's decision, he grabbed Tilda's jar too knowing she'd check, knowing she'd make his life hell if he didn't follow her exact instructions. His footsteps on the old wood sounded like a funeral march, slow and measured. Each step creaked slightly—the third, the seventh, and the tenth, Eliza noted automatically.

Bruno tensed beside her, a low whine escaping his throat. His ears swiveled toward the stairs, tracking something, and his body shifted into what Eliza recognized as his alert stance.

"What is it, boy?" she asked, her hand finding his collar.

Before Bruno could offer more warning, they heard Charlie's voice from above, tight with fear: "Mrs. Crane? Your tea is—oh my God. Oh my God!"

The crash of the tray was thunderous in the morning quiet. China shattered, silver rang against wood, and Charlie's scream echoed through the inn like a siren.

Eliza ran for the stairs, muscle memory from eight years of police work taking over. Bruno stayed at her heel, trained to follow but not interfere. She took the stairs two at a time, noting absently that Charlie had been right—the third, seventh, and tenth steps did creak. The hallway at the top was dim, lit only by a small window at the end that looked out onto the rain-swept street.

The private parlor door stood wide open like a mouth frozen in surprise.

The scene inside was almost peaceful, except for Charlie pressed against the doorframe, hyperventilating, his hands clutching the wood so hard his knuckles were white. The tea service lay scattered across the Persian rug—a nineteenth-century Tabriz that Millie had inherited from her grandmother. Tea was spreading in a dark stain, and broken china glinted like teeth in the morning light.

Tilda Crane sat in the wingback chair by the window, her posture perfect, her eyes open and staring at nothing. The rain on the window behind her created moving shadows across her face, giving the illusion of expression where there was none. Her fingers still curled around a delicate china cup, frozen in an eternal toast. On the plate beside her, a single lemon scone sat with one bite missing, its signature glaze pooling like liquid sunshine.

The room smelled of lemon, Earl Grey, and underneath it all—cutting through the comfortable scents like a blade—the distinct smell of bitter almonds.

Eliza's detective instincts kicked in, cataloging details with the automatic precision of eight years in Portland homicide. The teacup in Tilda's hand was from the Spode collection—she could see the blue flowers clearly, no chips or cracks, positioned as if Tilda had been about to take another sip. The angle suggested Tilda had been relaxed, unsuspecting. No defensive wounds on her visible skin, no signs of struggle. The chair hadn't moved—the indentations in the Persian rug showed it had been in the same position for hours.

The morning light from the window created a tableau that would have been peaceful if not for the absolute stillness of death. Tilda's tweed suit showed no wrinkles beyond normal wear, her pearl necklace sat perfectly centered. Even her hair, that silver chignon she spent an hour perfecting each morning according to town gossip, remained intact. Only her face betrayed the violence of her end—the slight blue tinge to her lips, the pupils fixed and dilated, the expression of surprise that suggested whatever she'd expected from this morning, death hadn't been it.

The sugar crystals scattered on the rug formed an almost perfect arc, as if someone had thrown them in haste or anger. Eliza counted approximately two tablespoons' worth, enough to thoroughly sweeten a cup of tea or, in this case, deliver a fatal dose of poison. The jar itself, crystal with its ornate silver lid, had rolled to rest against the settee's carved leg, leaving a thin trail of white crystals like a comet's tail across the dark wool.

Bruno growled low in his throat, hackles raised as he stared at the body. His training kept him back, but every line of his body radiated tension.

Tilda Crane's reign of terror over Ashford Creek had come to an abrupt end.

And as Eliza looked at the scattered sugar crystals glinting on the carpet like a constellation of guilt, the overturned jar that had rolled under the settee, and the expression of surprise frozen on Tilda's face, she realized that someone in this inn had just committed murder.

The question was: who had Tilda pushed too far?

Thunder cracked overhead, rattling the old windows in their frames, and the lights flickered once, casting shadows that seemed to dance around Tilda's still form. For a moment, in the shifting light, Tilda's expression seemed to change— surprise to accusation, as if even in death she was cataloging one last secret.

"Nobody move," Eliza commanded, her voice carrying the authority of her former career. The cop she'd tried to leave behind in Portland was suddenly, fully present. "Charlie, call 911. Everyone else, stay exactly where you are."

But as she turned to secure the scene, something made her freeze. She noticed something that made her blood run cold, a detail that would trouble her through the investigation to come.

The parlor's service door—the one that led to the back stairs, the one that should have been locked—stood slightly ajar. The darkness beyond it seemed to breathe.

Someone had been here. Someone had watched Tilda die.

And that someone was still in the inn.

CHAPTER 3

SECRETS IN THE STEAM

*T*he Ashford Creek Police Department consisted of exactly four people, and Sheriff Wade Colton was worth at least three of them on his own. He arrived within seven minutes of Charlie's call, rain streaming off his brown sheriff's hat like a waterfall, his presence immediately transforming chaos into something manageable.

Eliza heard him before she saw him—the authoritative tread of his boots on the inn's front steps, the low rumble of his voice directing his deputies, the way the crowd noise below shifted from panic to nervous compliance. Wade had that effect on people. At six-foot-two with shoulders that suggested his college football days weren't entirely behind him, he commanded attention without trying. But it was his eyes—steady gray, patient but sharp—that really did the work.

"Nobody leaves," he announced, his deep voice carrying through the establishment like rolling thunder. "Deputy Lang, secure the exits. Deputy Morris, start a sign-in sheet. Everyone who was here when it happened stays here."

Deputy Lang, young and eager with academy polish still

on him, immediately moved to the front door. Deputy Morris, older and more weathered, pulled out a notebook and began corralling the tourists who were edging toward escape.

Eliza stood guard at the parlor door, Bruno sitting at attention beside her. She'd already prevented three people from contaminating the scene—Patsy Doyle ("I just need to see if she's really..."), Dr. Pemberton ("I'm a doctor, I should check for signs of life"), and Marina, who'd appeared silently on the stairs without explanation, her approach so quiet even Bruno had only noticed her at the last second.

"Eliza," Wade said, climbing toward her. His eyes held a mixture of respect and resignation, the look of a man who'd just had his morning complicated in a familiar way. "Should have known you'd be here."

"Pure coincidence," she said.

"With you, it never is." He studied the scene from the doorway, his weathered face growing more grave with each detail. She watched him catalog everything—the position of the body, the scattered tea service, the morning light playing across Tilda's frozen expression. His hand moved unconsciously to his belt where his radio sat, then away, a tell that he was thinking hard.

"Tell me what you saw," he said.

Eliza gave him the rundown: Tilda's threats, the mysterious jar of "special sugar," Charlie's discovery of the body, the service door ajar. She used her cop voice, the one she'd thought she'd retired—just facts, no interpretation, each detail in chronological order. Wade listened without interrupting, occasionally nodding, his eyes never leaving the scene.

"This jar," he said when she finished. "Where is it now?"

Eliza pointed to where it had rolled under the settee, just

visible in the shadow. "Nobody's touched it since Charlie dropped the tray."

Wade pulled on latex gloves from his belt pouch—he always carried them, a habit from thirty years of law enforcement. He moved into the room with careful steps, avoiding the broken china, and crouched by the settee. His knees popped audibly, and he grimaced.

"Getting too old for this," he muttered, carefully retrieving the jar. A few crystals still clung to the rim, catching the light like tiny diamonds. He sniffed carefully, his training showing in the way he wafted the scent rather than breathing directly, then pulled back sharply. "Cyanide, most likely. The bitter almond smell is distinctive. Seen it twice before—once in Portland during that insurance fraud case, once here about fifteen years back."

"She brought it herself," Eliza said. "Called it her special sugar blend. Insisted Charlie use it on her scone."

Wade's eyebrows rose, creating deep lines in his forehead. "She brought her own murder weapon?"

"That's what it looks like. But Wade..." Eliza lowered her voice, glancing back at the dim hallway. "That service door was open. Someone else was here."

Wade moved to the service door, examining it without touching. The old brass hinges were well-oiled—Millie's attention to detail—and wouldn't have squeaked. Someone could have stood there, watching, without anyone knowing.

Before Wade could respond, a commotion erupted downstairs. Deputy Morris's voice rose above the noise, surprisingly commanding for such a soft-spoken man: "Ma'am, you can't go up there!"

Marina appeared on the landing, having somehow slipped past the deputy. She moved like water, silent and fluid, but her usual composure had cracked. Her elegant hands trembled as she clutched her leather bag—expensive, Italian, the kind that cost more than most people's rent. Her dark eyes darted between Wade and Eliza.

"Sheriff, I need to speak with you privately," she said. Her accent, which Eliza hadn't noticed before, showed slightly—just a hint of something West Coast, maybe Seattle. "It's about Tilda. About why she—" She stopped, noticing Eliza, and her expression shuttered. "Alone, please."

Wade studied her for a long moment, his cop eyes taking in details—the slight smudge in her lipstick, the way her right hand kept moving to her bag, the tension in her shoulders. "In a minute, Ms...?"

"Blackwood. Marina Blackwood." The name came out practiced, automatic.

"Ms. Blackwood. Please return downstairs. I'll speak with everyone shortly."

Marina hesitated, her gaze flicking to the parlor door where Tilda's foot was just visible. Something passed across her face—not grief exactly, but something more complex. Relief mixed with fear, perhaps. Then she descended, her heels silent on the stairs that had creaked under Charlie's feet.

Wade turned back to the parlor, pulling out his phone. "I need to call the state police. This is beyond our usual—"

"You can handle this," Eliza said quietly. "You've done it before."

"Not with half the town as suspects," Wade replied, but he pocketed his phone. Instead, he pulled out a digital camera and began his methodical documentation. Each angle, each piece of evidence, each detail captured with the patience of someone who knew that murders were solved in the details, not the drama.

"Eliza, I need you downstairs too," he said without looking up from his work. "This is an active crime scene."

"Of course." She started to go, then paused. "Wade, there's something else. Charlie mentioned Tilda was expecting someone at eleven. It's only ten-thirty."

Wade checked his watch, a sturdy Timex that had survived three decades of police work, frowning. "So either she decided to sample her own poisoned scone before her guest arrived, or—"

"Or someone else knew about the poison and made sure she ate it first," Eliza finished.

Their eyes met, and she saw him mentally shift from small-town sheriff dealing with a sudden death to investigator working a murder case. It was like watching a blade being drawn from a sheath—sudden, sharp, and somehow inevitable.

Downstairs, the tea room had transformed into a makeshift interrogation center. Deputy Lang had closed the curtains, giving the room an underwater quality in the gray morning light. Deputy Morris had commandeered the largest table and was methodically taking names and contact information, his printing neat and precise. The tourists—a family of four from Connecticut and an elderly couple from Boston —huddled by the door looking bewildered and slightly offended, as if murder was not what they'd paid for in their Ashford Creek vacation packages.

The locals had instinctively separated into their usual groups, but with a new wariness. They watched each other now with different eyes—not neighbors, but suspects.

Millie stood behind the counter, mechanically polishing the same teacup over and over, the motion hypnotic. The cup was one of her grandmother's—bone china so thin you could see light through it. "I can't believe she's dead," she kept saying to no one in particular. "In my inn. In grandmother's parlor. The Queen stayed in that room in 1959. Did you know that? The Queen, and now..."

Charlie sat in the corner, still pale and shaking, his culinary school uniform now splattered with tea stains that looked disturbingly like blood in the dim light. Owen stood beside him, arms crossed, expression unreadable. But Eliza noticed how he'd positioned himself—between Charlie and everyone else, protective. Every few seconds, Owen's eyes would flick to the stairs, then to the exits, like he was calculating distances, planning escapes or defenses.

"Where did the jar come from?" Deputy Morris was asking Charlie, his voice gentle but insistent. "Did Mrs. Crane give it directly to you?"

"Y-yes," Charlie stammered. His hands twisted in his lap, leaving flour residue on his dark pants. "She pulled it from her purse. Said to use it on her scone specifically. Said it would enhance the flavor profile." He laughed, a broken sound. "Flavor profile. She murdered herself over a flavor profile."

"You did exactly what she requested," Owen said firmly, his hand landing on Charlie's shoulder. "If anyone's responsible, it's—" He cut himself off, jaw clenching.

"It's who?" Morris pressed, pen poised.

Owen's jaw tightened further, the muscles visible beneath his weathered skin. "Nothing. I misspoke."

Eliza settled at her previous table, Bruno alert beneath it. His ears swiveled constantly, tracking every movement, every voice. She watched the room's dynamics with her investigator's instincts, cataloguing every nervous tic and furtive glance.

Patsy Doyle kept checking her phone, her thumb moving in repetitive swipes even though the screen was dark. Dr. Pemberton had developed a suspicious interest in the window, despite the rain obscuring any view. He'd adjusted his glasses seventeen times in the past minute—Eliza had counted. Marina sat alone, her tea untouched and now certainly cold, staring at something in her bag with an expression of profound loss.

Wade's interview technique hadn't changed much since Eliza had known him in Portland, where their paths had crossed on several cases. He had a way of creating silence that made people want to fill it, a patient stillness that suggested he had all the time in the world to wait for the truth. She watched him now as he observed the room, his gray eyes taking in every nervous gesture, every exchanged glance, every tell that might lead to answers.

The inn itself seemed to be holding its breath. The usual sounds—the comfortable clink of china, the whisper of turning newspaper pages, the gentle bubble of conversation—had been replaced by a watchful quiet. Even the building seemed to sense the weight of what had happened. The old radiators, usually prone to cheerful clanking, had gone silent. The grandfather clock in the corner, a donation from the founding family that had kept perfect time for over a century, seemed to tick more slowly, each second drawn out like taffy.

Eliza noticed how people had unconsciously arranged themselves into camps. The locals clustered together near the windows, as if proximity to escape routes might offer comfort. The staff—what remained of them—huddled near the kitchen door, their usual efficient movements replaced by uncertain stillness.

Dr. Pemberton hadn't moved from his corner table in

forty-five minutes, but his coffee cup had been refilled three times—Eliza had counted. His hands, surgeon's hands that she'd seen steady as stone during medical emergencies, trembled slightly each time he lifted the cup. The newspaper in front of him hadn't been turned in all that time, though he maintained the pretense of reading, his eyes scanning the same headline over and over.

The Henderson sisters whispered to each other in the rapid-fire shorthand of siblings who'd spent seventy years together. Their Pomeranians, usually perfectly behaved, whined and pulled at their leashes, sensing the distress their owners tried to hide. Mrs. Henderson's hands kept moving to her purse, checking for something—her phone, perhaps, or just the nervous gesture of someone who needed to be doing something, anything, other than sitting still while murder hung in the air like morning fog.

Tilda had been systematically destroying lives, and everyone in the room knew it. The Henderson sisters' antique shop had been under siege for months over a Victorian armoire that Tilda claimed was a fake—a claim that, if proven, would ruin their reputation with collectors from Boston to Burlington. Tom Garrett faced even worse—Tilda's accusations about overcharging seniors and her threats to report him to the state board could end his thirty-year career with a single phone call. And Rebecca Harris, who'd arrived just minutes before the discovery, kept her distance from her son Charlie, as if proximity might reveal whatever secret had brought her here this morning—her timing either terrible or suspicious.

Rebecca was a small woman, neat and contained, but her hands betrayed her—they kept moving to her grandmother's ruby ring, twisting it, a gesture Eliza recognized as severe anxiety.

"Ladies and gentlemen," Wade announced, having come back downstairs. His presence immediately commanded attention, conversations dying mid-sentence. "I need to interview each of you individually. We'll use the library. Deputy Lang will call you one at a time."

"This is ridiculous," Patsy burst out, her voice climbing to a pitch that made Bruno's ears flatten. "Tilda poisoned herself! She brought the jar, she insisted on using it. Case closed. We all saw it. Charlie's not to blame—she is!"

"Then why was the service door open?" Eliza asked mildly.

Everyone turned to stare at her. The question hung in the air like an accusation.

Patsy flushed. "What door?"

"The parlor has two entrances," Eliza explained, using her teaching voice, the one that had served her well in countless witness interviews. "The main door from the front stairs, and a service door that connects to the back stairs—the ones staff use. That door was open when we found her, but Charlie came up the front stairs."

"So?" Tom Garrett asked, but his voice had an edge of worry.

"So someone else was in that room. Either while Tilda was dying, or just after."

A ripple of unease went through the crowd like wind through wheat. People shifted, looking at each other with new suspicion. The Henderson sisters actually scooted their chairs slightly apart, as if suddenly unsure of each other.

"That's enough speculation," Wade said firmly, though Eliza caught the slight nod he gave her—approval and warning mixed. "Mr. Harris, you're first."

As Charlie was led away, walking like a man heading to execution, Millie approached Eliza's table. She'd stopped polishing the cup, but her hands still trembled slightly.

"The service door," she whispered, leaning close enough that Eliza could smell her rose hand lotion mixed with nervous sweat. "I locked it this morning. I always lock it when we're using the parlor for special guests. It's part of my routine—check the flowers, adjust the curtains, lock the service door."

"Who has keys?"

"Just me, Owen, and Charlie. We keep a spare in the Kitchen, but..." She frowned, creating lines around her mouth that hadn't been there this morning. "Actually, I haven't seen it in a few days. I noticed on Monday when I went to get it for the cleaning service."

Before Eliza could respond, Bruno suddenly stood, ears pricked forward, body tense. He was staring at Marina's table with the fixed attention that meant he'd noticed something important. The woman had pulled something from her bag— a photograph, old and creased along the edges. She studied it intently, her lips moving as if in prayer or curse.

Eliza rose and crossed to her, Bruno padding alongside. Marina didn't look up until Eliza's shadow fell across the photograph.

"Ms. Blackwood?"

Marina startled, quickly shoving the photo back in her bag. But not before Eliza caught a glimpse: a group of young women in front of what looked like the Teacup Inn, circa twenty years ago, the colors faded but the faces clear. One of them could have been a younger Marina—same bone structure, same elegant posture. Another looked remarkably like Tilda, though decades younger and actually smiling.

"You knew her," Eliza said quietly, sitting down uninvited. "From before."

Marina's composure finally cracked completely. Her face crumpled like tissue paper, years of practiced control dissolving. "You don't understand. Tilda destroyed my life twenty years ago. My business, my marriage, everything. All because I had something she wanted."

"What did she want?" Eliza asked.

Marina laughed bitterly, the sound sharp as broken glass. "A recipe. Can you believe it? A stupid recipe for lemon scones that won a national competition. She accused me of stealing it from her, launched a campaign that ruined my bakery's reputation. Health department inspections every week, rumors about expired ingredients, anonymous reviews online before online even mattered." Her hands clenched. "I had to leave town, change my name, start over. I lost everything because of a few cups of flour and sugar."

"And you came back now because...?"

"Because I heard she was finally going to get what she deserved. Someone sent me a letter saying Tilda's crimes would be exposed at the town meeting. That justice would be served." Marina's eyes glittered with unshed tears. "I wanted to see it happen. I wanted to watch her fall."

"Who sent the letter?"

"I don't know. It was unsigned. Block printing, generic paper."

Eliza felt the pieces clicking together, but the picture was still incomplete. "Marina, I need to see that letter."

"I burned it," Marina said quickly. Too quickly. Her tell was subtle—the slight touch to her bag, unconscious protection of something still there.

Before Eliza could press further, a scream echoed from the

Kitchen. Not terror this time—surprise and disgust mixed. Everyone jumped up, chairs scraping against wood, rushing toward the sound.

They found Rebecca Harris standing by the pantry, pointing at the floor with a shaking hand. A steady drip of red was pooling beneath the door, viscous and spreading.

Owen pushed past everyone with military efficiency and yanked the door open. A body tumbled out—

But it wasn't a person. It was one of Millie's cloth napkins, soaked in what looked like blood but smelled like—

"Raspberry jam," Owen announced, holding up the dripping fabric with two fingers, his expression disgusted. "Someone's idea of a joke."

But Rebecca wasn't looking at the napkin anymore. She was staring into the pantry itself, where someone had written on the back wall in the same red jam, the letters dripping like something from a horror movie: SHE KNEW TOO MUCH. THE TRUTH DIES WITH HER.

CHAPTER 4

THE SERVICE DOOR

"Thursday is today," Patsy breathed, her face pale. "That's when Tilda was going to reveal her 'proof.'"

Wade pushed through the crowd, his expression thunderous. "Everyone out of the Kitchen. Now."

As people filed out, Eliza noticed Charlie wasn't among them. "Where's Charlie?" she asked Millie.

"Still being interviewed, I think—" Millie stopped, frowning. "No, wait. Wade just sent him to fetch his notebook from the library."

They found Charlie in the library, standing frozen over Wade's interview notes. The library was a small room, really just a converted parlor, but Millie had filled it with books donated by guests over the years. Charlie stood by the writing desk, his face had gone from pale to green, like old cheese.

"Charlie?" Millie rushed to him. "What's wrong?"

He held up a piece of paper with trembling hands. It wasn't from Wade's notebook. It was a note, written in Tilda's distinctive handwriting—sharp, angular, unmistakable:

Marina Blackwood is really Mary Brennan. She killed her husband in Seattle five years ago. Suspected poisoning but never proven. She's here for revenge because she thinks I'm responsible for his death. But she's wrong. The real killer is someone she'd never suspect. Someone who's been here all along. If something happens to me, check the sugar jar—but not the one I brought. Check the one that was already here.

Eliza's blood ran cold. "There were two jars?"

Charlie nodded miserably. "Tilda brought one, but there was already one in the parlor. The tea service we set up this morning—it had a matching sugar jar. I thought it was empty, but..."

"But you used Tilda's jar, right?" Eliza pressed.

"I... I think so? They looked the same. Crystal with silver lids. I grabbed one from the tray, but in the nervousness of it all..." His voice trailed off, hands wringing.

Wade appeared in the doorway, having heard the commotion. He read the note, his expression darkening like storm clouds gathering. "Where's Ms. Blackwood?"

They rushed back to find Marina's table empty, her teacup cold and abandoned, her coat gone. The front door stood slightly open, rain blowing in, creating puddles on Millie's polished floor.

"She ran," Deputy Morris reported, slightly out of breath. "Must have slipped out during the pantry commotion. I tried to follow but she had a head start."

"Find her," Wade ordered. Then, to the room at large: "Nobody else moves."

But Eliza was already moving, Bruno at her side. Because she'd noticed something others hadn't—wet footprints leading not out the front door, but up the back stairs. The prints were small, elegant—Marina's expensive Italian boots. She hadn't fled.

She'd gone back to the scene of the crime.

Eliza climbed the service stairs quietly, Bruno padding silently behind her. His training kicked in—he knew when to be invisible. The old wood was damp from various feet, muffling their approach. The door to the parlor stood open, afternoon light struggling through rain-streaked windows.

Inside, Marina knelt by Tilda's chair, searching frantically through the dead woman's pockets. Her elegant composure was completely gone—she looked desperate, wild, her perfect hair coming loose from its chignon.

"Looking for this?" Eliza asked.

Marina spun around. In Eliza's hand was a small key, one she'd noticed earlier attached to Tilda's bracelet—a detail her detective's eye had catalogued automatically.

"That's not—" Marina started.

"Your husband's safety deposit box key? The one Tilda somehow had? Yes, I think it is." Eliza stepped into the room, keeping distance between them. "She didn't destroy your business because of a recipe, did she? She did it because your husband was embezzling from his company—Tilda's late husband's company. And when you found out and threatened to expose him, he tried to poison you. But you switched the cups, didn't you? He died instead."

Marina's face crumbled completely, years falling away until she looked young and terrified. "It was self-defense. He was going to kill me and run away with her—with Tilda. They'd been having an affair for years. She provided the poison. I just... made sure he drank it instead of me."

"And you came back to Ashford Creek to what? Kill her the same way?"

"No!" Marina protested, tears flowing freely now. "I came back to see her exposed. That letter promised she'd finally pay for her crimes. I wanted to watch her fall. I wanted to see her face when everyone knew what she really was."

"Then who killed her?"

Before Marina could answer, footsteps thundered up both staircases. They were trapped between Wade's deputies coming up the front and someone else on the service stairs.

But as Wade and his deputies burst in from both doors, Eliza noticed something that made her stomach drop. Bruno was growling at the window—the one that overlooked the inn's Kitchen garden.

Down below, barely visible through the rain, a figure in a dark raincoat was burying something beneath the rosebushes. The figure was too far away to identify clearly, but something about the movement was familiar—controlled, efficient, military.

"Wade," Eliza said urgently. "The real killer is still here."

CHAPTER 5

BITTER TRUTHS

*W*ade sent Deputy Morris racing down to the garden while Marina was cuffed and led away. Morris, despite being in his fifties with a bad knee from his high school football days, moved with surprising speed when motivated. The rest of them watched from the parlor window as he disappeared into the rain, which had intensified to near-horizontal sheets.

The inn's garden, usually Millie's pride and joy, looked like a crime scene from a gothic novel. The heritage roses were beaten down, their pink and yellow blooms scattered like confetti at a funeral. The herb garden's neat borders had dissolved into mud. And there, near the oldest rosebush—a climber that had been planted when the inn was built—the earth was clearly disturbed.

"He's gone," Morris's voice crackled over Wade's radio. "But Sheriff, you need to see this."

By the time they reached the rosebushes, Morris had already begun excavating, his hands gentle despite the urgency. The rain had plastered his uniform to his body, making him look like a drowned scarecrow. He'd found a bundle wrapped in Kitchen plastic—the heavy-duty kind Millie used for storing holiday decorations.

"Don't touch it directly," Wade warned, pulling on fresh gloves.

Inside was an apron—one of the inn's, with "Teacup Inn" embroidered on the front in Millie's grandmother's distinctive script. The fabric was stained with white crystalline residue that the rain hadn't managed to wash away. Even from a distance, Eliza could smell it—bitter almonds, faint but unmistakable.

"Cyanide," Wade said grimly after a careful sniff. He sealed the apron in an evidence bag, rain pattering against the plastic. "Someone was covering their tracks."

They trudged back inside, a procession of soaked and shaken people. The inn felt different now—no longer a cozy refuge but a place where someone had methodically planned and executed murder. The tourists had been allowed to leave with strict instructions to remain available, but the locals were required to stay.

They were back in the tea room now, the afternoon growing dark as the storm intensified. The power had flickered twice already, and Millie had lit candles on each table, giving the room an inappropriately romantic atmosphere for a murder investigation. The dancing shadows made everyone look suspicious, faces shifting between light and dark like their secrets.

Marina sat in custody at a corner table, her expensive clothes now rumpled, her perfect makeup smeared. Deputy Lang sat across from her, ostensibly guarding but really just looking uncomfortable. Marina had been determined a flight risk but not yet formally arrested for Tilda's murder—

multiple witnesses confirmed she'd never left the main tea room until after Tilda's death. Her wet footprints on the back stairs proved she'd returned to search, not to kill.

"The apron changes things," Eliza said to Wade quietly, standing near the Kitchen door where they could observe everyone. "Whoever wore it had access to the Kitchen, knew about the poison, and was in the parlor."

"That's half the people here," Wade pointed out, frustration creeping into his usually steady voice. "All the staff, plus anyone who's been a regular. The inn's not exactly Fort Knox. Millie's never turned anyone away from her Kitchen."

As if to prove his point, Mrs. Henderson had wandered behind the counter to help herself to more hot water, moving with the confidence of someone who'd done it a hundred times before.

Bruno, who'd been sniffing around the room in an ever-widening pattern, suddenly stopped at Owens feet and sat. His old police signal for alerting to evidence. His tail was still, ears forward, completely focused.

Owen looked down, expression neutral as always, but Eliza caught the slight tension in his shoulders. "Smart dog."

"He is," Eliza agreed, keeping her voice conversational. "What's he smelling, Owen?"

Owen lifted his shoe—a practical work boot, worn but well-maintained. A white crystal was embedded in the tread, glinting in the candlelight. "Sugar," he said, voice flat. "From this morning's prep. Unless you think it's something else?"

The room had gone quiet, everyone watching. The candle-light made the crystal look like a tiny star against the dark rubber sole.

Wade bagged the shoe immediately, his movements effi-cient but somehow ominous. "We'll test it."

Owen surrendered it without protest, oddly calm for someone who'd just become a prime suspect. He stood in his sock feet, toes visible through a hole he probably hadn't known about. The small vulnerability made him seem more human, less like the controlled military machine he usually projected.

"Where were you when Tilda died?" Wade asked, pulling out his notebook.

"Kitchen, prepping for lunch. Charlie can confirm—he was in and out."

"Actually," Charlie said miserably from his corner table, his voice small in the large room, "you left for about ten minutes. Said you needed air. That was right before I went up with the tea."

Owen's calm finally cracked, just a hairline fracture but visible. His hands clenched and unclenched at his sides. "I stepped out back for a smoke. Is that a Crime?"

"Depends what you were smoking," Wade said evenly.

The tension ratcheted higher, the air thick enough to cut. Eliza watched the dynamics shift—people edging away from Owen, suspicious glances, whispered speculation. But something felt wrong. Too neat. Too obvious. Like someone was painting by numbers, and Owen was meant to be colored guilty.

"Millie," she said suddenly, an idea forming. "You said the spare key to the service door went missing. When did you notice?"

Millie thought, absently straightening silverware that didn't need straightening. "Monday? No, Sunday. After church service. We had Judge Morrison's anniversary tea, and I went to get the key to lock up, but it wasn't on the hook."

"Who was here Sunday?"

"Everyone," Millie said helplessly, gesturing at the room. "We had forty people for the anniversary, and the Kitchen was chaos. Anyone could have taken it."

Dr. Pemberton cleared his throat, the sound sharp in the tense atmosphere. He'd been so quiet that everyone had almost forgotten him, hidden in his corner like a turtle in its shell. "I may have seen something relevant." All eyes turned to him. He adjusted his glasses—a nervous habit Eliza had been counting. This was adjustment number forty-three since the investigation began. "Sunday afternoon, I saw Tilda leaving the inn through the back entrance—the staff entrance. She looked... furtive."

"Why didn't you mention this earlier?" Wade demanded, his patience finally fraying.

"I didn't think it relevant until now. But if she took the key..."

"She could have planted the poison herself," Patsy finished eagerly, practically bouncing in her seat. "Set someone up to take the fall."

"But why would she poison herself?" Rebecca Harris asked. Her voice was steady, but her hands weren't—they kept moving to her grandmother's ring, twist, twist, twist.

"She wouldn't," Eliza said, pieces clicking together in her mind. "Not intentionally. Which means—"

The lights went out completely.

Several people screamed. A chair crashed over—the sound explosive in the darkness. In the chaos, Eliza heard rapid footsteps, a door slamming, breaking glass from somewhere upstairs.

"Everyone stay still!" Wade shouted, his voice cutting through the panic.

Emergency lighting flickered on, casting eerie shadows

that made everyone look like suspects in a German expressionist film. The Henderson sisters were clutching each other, their faces pale as moonlight. Tom Garrett had knocked over his chair and stood frozen, half-crouched like he didn't know whether to run or hide. Charlie was pressed against the wall, eyes wide, breathing too fast.

And Owen was gone.

"The Kitchen," Wade barked, already moving.

They found the back door hanging open, rain driving in like an accusation. The wind had scattered papers from the counter, creating a snow of receipts and order tickets. Owen's remaining shoe sat abandoned on the threshold, looking somehow sadder than a pair would have.

But more concerning was what they found on the Kitchen counter: Millie's recipe box, forced open, its tiny lock twisted beyond repair. Papers were scattered everywhere—decades of carefully preserved family recipes spread like secrets across the stainless steel.

"No," Millie gasped, rushing to gather them. Her hands shook as she sorted through the papers, some so old the ink had faded to brown. "These are grandmother's recipes. They're irreplaceable—" She stopped, face paling to match the papers. "The lemon scone recipe. It's gone."

"But you said it was in the bank," Eliza said, confused.

Millie's face flushed. "I... I took it out yesterday. After Tilda's threats, I wanted to make sure it was really mine, that grandmother's notes were authentic. I was going to put it back today, but then..." She gestured helplessly at the chaos around them. "I never thought anyone would break into my personal recipe box. It's been in my family for seventy years."

"Owen took it?" Charlie asked, confused. "Why would he—"

48

"Why would Owen care about—" Eliza started, then stopped. Because there, caught on a splinter of the broken recipe box, was a torn piece of paper. She recognized Tilda's handwriting immediately—the same sharp angles, the same aggressive periods:

O.K. — Thursday, 11 a.m. Bring the proof about M.H. or I tell everyone about Fort Bragg.

"O.K.," Wade read. "Owen Kraft."

"M.H.," Millie whispered, her hand going to her throat. "That's me. Millicent Hart."

Eliza's mind raced, connections forming like a spider's web. "Tilda wasn't just threatening people randomly. She was collecting meetings. Marina said Tilda was meeting someone. This note proves it was Owen. But what proof about Millie?"

"I don't understand," Millie said tearfully. "What could Owen know about me? He's been nothing but loyal for three years. I gave him a chance when no one else would—"

Before anyone could answer, Bruno began barking urgently at the pantry door. Not his alert bark—his warning bark. The deep, aggressive sound he only made when there was immediate danger. Someone was in there.

CHAPTER 6

THE LOCKET IN THE GARDEN

*W*ade drew his service weapon—a Glock he'd carried for fifteen years, the metal worn smooth where his palm rested. "Police! Come out slowly!"

The door creaked open like a scene from a horror movie. Owen emerged, hands raised—but he wasn't alone. He was supporting someone, someone who'd been hidden in the pantry all along, someone small and shaking.

It was a young woman, maybe twenty-five, with Owen's same dark eyes and stubborn jaw. But where Owen was solid and controlled, she looked fragile, days of hiding written in the hollows of her cheeks and the tremor in her hands. Her clothes were wrinkled, her dark hair tangled, and she smelled of the mustiness that came from hiding in small spaces.

"My daughter," Owen said quietly, his voice holding a defeat Eliza had never heard from him. "Sarah. She's been living in the crawlspace under the inn for three days."

The room exploded in shocked voices, but Wade silenced them with a gesture. "Explain. Now."

Owen's shoulders sagged, the military bearing finally failing. "Sarah was at Fort Bragg with me. She was the real whistleblower—reported command for embezzlement. A major was skimming from the mess hall budget, selling supplies on the black market. Sarah had documented everything, had proof. But they flipped it, made it look like we were the thieves."

Sarah spoke for the first time, her voice hoarse from disuse. "Dad took the dishonorable discharge to protect me. Said he did it alone. But they still came after me—trumped up charges, threats. I've been running ever since."

"And Tilda found out," Eliza said, understanding dawning.

"She saw Sarah sneaking in Sunday night," Owen confirmed, his arm tightening protectively around his daughter. "The crawlspace has an old access from when they did the plumbing in the fifties. Sarah knew about it from when I showed her the inn's layout—habit from the military, always know your exits. Tilda threatened to call the MPs unless I helped her."

"Helped her how?" Wade asked, though his expression had softened slightly. He had a daughter too, away at college.

"She wanted dirt on Millie—specifically, proof that Millie's grandmother stole the lemon scone recipe from Tilda's family fifty years ago."

Millie gasped, her hand flying to her heart. "That's a lie! Grandmother created that recipe! She won awards—"

"I know," Owen said firmly. "But Tilda had forged documents, fake letters. She'd been building this false narrative for years. She was going to present them today unless I gave her real proof—proof I didn't have because it doesn't exist."

"So you poisoned her?" Wade asked, though doubt had crept into his voice.

"No!" Sarah spoke with surprising force for someone so

fragile-looking. "Dad would never. He was going to run, take me with him. We were packing when we heard the scream."

"Then who—" Wade started.

"Wait," Eliza interrupted, a crucial detail clicking. "Sarah, you've been hiding here three days. You must have seen things, heard things."

Sarah nodded slowly, her eyes darting nervously around the room. "Yesterday, I heard Tilda on the phone. She was in the parlor—the sound carries through the old radiator pipes. She said, 'I know what you did to Martha Harris twenty years ago. Bring fifty thousand to the parlor Thursday or everyone knows.'"

Rebecca Harris went white as bone. The ring she'd been twisting slipped off her finger and rang against the floor like a bell. "Martha was Charlie's aunt. She died in a car accident twenty years ago."

"It wasn't an accident," Charlie said suddenly, voice hollow. Everyone turned to stare at him. His face had taken on a gray cast, like old newspaper. "I found out last year. Went through Mom's old letters when I was looking for family recipes for a school project. Martha was having an affair with someone prominent. She threatened to go public. The accident... the brake lines were cut."

"Charlie," Rebecca breathed, reaching for her son. "Why didn't you tell me?"

"Because the letters implicated you, Mom!" Charlie's voice cracked like he was thirteen again. "They made it sound like you knew, like you helped cover it up to protect the family reputation. I couldn't—I couldn't ask you if you were—"

"A murderer," Rebecca finished, her voice barely a whisper. She sank into a chair like her strings had been cut. "I didn't know. I suspected, but I never knew for sure. And I never,

ever would have hurt Martha. She was my best friend before she was my sister-in-law."

"But Tilda thought you did," Eliza said, pieces clicking with terrible clarity. "She was blackmailing you too."

"She was blackmailing everyone," Patsy said bitterly, her usual composure completely gone. "Tom about watered-down medications. The Hendersons about selling forgeries. Dr. Pemberton about—"

"Enough," Pemberton said sharply, but his voice shook. "Yes, she had dirt on all of us. That's what she did—collected secrets like weapons."

Wade looked overwhelmed, running his hand through his hair in a gesture Eliza had seen when cases got too complex. "So everyone had motive."

"But not everyone had opportunity," Eliza pointed out. "Let's think about this. The poison was in a sugar jar—but which jar? Charlie, you said there were two?"

Charlie nodded miserably. "Tilda's, and the one already on the tea service."

"Who prepared the tea service?"

"I did," Owen said. "Early this morning, around six. Set it all up in the parlor."

"And I checked it," Millie added. "Around nine. Everything was perfect—wait." Her face changed, memory dawning. "The sugar jar was full. I noted it specifically because we'd been running low. I thought Owen had filled it."

"I didn't," Owen said with certainty. "I left it empty, planning to fill it later."

"But you didn't fill it?"

"No, I assumed someone else had."

Eliza felt the truth hovering just out of reach, like a word on the tip of her tongue. "So someone filled it between nine and when Charlie served the tea. Someone who knew Tilda would use the sugar, not her own."

"But Tilda insisted on her own jar," Charlie protested.

"Did she?" Eliza asked. "Or did she just insist on her special sugar being used? Charlie, think carefully. What exactly did she say?"

Charlie's brow furrowed in concentration. The candles flickered, making shadows dance across his face. "She said... she said 'Make sure to use the special sugar on my scone. It's already up there.'"

"Already up there," Eliza repeated. "She thought her jar was already in the parlor. Someone had switched them."

"But who?" Wade demanded.

Bruno had been sniffing around the group, and now he sat again—this time at Rebecca's feet. But he wasn't alerting. He was comforting, the way he did with victims, not perpetrators. His tail wagged once, gently, and he leaned against her leg.

And suddenly, Eliza knew.

"Charlie," she said gently. "You didn't go up the front stairs with the tea, did you? You used the service stairs. That's why the door was open."

Charlie went very still, like a rabbit sensing a hawk.

"You had the missing key," Eliza continued, her voice soft but inexorable. "You took it Sunday to get into the parlor. You knew about Tilda's plan to bring poisoned sugar—you'd overheard her on the phone, planning to frame someone for attempted murder. But you switched the jars. Put her poison in the house jar, left an empty one for her to bring."

"That's insane," Charlie said, but his voice shook like leaves in a storm.

"You knew she'd use the sugar already there if she thought

it was hers. She was arrogant that way. And you knew she was going to destroy your mother with those accusations about Martha Harris. You couldn't let that happen."

"Charlie?" Rebecca stared at her son in horror. "Is this true?"

Charlie's composure finally shattered like the china in the parlor. Tears streamed down his face, and his whole body shook with suppressed sobs. "She was evil!" he burst out. "She destroyed everything she touched! Marina's life, Owen's career, and she was going to destroy you, Mom. Make everyone think you were a murderer!"

"So you became one instead?" Wade asked quietly.

"I didn't mean for her to die!" Charlie sobbed, his words coming in rushes between gasping breaths. "I thought—I thought she'd just get sick. Scare her, make her back off. I didn't know how much poison she'd brought. I didn't know it would kill her so fast."

"You were trying to protect everyone," Eliza said. "But Charlie, you also wrote the threatening message in the pantry, didn't you? To throw suspicion elsewhere?"

He nodded miserably, looking younger than his nineteen years. "I panicked. I'm sorry. I'm so sorry."

Rebecca pulled her son into her arms, both of them crying now. The room stood in stunned silence, the only sound the rain against windows and the soft sobbing of mother and son.

Wade looked older suddenly, the weight of the situation visible in the lines of his face. "Charlie Harris, you're under arrest for the murder of Tilda Crane."

"No!" Rebecca cried out, her composure finally shattering completely. "This is all my fault! All of it!" She stumbled backward toward the stairs, sobbing.

"Rebecca, wait—" Wade started, but he had to secure

Charlie first. His hand moved to his belt, fingers finding the familiar metal of his handcuffs. But as he unclipped them, the lights went out again. This time, they heard a crash from upstairs—from the parlor.

Several people screamed. A chair crashed over in the darkness. Eliza heard rapid footsteps, a door slamming, glass breaking somewhere.

"Everyone stay still!" Wade shouted, his voice cutting through the panic.

They stood frozen in the darkness for what felt like an eternity but was probably only three or four minutes. The sound of rain against windows mixed with heavy breathing and someone's muffled sobbing. Wade's flashlight finally clicked on, sweeping the room.

"Stay here," Wade ordered, but Eliza was already moving, Bruno beside her.

They reached the parlor to find the window broken, rain driving in like an accusation. The curtains whipped in the wind like ghosts. Tilda's body remained in the chair, but something was different. A piece of paper was pinned to her chest—a paper that hadn't been there before.

Eliza read it by flashlight, her blood running cold:

Wrong killer. The boy's protecting someone. The real murder happened twenty years ago. Martha Harris didn't die in a car accident. She was murdered. And her killer just confessed.

"Eliza!" Wade's voice from below, urgent and shocked. "Rebecca's gone!"

They found her in the garden, kneeling in the rain where the apron had been buried. She was soaked through, her neat appearance destroyed, but she seemed calm. In her hands, she held a second bundle—this one wrapped in oilcloth, preserved for two decades.

"I kept it," she said numbly as they approached, rain mixing with tears on her face. "All these years, I kept the evidence. Because I thought someday I'd be brave enough to use it."

Wade knelt beside her, gently taking the bundle. Inside was a brake line, clearly cut, and a note in Tilda's younger handwriting: This should solve your Martha problem. You owe me.

"But I never asked her to," Rebecca said, her voice breaking completely. "Martha was going to leave town, start over. She wasn't going to expose anyone. But Tilda... Tilda thought she was doing me a favor. Protecting the family reputation. She killed Martha and expected me to be grateful."

"You've been living with this for twenty years," Eliza said softly, rain plastering her hair to her head.

"And Tilda held it over me the whole time. Not blackmail, exactly. Just... reminders. Little comments. 'Remember what I did for you.' 'Family loyalty is so important.' Until this week, when she finally demanded payment." Rebecca looked at her son, who had followed them out, Wade's cuffs still dangling from his wrist. "That's why I brought this evidence today—I was finally going to confront her at the meeting tonight. Charlie must have overheard more than I thought. He knew my plans. He tried to protect me by..." She broke down completely.

The rain had become a deluge, turning the garden into a mudscape that seemed appropriate for the unearthing of old secrets. The heritage roses, Millie's pride and usually standing tall even in storms, were beaten down, their petals scattered like confetti at a funeral no one wanted to attend. The smell of wet earth mixed with the lingering scent of roses created an oddly funereal perfume, sweet decay and fresh rain mingling into something that would forever remind Eliza of this moment.

Rebecca knelt in the mud, her neat appearance completely destroyed. Her usually perfect hair hung in wet strings, her makeup had run in dark rivers down her cheeks, and her clothes were soaked through. But there was something almost peaceful in her expression, as if confession had lifted a weight she'd carried so long she'd forgotten what it felt like to stand straight.

The evidence in her hands was wrapped with the kind of care usually reserved for holy relics. The oilcloth was old but well-maintained, the kind that might have wrapped fishing gear or hunting supplies two decades ago. Inside, the brake line was corroded but clearly cut—the edges too clean to be anything but deliberate. The note, protected by a plastic bag that had gone yellow with age, was still readable despite the years.

"I found them in my husband's things after he died," Rebecca said, her voice steady now that the worst was out. "He'd been having an affair with Martha—his own brother's wife. She was going to tell me, that's why she called that night. Said she had something important to discuss, something that couldn't wait. But she never made it."

Charlie stood beside his mother, the rain plastering his hair to his head, is face stripped of any pretense of adulthood. The expression on his face was something Eliza recognized from her years in Portland—the look of someone recalculating everything they thought they knew about their world. Every memory was being reexamined, every family story reevaluated in the harsh light of this new truth. His father had betrayed not just his mother, but his uncle too—a double betrayal that made the family gatherings, the shared holidays, all of it a lie.

"Tilda called me the next day," Rebecca continued. "Said she was sorry for my loss, but that Martha had been troubled, unstable. That the accident was probably for the best, that some secrets should die with the people who carry them. I knew then. The way she said it, the satisfaction in her voice. She'd done something. But I was a coward. I had Charlie to think about, a business to run, my brother-in-law who'd just lost his wife, a life to maintain. So I kept quiet and kept the evidence, telling myself that someday I'd be brave enough to use it."

Eliza had been studying Rebecca throughout her confession, and now she noticed something that made her step closer. "Rebecca, you have something on your face."

Rebecca touched her cheek, confused. Her fingers came away with a black smudge—the kind that came from permanent marker. More telling, there was a matching streak of black on her palm, and when she'd touched her face, she'd transferred it. The same deep black as the writing on the note pinned to Tilda's body.

"You wrote the note during the blackout," Eliza said quietly. "With a marker from the parlor desk."

Rebecca's shoulders sagged in defeat. "When the lights went out," she continued, her voice hollow, "I knew Charlie was about to be arrested for something I'd caused. I couldn't let that happen. I slipped upstairs in the darkness—I know this inn like my own home, every creaking board. I found the marker in the desk drawer and wrote that note, then pinned it to her. I wanted everyone to know the real murder was Martha's, twenty years ago. I wanted them to know my boy was just trying to protect me from the truth." She looked at Wade. "I'm sorry for tampering with the scene. But I couldn't let Charlie take the blame alone."

Wade's expression was unreadable. "You wrote the note during the blackout?"

"Yes. I had to make sure everyone knew there was more to this. That the real crime happened twenty years ago."

Wade stood in the rain, looking between mother and son, the weight of Solomon on his shoulders. "So Charlie poisoned Tilda to stop her from revealing that Tilda herself was a murderer?"

"The irony," Dr. Pemberton said from the doorway, having ignored Wade's order to stay put, "is that Tilda finally got justice. Just not the kind she expected."

"There's no justice in any of this," Wade said heavily. "Just tragedy all the way down, like Russian nesting dolls of pain."

But as they stood in the garden, rain washing away twenty years of secrets, Eliza noticed something that changed everything.

Bruno was alerting again—but not to any person. He was focused on the rosebush itself, nose pointing like an arrow at the base where something metallic gleamed among the roots. His tail was rigid, his whole body tense with discovery.

The metallic gleam in the rosebush turned out to be a small silver locket, tarnished with age but still intact. Wade extracted it carefully with gloved hands, the rain making everything slippery and difficult. The locket was heart-shaped, Victorian in style, with delicate etching that had survived two decades in the earth.

Bruno sat perfectly still, his alert posture rigid despite the rain soaking through his coat. His training held even in the storm—once he'd indicated evidence, he wouldn't move until released. Eliza gave him the command to relax, and he shook himself, sending water everywhere, but his eyes remained fixed on Wade's hands.

"Let me see," Rebecca said, reaching with trembling fingers.

Wade opened the locket with careful pressure. The hinge protested but held. Inside was a photograph, protected by glass that had somehow remained uncracked. Two young women smiled at the camera—one clearly Martha Harris, young and vibrant with eyes that matched Charlie's. The other face had been carefully cut out with surgical precision, leaving a perfect oval void.

"That's Martha's locket," Rebecca said, her voice hollow with shock. "She was wearing it when she died. She never took it off—it was her grandmother's. How did it get here?"

CHAPTER 7

THE LAST CUP

$\mathcal{T}$he question hung in the air like the rain, persistent and unanswerable. The locket shouldn't exist. It should have been destroyed in the accident, or buried with Martha, or at the very least, lost to time. Its presence here, in Millie's rose garden, suggested something far more complex than they'd imagined.

"Someone saved it," Eliza said slowly, her detective mind working through possibilities. "Someone was at the accident scene. Someone who knew what really happened."

"But the police report—" Wade started.

"Could have been altered. We already know Tilda had connections, money to throw around." Eliza studied the locket, noting the careful way the photo had been cut. "This wasn't random. Someone wanted to preserve Martha's image but eliminate the other person."

They stood in the rain, a bedraggled group of suspects and investigators, all soaked through and shivering. The storm had turned cold, more like October than late spring, and

Charlie was shaking so hard his teeth chattered. Rebecca had her arm around him, but she looked ready to collapse herself.

"Everyone inside," Wade commanded. "We're solving this tonight, but not if half of you die of pneumonia."

They trooped back into the inn, leaving puddles in their wake. Millie immediately began distributing towels she'd gathered, her innkeeper instincts overriding the surreal situation. The tea room felt different now—charged with the weight of revealed secrets and the promise of more to come. The candles had burned lower, creating pools of wax that looked like frozen tears.

Charlie sat with Deputy Morris, having confessed but not yet formally arrested. The handcuffs remained off, a small mercy from Wade who seemed to be weighing justice against tragedy with every decision. Rebecca stayed close to her son, mother and son bound by their mutual desire to protect each other and their shared guilt over actions taken and not taken.

Sarah and Owen huddled near the Kitchen, her exhaustion evident in every line of her body. Three days of hiding in crawlspaces had taken their toll—she looked like she might collapse at any moment. Owen kept a protective arm around her, but his own strength was flagging. The soldier's bearing that had kept him upright through everything was finally failing.

Marina sat alone at her table, guarded by Deputy Lang who looked increasingly uncomfortable with his job. She'd stopped crying, but her face held a bleakness that was worse than tears.

"We need to piece this together properly," Wade said, exhaustion clear in his voice. He'd been sheriff for fifteen years, but nothing had prepared him for this—a murder with three potential killers and a victim who was herself a murderer. "Charlie, tell us exactly what you did. Every detail."

Charlie wiped his eyes with the towel Millie had given him. When he spoke, his voice was thin but steady, like he'd moved past panic into a numb acceptance. "Sunday night, I couldn't sleep. I kept thinking about what Tilda had said to Mom at the grocery store—these hints about Martha, about family secrets. So I went for a walk around two AM. I saw Tilda's car at the inn, which was weird."

"The inn was closed," Millie said, frowning.

"That's what I thought. So I used my key and came in the back way. I heard voices from upstairs—Tilda was on the phone in the parlor. The acoustics in this old place are weird; if you stand in the right spot in the Kitchen, you can hear everything from the parlor through the radiator pipes."

Sarah nodded confirmation. "It's true. I heard things too."

Charlie continued, his hands twisting the towel. "She was talking about bringing 'special sugar' to her Thursday meeting teach someone a lesson. She said something about frame insurance, about making sure she couldn't be blamed. I thought she was going to poison someone today and make it look like an accident or frame them for attempted murder."

"So you decided to beat her to it," Wade said.

"I panicked. I took the service key from the hook—I knew where Millie kept it. This morning, really early, like five AM, I went up to the parlor. I was just going to check, you know? See if she'd left anything. But then I found this note." Charlie pulled a crumpled paper from his pocket—another piece of evidence he'd hidden. Wade took it, read it, and his expression darkened further.

The note was in block printing, not Tilda's handwriting:

"For Tilda—Your special sugar is already in place. Use it generously. Justice is patient but not indefinite. —M.C."

"M.C.," Eliza breathed, then paused. "Wait. What was Martha Harris's maiden name?"

Rebecca looked up, confused by the question. "Caldwell. Martha Caldwell. She kept her maiden name professionally even after marrying my brother."

"M.C.," Wade said slowly. "Martha Caldwell."

"But that's impossible," Rebecca said. "Martha's been dead for twenty years."

"Or someone wants us to think she sent it," Wade said. "Charlie, what did you do when you found this note?"

Charlie's face crumpled. "I thought someone else was planning to poison Tilda. So I... I went to her usual table in the tea room. She always sat at the same place for her morning meetings, had for years. There was a small jar there, crystal with a silver lid, just like the ones we use for the private parlor. I thought it was Tilda's poison."

"But it wasn't," Eliza said, understanding dawning.

"I took it and put it in the house sugar jar in the parlor. I figured if she was planning to poison someone, she deserved to get a taste of her own medicine. Not to kill her!" His voice cracked. "Just to make her sick, scare her, make her back off from Mom."

"But you put cyanide in the jar," Wade said.

"I didn't know it was cyanide! I thought it was something milder, something to cause stomach upset maybe. Like ipecac or something. I never meant—" He broke off, sobbing again.

Eliza had been thinking, and something didn't add up. "Charlie, you said you took sugar from Tilda's usual table. But Tilda brought her jar with her this morning. So whose sugar did you actually take?"

Charlie went pale. "I... I don't know."

"Someone else planted poison," Eliza said. "Before you, before Tilda. Someone who knew exactly what would happen." She turned to the room. "Someone who's been planning revenge for twenty years."

Sarah Kraft, who'd been silent in her corner, suddenly spoke. Her voice was stronger now, as if telling the truth had given her energy. "There's something else. When I was hiding in the crawlspace, I found old blueprints. Original ones from when the inn was built. There's a sealed room in the basement that's not on any current floor plan."

Millie gasped, her hand flying to her throat. "Grandmother always said there were secrets in the foundation, but I thought she meant metaphorically."

"Show us," Wade ordered.

They descended into the basement, a procession of suspects and investigators. The basement was exactly what you'd expect in a Victorian inn—stone foundation, wooden beam ceiling, the musty smell of age and damp. Sarah led them past the modern utilities to what appeared to be a solid wall. But Bruno immediately began pawing at one corner, his nose working furiously.

"Here," Sarah said, running her hands along the wall. "There's a seam."

Owen produced a crowbar from the utility closet—he knew where everything was in this inn, three years of working here evident in every movement. The paint had sealed the edges, decades of layers creating a barrier. It took effort, Owen and Wade working together, before the hidden door finally gave way with a groan that sounded almost human.

The door opened to reveal a small room, musty with age

but surprisingly dry. A single bulb hung from the ceiling—someone had wired it recently, the electrical work modern. Inside was a desk, covered in papers, photographs, and newspaper clippings—all about Martha Harris's death.

But more shocking was what sat in the corner: a bed, recently slept in, with a neat stack of clothes beside it. Someone had been living here.

"Someone's been staying in the inn," Millie whispered, horrified. "In my own basement."

The walls were covered with surveillance—photos of Tilda taken from various angles over what looked like years. Tilda at the grocery store. Tilda at town meetings. Tilda at the inn. Some were date-stamped going back five years. Others were as recent as yesterday.

Eliza examined the papers on the desk. They were detailed notes about everyone in Ashford Creek—their routines, their secrets, their vulnerabilities. Tilda featured prominently, with twenty years of observations. Every cruel thing she'd done was documented, every person she'd hurt catalogued.

The most recent entry was from yesterday: Tomorrow, it ends where it began.

"This is..." Wade picked up a photograph. It showed the tea service in the parlor, with a clear shot of someone adding something to the sugar jar. The timestamp was 4:47 AM—before Charlie's visit.

"So Charlie really did poison Tilda," Rebecca said, her voice hollow, "but with poison someone else planted, expecting Tilda to serve it to someone else."

"The question is who," Wade said.

Bruno had moved to the bed, sniffing intently. He pawed at the pillow, and something crinkled. Eliza lifted it to find an envelope addressed to "The Truth Seekers of Ashford Creek."

Inside was a confession, but not the one they expected. Eliza read it aloud, her voice steady despite the shock:

My name is Margaret Caldwell—Martha's younger sister. Everyone thinks I died in foster care after Martha's death and our parents' deportation. But I survived. I changed my name, my face, my entire identity. I became Marina Blackwood, among others.

For twenty years, I've waited. I knew Tilda killed my sister. I knew Rebecca suspected but did nothing. I knew this entire town chose comfortable lies over justice for an orphaned immigrant girl.

I came back for the antique fair because I knew Tilda would be at her most vulnerable—her reputation on the line, her control slipping. I planted the cyanide, knowing her patterns, knowing she always tested her "special ingredients" herself first. But I wanted her to know why she was dying. I wanted her to see Martha's face in mine.

The boy complicated things by switching the jars, but the result was the same. Tilda Crane is dead by the poison she so loved to metaphorically spread. Justice is served.

I'll be gone by the time you read this. Don't look for Margaret Harris or Marina Blackwood. Both are ghosts now.

But know this—Martha Harris mattered. Her life had value. And her death has finally been avenged.

"Marina is Martha's sister?" Patsy gasped from the doorway—the entire group had followed them down, unable to stay away.

"That's why she looked familiar," Millie said slowly. "She has Martha's eyes. The same shape, the same unusual green color."

Wade immediately radioed his deputies. "Find Marina Blackwood. Now."

But Eliza was studying the photograph of the sugar jar more carefully. The person in the image was partially reflected in an antique mirror on the parlor wall—distorted but clear enough. "Wade, look at this. The person adding the poison—you can see their reflection in the mirror."

Wade looked closer, pulling out his reading glasses. "That's not Marina."

The reflection was distorted but clear enough: a man's profile, familiar and unexpected. The distinctive nose, the way he held his shoulders, even the characteristic way he tilted his head when concentrating.

"Dr. Pemberton," Eliza said.

Everyone turned to where the doctor had been standing, but he was gone. His absence was like a shout in the sudden silence. They heard a car engine starting outside, tires squealing on wet pavement.

"He's running!" Charlie shouted.

Wade was already on his radio, calling in roadblocks. "All units, be on the lookout for Dr. Pemberton's blue Volvo, license plate—" He rattled off the number from memory, a small-town sheriff who knew every car in his jurisdiction.

Within minutes, word came back—Pemberton had been stopped at the town limits, caught at the very boundary between Ashford Creek and the outside world.

They brought him back to the inn in cuffs, a shocking sight for someone who'd been the town's respected physician for thirty years. He looked older, defeated, all his pompous authority drained away like water from a broken cup. His usually perfect hair was disheveled, his glasses askew, and his hands—surgeon's hands that had saved lives—shook with tremors.

"Why?" Wade asked simply.

Pemberton's laugh was bitter, broken. "Why? Because Tilda destroyed everything she touched. Martha Harris was my patient. She came to me, pregnant and scared, begging for help. The baby's father was prominent—a married man, someone important in town. It wouldn't do for a scandal. "Tilda convinced me to break confidentiality. Said it was for Martha's own good. Said the father had a right to know. I was young, stupid, believed in hierarchies and social order."

"You told the father," Eliza said quietly.

"I told Tilda who the father was, and she told him. He arranged the accident. Cut her brake lines. Martha died because I broke my oath, because I trusted Tilda Crane." Tears ran down his face, mixing with rain residue. "I've been drowning in that guilt for twenty years."

"So you decided to kill Tilda."

"When Margaret contacted me—yes, I knew who Marina really was—she didn't hide it from me. She said she had a plan for justice. I saw a chance for redemption." He looked at his cuffed hands. "I planted the first poison, the real poison, knowing Tilda's habits. She always came early on Thursdays to set up her power plays. She always tested anything she planned to serve, paranoid about her own tricks being turned on her."

"You've been living with this guilt for twenty years," Eliza said.

"Living with it? I've been drowning in it. Every patient I saved felt like penance that was never enough. When Margaret told me her plan, I saw a chance to finally balance the scales."

"You let Charlie think he was a murderer," Rebecca said, furious, mother's rage giving her strength.

"The boy was trying to protect you," Pemberton said.

"Noble, if misguided. He would have been charged with manslaughter at worst, probably gotten probation. Meanwhile, the real killer—Tilda's own arrogance—did her in."

"Except you're the real killer," Wade said. "You put the cyanide there."

"I put medicine there," Pemberton corrected with a ghost of his old precision. "Tilda turned it into poison by being herself."

The legal arguments would be complex, Eliza knew. Charlie had switched jars with intent to harm. Pemberton had planted the poison. Marina/Margaret had orchestrated it all. But ultimately, Tilda had insisted on using what she thought was her own weapon.

"Where is Marina now?" Wade asked Pemberton.

"Gone. She slipped away during all that confusion with the pantry. Her revenge was complete. Twenty years of planning for ten seconds of watching Tilda realize she'd been poisoned by her own weapon."

But Bruno was alerting again, this time at the kitchen door. When they opened it, Marina stood there, soaking wet, looking nothing like the composed woman from this morning. Her elegant clothes were plastered to her body, her makeup completely gone, revealing a face that looked younger and infinitely sadder.

"I couldn't leave," she said simply. "Not without visiting Martha's grave. Twenty years, and I never got to say goodbye to my sister properly. But standing there in the rain, I realized I couldn't run. Not again." As he read her rights, she looked at Rebecca. "You should have helped her. She trusted you."

"I know," Rebecca whispered. "I've lived with that failure every day."

"And you?" Marina looked at Charlie. "You have your

mother's protective instincts but also her weakness—the inability to act when it mattered most."

"That's enough," Wade said, leading her away.

But Marina turned back one more time. "I left something else in that room. Under the mattress. You should see it before you decide who's really guilty here."

Wade sent Deputy Morris to check. He returned with a manila folder—thick, worn, held together with rubber bands. Inside were documents, photos, evidence spanning twenty years.

"These are..." Wade's voice trailed off as he examined them.

The documents told a story of systematic cruelty that spanned decades. Each folder was meticulously labeled in Tilda's distinctive handwriting—names, dates, amounts. The Henderson sisters had been paying her five hundred dollars a month for three years to keep quiet about a forged Tiffany lamp they'd sold to a collector from Boston. Tom Garrett's payments were irregular but larger—sometimes two thousand, sometimes five, corresponding to shipments of medications that were approaching expiration but relabeled with fresh dates.

But it was the folder labeled "Martha Harris" that made everyone in the room step back. Inside were photographs—Martha with her lover, taken with a telephoto lens through bedroom windows. Bank statements showing deposits from him to her account. Medical records that should have been confidential, including the pregnancy test results. And at the bottom, a receipt from an auto parts store for brake line tools, dated three days before Martha's death, paid for with Tilda's credit card. She didn't just arrange Martha's death—she planned it for months."

"She documented her own crime," Wade said, disbelief clear in his voice. "Why would she keep this?"

"Insurance," Marina said quietly from her corner. "That's how she thought. Everyone was potentially an enemy, so she kept evidence on everyone, including herself. If someone tried to expose her, she could claim they were framing her, that they'd planted the evidence. She'd have revealed just enough to make herself look like a victim of an elaborate setup."

"There's more," Morris said, pulling out newer documents. "Tilda's been blackmailing half the town for decades. But look at this—she was embezzling from the town council, from the church, from every charity she ever ran."

Margaret pulled out another folder, this one labeled "Emergency Exit." Inside were plane tickets to the Cayman Islands, dated for Thursday afternoon. Bank routing numbers for offshore accounts. A new identity complete with passport and driver's license—Helen Crawford, a widow from Connecticut with no children and no ties.

"She was never going to reveal anything at the town meeting," Eliza said, understanding dawning. "She was going to disappear. Take everyone's money and run."

"But not before one final score," Wade said, pulling out a draft email on Tilda's personal stationary. It was addressed to the town council, scheduled to be sent Thursday morning: "Due to family emergency, I must leave immediately. I've left important documents in the town hall safe that must be reviewed by state authorities. The truth about Ashford Creek's corruption must come to light."

"She was going to frame everyone for her crimes," Dr. Pemberton said, his face pale. "Leave us to deal with the accusations while she vanished with the money."

The room stood in stunned silence as the full scope of

Tilda's plan became clear. She'd spent twenty years gathering weapons, and she'd planned to fire them all at once, leaving the town to destroy itself while she escaped to a new life built on their ruins.

"Then why bring poison?" Rebecca asked.

Eliza thought about it, pieces clicking. "Insurance. If someone tried to stop her, she'd poison them and claim self-defense. She'd done it before—there are three other deaths here over the years that look suspicious in hindsight."

The inn stood in shocked silence. Three killers, in a way—Marina who planned it, Pemberton who enabled it, and Charlie who executed it unknowingly. And at the center, Tilda herself, whose cruelty had sewn the seeds of her own destruction.

"What happens now?" Millie asked quietly.

Wade looked exhausted beyond measure. "Now we let the lawyers sort it out. Three people conspired to kill a woman who was also a murderer. I don't even know where to begin with the charges."

"Maybe," Eliza said quietly, "we begin with the truth. All of it. Let the town know who Tilda really was. Let them know about Martha. Let justice be served with full knowledge, not comfortable lies."

Thunder rumbled overhead, softer now, the storm finally passing. Through the windows, they could see breaks in the clouds, stars beginning to appear.

"It's Thursday," someone said. "The town meeting is in two hours."

Wade straightened his shoulders. "Then we'd better get ready to tell them everything."

* * *

THURSDAY EVENING ARRIVED with unexpected sunshine breaking through the clouds, as if nature itself wanted to witness Ashford Creek's reckoning. The Town Hall, a Greek Revival building that had served the community since 1853, was packed beyond capacity. People stood in the aisles, lined the walls, and spilled out onto the front steps where someone had set up speakers to broadcast the proceedings.

Wade stood at the podium where Tilda had planned to stand, still in his sheriff's uniform, still damp from the afternoon's rain. Beside him, a table held the evidence boxes, each one labeled and sealed, waiting to tell their part of the story.

"Folks," Wade began, his deep voice carrying even to those outside. "What I'm about to tell you isn't easy to hear. But after twenty years of secrets, this town deserves the truth."

He started with Martha Harris, projecting her photograph onto the screen behind him—young, smiling, full of life. "Martha Harris died twenty years ago in what we believed was an accident. It wasn't. She was murdered by Tilda Crane, who cut her brake lines because Martha was pregnant and threatening to expose an affair."

The gasps rippled through the crowd like wind through wheat. Mrs. Henderson clutched her sister's hand. Tom Garrett removed his glasses, cleaning them with shaking hands.

"But that was just the beginning," Wade continued. He detailed Tilda's twenty-year reign of blackmail, each revelation landing like a physical blow on the assembled crowd. The forged documents about Millie's grandmother's recipe. The false evidence she'd planted about various citizens. The money she'd extracted—nearly half a million dollars over two decades.

"She was planning to leave town," Wade said simply. "Take

your money and disappear, leaving you all to deal with the chaos she'd created."

The crowd erupted in voices—anger, relief, confusion mixing into a cacophony that Mayor Doyle had to gavel into order.

"The poison that killed her—she brought it herself," Wade continued once quiet returned. "She intended to use it on someone else. Instead, through a series of events I can only describe as poetic justice, she ingested it herself."

He explained the complicated web of Charlie's attempt to protect his mother, Dr. Pemberton's involvement, and Margaret Harris's twenty-year quest for justice. The crowd listened in stunned silence as the full story unfolded.

"Three people have been arrested," Wade said. "The district attorney will sort out the charges. But what matters now is what we do next."

He paused, looking out at the assembled faces—his neighbors, his community, the people he'd sworn to protect and serve. "We can let this destroy us, let suspicion and blame tear apart what's left of our community. Or we can choose to rebuild, to be honest with each other, to create the town we always pretended we were."

The silence stretched until Millie Hart stood up, still wearing her inn apron, her face tear-stained but determined. "I propose we start fresh. All of it. The secrets Tilda collected die with her. We support the Harris family, we forgive each other's mistakes, and we move forward. Together."

"But what about the money she stole?" someone called out.

"We'll work with the district attorney and file civil suits to recover the extorted funds," Mayor Doyle said, standing. "Her estate will go through probate, and we'll petition the court for restitution. It may take months, maybe longer, but we'll fight to get every penny back. And if there's anything left after victims are compensated, I propose we request it be used to create a memorial scholarship in Martha Harris's name."

Tom Garrett stood next, his pharmacist's coat still on. "I want to apologize. To all of you. I did things I'm not proud of to keep Tilda quiet. But no more. From now on, transparency. And seniors get a permanent discount at my pharmacy."

One by one, people stood. The Henderson sisters admitted their antique might indeed be a reproduction. Sally Brennan, the nurse practitioner who worked with Dr. Pemberton, announced she'd keep the practice open. "I've been here five years. I know all of you. We'll manage just fine."

Owen Kraft stood, glancing at Millie for permission before speaking. "If Millie agrees, the inn could host a free community dinner next Thursday—to remember that we're neighbors, not enemies."

Millie nodded immediately. "Of course we will. The inn was built to bring people together. It's time we remembered that."

By the time the meeting ended, something had shifted in Ashford Creek. The perfect facade had cracked, but what emerged wasn't ugliness—it was humanity. Flawed, complicated, but ultimately forgiving humanity.

As people filed out into the evening sunshine, Eliza heard snippets of conversation: "Can you believe Tilda was going to run?" "Poor Martha. All these years..." "Maybe we needed this. Maybe we needed the truth." And from Mrs. Henderson to her sister: "You know, I'm almost glad that armoire is fake. The insurance value was giving me ulcers." They laughed— actual, genuine laughter—and Eliza realized that Ashford Creek might actually emerge from this stronger than before.

EPILOGUE

SIX MONTHS LATER

*T*he Teacup Inn was quiet on a Thursday morning, exactly six months after Tilda Crane's death. Eliza sat at her usual table, Bruno dozing at her feet, writing in her notebook. She was documenting everything, not for publication but for clarity—her own need to understand how a town's silence had led to such tragedy.

The legal aftermath had been surprisingly merciful. The district attorney, faced with the complexity of the case and the public revelation of Tilda's crimes, had offered plea deals all around. Charlie received two years probation and community service—teaching cooking classes to underprivileged youth. Dr. Pemberton lost his medical license but avoided jail time due to his age and cooperation. Margaret Caldwell—she'd legally reclaimed her real name—was serving eighteen months in minimum security, with the possibility of early release.

The town had been shocked by the revelations at the emergency meeting. Learning that their social leader had been a murderer, blackmailer, and thief had shaken Ashford Creek to its foundation. But in typical small-town fashion, they were rebuilding, carefully, with more honesty than before.

"Your tea," Millie said, setting down the familiar cup. "And Owen's new lemon scones. He's calling them 'Truth Scones'— completely transparent recipe, no secrets."

Indeed, Owen had posted the recipe in the window for anyone to copy. The secret, it turned out, was not in hidden ingredients but in the technique—something that couldn't be stolen, only learned.

"Sarah?" Eliza asked. "How is she?"

"Thriving, actually. The military review board overturned her case thanks to all the publicity. She's officially cleared and working with Owen in the kitchen. They make a good team." Millie smiled. "She's even started dating Tom Garrett's son— the one who just graduated from UVM. The town really rallied around her once they knew the truth."

Charlie appeared in the doorway, broom in hand. His community service included helping at the inn, and he'd thrown himself into it with dedication. "Ms. Prescott, Bruno's treat?"

Bruno's tail thumped hopefully. Charlie had taken to bringing homemade dog biscuits, his way of making amends to everyone, even the dog who'd helped expose him.

"Thank you, Charlie," Eliza said, watching him carefully give Bruno the treat. "How are you doing?"

"Better," he said simply. "The kids at the community center don't know about... everything. To them, I'm just the guy who teaches them to make cookies. It's nice."

Rebecca arrived for her weekly visit with Charlie, and

Eliza watched mother and son embrace. They were healing, slowly, the kind of healing that comes from truth rather than comfortable lies.

Sheriff Wade entered, looking less exhausted than he had two weeks ago. "Morning, Eliza. Any new mysteries to solve?"

"Just the usual. Mrs. Henderson thinks someone's stealing her garden gnomes."

"Raccoons," Wade said immediately.

"That's what I told her. She wants a full investigation."

They shared a smile—normal problems, small-town concerns. It was refreshing after the intensity of Tilda's murder.

"You know," Wade said, settling into the chair across from her, "the town council wants to create an official position. Part-time investigator, help me with the complex cases. Interested?"

Eliza looked around the inn—at Millie humming as she served customers, at Owen and Sarah laughing in the Kitchen, at Charlie carefully sweeping the entrance. The town had survived its trial by poison. People were choosing honesty over comfortable lies, community over isolation.

"Ask me after I solve the gnome case," she said.

Bruno woofed in agreement, and Wade laughed—the first real laugh she'd heard from him since this all began.

Outside, the sun shone on Main Street, warming the cobblestones and bringing out the spring flowers. The Teacup Inn's windows gleamed, reflecting not the past but the possibility of the future.

In her notebook, Eliza wrote: Case closed. But in a town like Ashford Creek, there's always another secret waiting to surface. The difference now is that the town faces them together, with truth as their witness and tea as their comfort.

She closed the notebook and sipped her tea. It was perfect —no secrets, no poison, just the honest comfort of a well-made cup.

For now, that was enough.

MILLIE HART'S GRANDMOTHER'S LEMON SCONES

The recipe that started it all—finally revealed after 70 years

Makes 8 scones

"The secret was never about hiding ingredients. It was about technique, timing, and putting love into every batch. Grandmother would be happy to know it's finally being shared." —Millie Hart

Ingredients:

- 2 cups all-purpose flour
- 1/3 cup granulated sugar
- 1 tablespoon baking powder
- 1/2 teaspoon salt
- Zest of 2 large lemons
- 6 tablespoons cold unsalted butter, cut into small cubes
- 1/2 cup heavy cream (plus extra for brushing)
- 1 large egg
- 2 tablespoons fresh lemon juice

- 1 teaspoon vanilla extract

For the Signature Glaze:

- 1 cup powdered sugar
- 3 tablespoons fresh lemon juice
- 1 tablespoon heavy cream
- Pinch of salt
- Optional: 1/4 teaspoon almond extract (the safe kind!)

Instructions:

1. **Preheat and Prepare:** Heat your oven to 425°F. Line a baking sheet with parchment paper.
2. **The Secret First Step:** Place your mixing bowl and pastry cutter in the freezer for 10 minutes before starting. Cold tools make all the difference.
3. **Mix Dry Ingredients:** In your chilled bowl, whisk together flour, sugar, baking powder, salt, and lemon zest.
4. **Cut in the Butter:** Add cold butter cubes. Using a pastry cutter or two knives, cut butter into flour until mixture resembles coarse crumbs with some pea-sized pieces. Work quickly—the butter must stay cold.
5. **Combine Wet Ingredients:** In a separate bowl, whisk together cream, egg, lemon juice, and vanilla.
6. **The Gentle Fold:** Make a well in the center of flour mixture. Pour in wet ingredients. Using a fork,

gently stir until dough just comes together. Don't overmix—this is crucial!

7. **Shape with Care:** Turn dough onto lightly floured surface. Gently pat into a circle about 8 inches across and 3/4 inch thick. Cut into 8 wedges.
8. **The Final Touch:** Place wedges on prepared baking sheet, 2 inches apart. Brush tops with cream and sprinkle with a little sugar.
9. **Bake to Perfection:** Bake 15-17 minutes until golden brown on top and bottom.
10. **Glaze While Warm:** Mix all glaze ingredients until smooth. Drizzle over warm scones.

Millie's Tips:

- Never overwork the dough—gentle hands make tender scones
- The dough should be slightly sticky; resist adding too much flour
- For best results, serve within 2 hours of baking
- Store leftovers in airtight container for up to 2 days

OWEN'S TRUTH SCONES

A new recipe for a new beginning—no secrets, just good technique

Makes 8 scones

"After everything that happened, I wanted to create something honest. These scones have no secret ingredients—just good technique and quality materials." —Owen Kraft

Ingredients:

- 2 cups all-purpose flour
- 1/4 cup sugar
- 2 teaspoons baking powder
- 1/2 teaspoon baking soda
- 1/2 teaspoon salt
- 1 stick (8 tablespoons) frozen butter
- 1/2 cup buttermilk
- 1 large egg
- 1 teaspoon vanilla
- Optional mix-ins: chocolate chips, dried cranberries, or fresh blueberries

Instructions:

1. **Heat oven to 400°F.** Line baking sheet with parchment.
2. **Grate the frozen butter** using a box grater—this is Owen's trick for perfect distribution without warming the butter.
3. **Mix flour, sugar, baking powder, baking soda, and salt** in large bowl.
4. **Add grated butter,** tossing with flour mixture to coat.
5. **Whisk buttermilk, egg, and vanilla** in small bowl.
6. **Combine wet and dry** until just mixed. Fold in any mix-ins.
7. **Pat dough** into 8-inch circle on floured surface. Cut into 8 wedges.
8. **Bake 18-20 minutes** until golden.

Owen's Note: "The frozen butter trick came from my army days—we had to get creative with field kitchens. Works every time."

DEATH AT THE SWEET FESTIVAL

PROLOGUE

THE SWEET FESTIVAL ALWAYS PROMISED JOY.

*B*y dawn, Ashford Creek's square already smelled of sugar and spice, the summer air carrying whispers of cinnamon, vanilla, and dark chocolate that would linger in the humid breeze for hours. Tents bloomed across Main Street like bright petals—striped canvas in blues and whites, festooned with strings of lights that wouldn't truly sparkle until dusk. Bakers bustled between their booths, balancing trays of fudge squares cut with mathematical precision, cookies arranged in perfect spirals, and glass jars filled with hand-pulled taffy that caught the morning light like stained glass.

Children pressed sticky noses to display cases, leaving fingerprints their mothers would apologetically wipe away. Old Mr. Keene sat on his usual bench, complaining about the price of hot chocolate while buying three cups. The Ashford Creek High School band warmed up near the gazebo, their practice scales mixing with the fiddle player who'd already started his set, creating a cacophony that somehow felt like home.

But behind the frosting and ribbons, behind the practiced smiles and cheerful greetings, tempers simmered hotter than any candy thermometer could measure.

In the preparation tent, rivalries sharpened like palette knives. Millie Hart from the Teacup Inn measured her chocolate roulade one more time, checking that the raspberry swirl spiraled with architectural precision. Two tables over, Patsy Doyle muttered about "fancy imports" while arranging shortbread that her grandmother's grandmother would have recognized. Young Daisy Langley's hands trembled as she placed orange-scented truffles in neat rows, each one a small prayer for approval.

Secrets slipped between whispered conversations like melted chocolate between fingers. Behind Grady's chocolate shop, a conversation held three nights ago still echoed— threats made, threats dismissed, threats that would soon prove more than idle talk. In the mayor's office, financial ledgers told stories that festival banners tried desperately to hide. And somewhere in a rented room at the Riverside Motel, a small vial marked "Reserve" waited in a toiletry bag, insurance against dangers both real and imagined.

At the center of it all sat the festival's crown jewel, its star attraction, the reason reporters from Boston had made the two-hour drive north—Antoine Duval, the world-renowned chocolatier whose tongue could detect a single grain too much salt, whose reviews could crown careers or crush them like cocoa beans under a grinder.

He arrived at precisely nine o'clock, as advertised. His car —a black Mercedes that looked absurd on Ashcreek's cobblestones—parked in the reserved spot marked with a gold ribbon. Antoine emerged like royalty stepping onto a stage he owned by divine right. The plum-colored jacket had been tailored on Newbury Street. The silk scarf draped with studied casualness. His silver hair combed back with the kind of precision that suggested a man who controlled every variable in his life.

To the gathering crowd, he was charm incarnate. He kissed Mae on both cheeks, making the diner owner giggle like a schoolgirl. He complimented Mrs. Henderson's brooch with such specificity that she nearly fainted. He paused at Tommy Morrison's maple candy booth, sampled a piece, and declared it "rustic perfection" loud enough for the Boston reporter to scribble it down.

But to the competing bakers, he was judgment personified, the Old Testament God of the food world, ready to cast them into outer darkness with a single raised eyebrow. They watched him move through the square, noting what drew his attention, what made him pause, what made his lips purse in that particular way that preceded either praise or damnation.

Jasper Price, who'd spent his children's college funds on imported Belgian chocolate and new copper molds, gripped his sample tray so tight the caramels began to sweat. He'd practiced his pitch seventeen times in the mirror that morning. "Sea salt from the coast of Brittany," he'd say. "Caramel cooked to exactly 244 degrees." He wouldn't mention the second mortgage. He wouldn't mention the creditors. He wouldn't mention that everything—absolutely everything— depended on the next two hours.

In the judging tent, volunteers arranged plates with the reverence of altar boys preparing communion. Each fork polished. Each napkin folded into perfect triangles. The mayor fussed with name cards, adjusting them by millimeters, as if perfect alignment might somehow prevent the disaster he felt building in his bones.

Someone in Ashford Creek already knew exactly what Antoine's verdict would be. They had tasted his criticism before, felt it strip away pride and profit in equal measure. They had watched him destroy with a smile, devastate with a shrug, ruin with words as precisely measured as any recipe. They had tried the proper channels—letters, lawyers, appeals to his humanity that assumed he possessed any.

And so they had prepared their own recipe, one that required no oven, no thermometer, no decades of training in Parisian kitchens. Just steady hands, careful timing, and the kind of bitter determination that comes when sweetness is no longer an option.

The ingredients were already in place. The method had been tested. The presentation would be flawless.

Antoine Duval had come to judge Ashford Creek's festival, to separate the amateur from the artisan, to deliver his verdicts with the authority of a man who had never doubted his own palate. He would taste. He would pronounce. He would smile that thin smile that meant either elevation or execution.

And then, between one breath and the next, between the moment the fork touched his lips and the moment his review would have been recorded, everything would change.

The Sweet Festival had always promised joy. Today, it would deliver death.

The church bells rang ten o'clock. The judging tent opened its flaps like a mouth ready to swallow reputations whole. And somewhere in the crowd, someone checked their watch and smiled.

The recipe was already in motion.

CHAPTER 1

SWEET FESTIVAL

*T*he town square of Ashford Creek smelled like heaven—if heaven were made of sugar, butter, and cocoa, with a dash of cinnamon thrown in by the Almighty for good measure.

Eliza Prescott stood at the corner of Main and Maple, taking in the transformation. The annual Sweet Festival had turned their usually sensible New England town into something from a confectioner's fever dream. Striped tents in candy-bright colors lined both sides of the square. Strings of lanterns bobbed overhead like illuminated pearls, swaying in the warm summer breeze that carried hints of fresh-cut grass from the library's lawn. Each booth spilled over with displays designed to tempt and torment in equal measure: glossy truffles stacked in architectural pyramids, fudge cut into squares so precise they could have been measured with calipers, and towers of cupcakes crowned with buttercream roses that looked too perfect to be edible.

"Don't even think about it," Eliza said, glancing down at Bruno. Her retired police dog had frozen in that particular stance that meant he'd spotted something worth investigating. His nose quivered, pointing toward Mrs. Henderson's booth where a tray of chocolate-dipped bacon sat cooling. His tail began its hopeful wag, the one that said he was absolutely a good boy who deserved treats.

"You're diabetic," Eliza reminded him, though the vet had said no such thing. "And you're on duty."

Bruno gave her the long-suffering look of a professional forced to work with amateurs. He'd been with the Portland PD for eight years before retirement, and he knew perfectly well when he was working versus when he was simply taking a walk. The distinction, in his mind, had everything to do with whether crime was actually afoot and nothing to do with what his human said.

Still, he resumed walking, though not without casting one longing look back at the bacon.

The festival drew everyone. Eliza recognized most of the faces—Ashford Creek wasn't large enough for true strangers —but today they all seemed transformed. Normally sensible adults wore chocolate-smeared grins like children. Tommy Morrison from the hardware store had powdered sugar in his beard. Margaret Bloom, who ran the library with military precision, clutched a candy apple with both hands, working her way around it with methodical bites.

"Eliza!" Mae's voice carried from her diner's outdoor booth. "You have to try my chocolate chess pie. Secret ingredient this year."

Eliza veered over, Bruno padding beside her in the shade. Mae's booth was doing steady business, her grandson Jason manning the register while she cut generous slices.

"Let me guess," Eliza said, accepting a small sample. "Bourbon?"

Mae's eyes sparkled. "How did you—never mind. You and that detective brain of yours."

The pie was silk on Eliza's tongue, the chocolate deep and complex with just enough bourbon to make it interesting without being overwhelming. "It's perfect, Mae."

"Don't let Antoine Duval hear you say that," Mae lowered her voice. "Perfect is a word he reserves for exactly three things in this world, and none of them are in Ashford Creek."

"Ah yes. Antoine Duval."

The festival's special guest judge had been the talk of the town for weeks. Eliza had googled him, of course, partly out of curiosity and partly out of habit—old detectives never really stopped investigating. Antoine Duval, fifty-three, born in Lyon but trained in Paris, relocated to Boston fifteen years ago. Three James Beard nominations. Two cookbook deals. One very expensive chocolate boutique on Newbury Street where a single truffle cost more than Eliza spent on lunch.

He was also, according to the food blogs, notoriously difficult. His reviews could make or break careers. Just last year, he'd written such a scathing review of a Cambridge bakery that they'd closed within six weeks. The words "aggressively mediocre" and "an insult to flour" had been involved.

"Speak of the devil," Mae muttered.

The crowd near the judging tent had thickened, phones coming out like weapons. The tent flap lifted, held by a nervous-looking volunteer, and Antoine Duval stepped into Ashford Creek's humble square as if it were a Parisian runway.

He looked exactly like his photographs, down to the calculated casualness of his appearance. Short and compact, maybe five-foot-seven in dress shoes. The plum-colored jacket was perfectly fitted, nipped at the waist, with working buttonholes that suggested actual tailoring rather than off-the-rack adjustments. His silver hair was swept back from a face that managed to be both handsome and sharp, like a knife decorated with gold leaf. The silk scarf at his throat was tied in something that wasn't quite an ascot but wanted to be when it grew up.

But it was his eyes that held Eliza's attention. Piercing blue, yes, but more than that—they were measuring eyes, calculating eyes, eyes that were already judging everything they saw and finding it wanting.

He moved through the crowd like a shark through a school of fish. A nod here, acknowledging the mayor's greeting without encouraging conversation. A slight smile there, accepting Mrs. Henderson's gushing compliments about his chocolate boutique without actually engaging. When Millie from the Teacup Inn approached, he actually paused, kissing her cheeks in the European style that made half the crowd swoon and the other half roll their eyes.

"Bonjour, madame," he said, his accent exactly French enough to be authentic without being incomprehensible. "The Teacup Inn, yes? I have heard excellent things about your petit fours."

Millie, who was normally as composed as a Victorian governess, actually blushed. "Oh, monsieur, you're too kind."

"I am never kind," Antoine replied with a smile that suggested this was both a joke and not a joke at all. "I am merely accurate."

Bruno pressed against Eliza's leg, a low rumble in his throat that wasn't quite a growl but wasn't friendly either. She touched his head lightly. He had always been an excellent judge of character, even better than she was sometimes. In Portland, he'd once refused to let a seemingly innocent witness pet him; the man had turned out to be running a multi-state fraud ring.

"Quite a show," Eliza murmured.

"That's all it is," said a voice beside her. "Show business."

She turned to find Colin Greer, a reporter she recognized from the Boston food scene. He was younger than she'd expected, maybe thirty, with the kind of carefully disheveled look that suggested he'd spent forty-five minutes making his hair look like he'd just rolled out of bed.

"You're covering this for the Globe?" she asked.

"Freelance," Colin said, pulling out a narrow notebook that had seen better decades. "Though the Globe might pick it up if Antoine does something particularly quotable. He usually does. Last month he called a soufflé 'a cry for help disguised as egg whites.' The quote went viral."

"You sound like a fan," Eliza observed.

Colin's smile was complicated. "I'm a reporter. I go where the story is. And Antoine Duval is always a story." He paused, watching as Antoine examined the judging tent with the intensity of a general surveying a battlefield. "Though between you and me, I think the real story isn't him. It's them."

He nodded toward the line of bakers near the tent, each guarding their entries like mother birds with particularly precious eggs.

Patsy Doyle stood at the front of the line, arms crossed over her flower-print apron that had probably been washed a thousand times but still looked crisp. Her gray hair was pinned back in a bun so tight it looked painful. She'd run Patsy's Pastries for thirty years, and her shortbread was legendary in three counties. But her expression as she watched Antoine suggested she'd rather be feeding him hemlock than cookies.

"He'll pick the fancy nonsense, you'll see," she said to no one in particular, though loud enough for everyone to hear. "Some foam or reduction or whatever they're calling showing off these days. People forget a cookie can stand on its own. Butter, flour, sugar. You don't need a chemistry degree."

"You need talent," Jasper Price said, materializing beside her like expensive cologne looking for a nose to offend. He'd reinvented himself for the festival—gone was his usual uniform of pumpkin-farm flannel and jeans with suspicious stains. Today he wore a vest that wanted desperately to be suave, paired with pants that had actual creases ironed into them. His hair was slicked back with enough product to survive a hurricane.

"I have talent," Patsy snapped. "What I don't have is pretension."

"Pretension," Jasper said, rolling the word around like he was tasting it, "is just another word for ambition, Patsy. Some of us want more than local fame."

He had set up his display with the precision of a museum curator. His sea salt caramels were arranged in a spiral pattern that drew the eye inward, each piece placed exactly one finger-width from its neighbor. The cards beside them didn't just list ingredients—they told stories. "Sel de Guérande, hand-harvested from the coast of Brittany." "Madagascar vanilla beans, aged three years." "Cream from Hendricks Farm's grass-fed Jersey cows."

What the cards didn't mention was that Jasper had mortgaged his future on this festival. Eliza had heard the rumors at Mae's Diner, where all of Ashford Creek's secrets eventually ended up, served alongside coffee and sympathy. The pumpkin farm was struggling. His wife had left six months ago, taking the kids to her mother's in Connecticut. If Antoine's blessing could turn his artisanal chocolate venture into something profitable, maybe he could win them back. If not...

"Did you really use cream from Hendricks Farm?" Daisy Langley asked, her voice soft but skeptical. She stood a little apart from the others, young enough to be Patsy's granddaughter, pretty in the way that made older women want to feed her and older men want to protect her. Her auburn hair was pulled back in a ponytail that made her look even younger than her twenty-three years.

Jasper's smile flickered. "Of course. Would I lie?"

The question hung in the air like burnt sugar.

Daisy turned away, focusing on her own display. Her truffles were arranged simply on white porcelain, no fancy patterns or elaborate cards. But even from a distance, Eliza could see they were beautifully crafted—each one perfectly round, the chocolate shells gleaming with a professional temper that spoke of real skill.

"Orange zest with dark chocolate," Daisy said when she caught Eliza looking. She picked up one truffle with special tongs, offering it. "Seventy percent cacao. I kept the sugar low. Chef Duval prefers bold flavors."

Eliza accepted the truffle, letting it rest on her tongue for a moment before biting down. The shell cracked perfectly, releasing a ganache that was silk and citrus and something darker, almost smoky. It was sophisticated without being pretentious, complex without being complicated.

"It's brave," Eliza said, meaning it.

Daisy's shoulders relaxed slightly. "Brave or stupid. I guess we'll find out."

"He makes everyone nervous," Millie said, joining them. She'd closed the Teacup Inn for the morning to focus on the competition, something she hadn't done in five years. Her chocolate roulade sat on its pristine white platter like a piece of edible architecture—the spiral perfect, the raspberry coulis drizzled with an artist's precision, the fresh raspberries placed like rubies.

"Keep Bruno well back, won't you?" Millie added with a smile that didn't quite hide her anxiety. "We don't need paw prints on ganache."

"Don't worry," Eliza said, patting Bruno's head. "He knows better."

Bruno sat obediently, though his eyes tracked the roulade with the intensity of a detective watching a suspect. His tail thumped once against the ground, stirring up a small cloud of dust that made Patsy sneeze.

"This is ridiculous," Patsy muttered. "We're acting like he's the Pope of Chocolate."

"He might as well be," said Grady from behind them.

Everyone turned. Grady rarely left his chocolate shop during business hours, and he'd never entered the festival competition. He stood at the edge of the group, arms folded, watching Antoine with an expression that could have curdled cream.

"Come to see the show, Grady?" Jasper asked with false cheer.

"Come to see justice," Grady replied cryptically. "One way or another."

Before anyone could ask what he meant, a hush fell over the crowd. Antoine had taken his seat at the judging table. The mayor, Harold Doyle, attempted to approach with what was clearly a prepared speech—Eliza could see the index cards in his sweating hands—but Antoine lifted one finger, just one, and Harold stopped mid-step like he'd hit an invisible wall.

"Merci," Antoine said smoothly. "But the sweets—they will speak for themselves."

He arranged himself in the chair with the precision of someone who knew that photographs were being taken. The plum jacket fell perfectly. The scarf draped just so. His hands—surprisingly delicate for a man, with manicured nails that caught the light—rested on the white tablecloth like they were posing for a portrait.

"We begin," he announced.

The first contestant, Mrs. Burnett from Burnett's Bakehouse, approached with a tray of cranberry-studded tarts. Her hands shook slightly as she set them down. Antoine's eyes swept over the presentation, taking in everything—the way the cranberries were placed, the consistency of the custard, the golden-brown of the crust.

He selected one tart with the kind of care usually reserved for defusing bombs. The crowd held its breath as he lifted it, examined the bottom for proper baking, then took a precise bite. His face revealed nothing as he chewed, swallowed, made a note in his leather-bound notebook.

Mrs. Burnett waited, her smile becoming more fixed with each passing second.

Finally, Antoine nodded. "The cranberry is aggressive. But the custard—the custard whispers. There is conversation here. Not harmony, but conversation."

Relief flooded Mrs. Burnett's face. In Antoine-speak, this was practically praise.

Next came George Whitman's brownies, the tops shiny as mirrors. George ran the local bank and treated baking like he treated loan applications—everything measured to the decimal point, no room for improvisation.

Antoine tapped the brownie top with his fork, listening to the sound it made. "The crust," he said, "it tries too hard. Like a teenager in his father's suit." He tasted, chewed, swallowed. "Overbaked by ninety seconds. The chocolate is good chocolate, but you have made it ashamed of itself. Flavor good. Texture too proud."

George's face went from pink to red to a kind of mottled purple. A ripple of nervous laughter spread through the crowd, cut short by the look on George's face. In any other context, being told your brownies were "too proud" would be absurd. Here, it felt like a professional death sentence.

Daisy's turn came next. She carried her plate of orange-dark chocolate truffles like a sacred offering, hands trembling slightly. Antoine selected one with surgical precision, examining its surface, the temper of the chocolate shell gleaming in the tent's light.

He bit down. The shell cracked audibly. His eyes closed as he tasted, and for a moment, the tent held its breath.

"Orange is bold," he finally said. "Cocoa is shy. But..." He paused, and Daisy looked like she might faint. "Charming. There is conversation here."

Daisy nearly collapsed with relief.

Patsy strutted forward with her shortbread, dropping the plate on the table with deliberate force. "No tricks," she declared. "Just cookies."

Antoine picked one up, turned it over, examining it like an archaeologist with a pottery shard. He bit. Chewed. His expression revealed nothing.

"Solid. Unfashionable." He set the remainder down. "But honest."

Patsy's chin lifted with pride.

Jasper was next, carrying his sea salt caramels like crown jewels. "Sel de Guérande," he said before Antoine even asked. "Hand-harvested. The vanilla—"

"I taste, not listen," Antoine cut him off.

He selected a caramel, bit it in half. His face immediately soured.

"Salt is aggressive. Sugar cowers. They fight instead of dance." He made a note. "Amateur."

Jasper's face went white, then red. He opened his mouth to argue, but Wade stepped forward slightly, and Jasper retreated.

Millie presented her chocolate raspberry roulade last, the spiral perfect, the presentation flawless.

Antoine cut a precise slice, tasted thoughtfully. "Technically competent. Visually appealing. But the raspberries..." He shook his head. "They drown the chocolate's voice. The chocolate should lead, the fruit should follow. Here, they battle for dominance."

Millie accepted the critique with grace, though Eliza saw her hands clench slightly.

"And now," Antoine announced, "the final entry."

A hush fell as he turned to the Blackout Velvet cake. Three layers of darkness, the ganache so glossy it looked wet. It sat on its pedestal like a beautiful threat.

"Whose is this?" Antoine asked.

"Mine," Maeve Nolan said from the back. "Maeve's Bakery on Cedar Street."

Antoine nodded, already cutting. The cake yielded perfectly to the knife, neither too firm nor too soft. He placed a wedge on his plate with the reverence usually reserved for religious artifacts.

"Ambition," he murmured, studying the layers. "Let us see if it is justified."

He lifted his fork, gathered a perfect bite—cake, ganache, all three layers represented. The tent seemed to lean in as he brought it to his mouth.

Antoine chewed slowly, deliberately. His eyes widened slightly. He took a second bite, larger this time.

"Enfin," he said softly. "Finally. Someone who understands that chocolate is not about sweetness. It is about truth. This cake tells the truth about cocoa, about butter, about—"

He paused, setting down his fork to make a note in his leather notebook. "This deserves proper consideration. I shall return to it." He stood, addressing the crowd. "Ladies and gentlemen, I need a few moments to cleanse my palate and consider my final judgments. Please, enjoy the festival. I shall return shortly."

He walked toward the tent's side entrance, his gait perhaps slightly unsteady—too much rich chocolate, Eliza thought. The crowd began to disperse, chattering excitedly about his reactions to their entries.

"Well," Mae said, "that was certainly dramatic."

"He's always dramatic," Patsy muttered. "Makes a show of everything."

Eliza was about to agree when they heard it—a crash from behind the tent, followed by someone screaming.

"Help! Someone help! There's something wrong with—oh God!"

The voice was young, terrified. Daisy's voice.

Eliza and Wade moved simultaneously, Bruno right beside them. They rounded the tent to find Daisy standing frozen, one hand over her mouth, pointing at the ground near the portable restrooms.

Antoine Duval lay crumpled on the grass, his body twisted unnaturally. His face was turned toward them, eyes wide and staring at nothing. Foam had dried at the corners of his mouth.

"Don't touch him," Eliza said sharply as Wade moved forward. But even from a distance, she could see the truth. The blue tinge to his lips. The stillness that was more than unconsciousness.

Wade knelt anyway, checking for a pulse with professional efficiency. After a moment, he looked up and shook his head.

"He's dead," Wade said quietly. Then louder, his sheriff voice taking over: "Everyone back. This is a crime scene."

CHAPTER 2

BITTER AFTERTASTE

"*N*obody moves," Wade said again, louder this time. "Nobody leaves this tent."

The festival crowd had become a crime scene audience in the span of thirty seconds. Some people were crying. Others stood frozen, unable to look away from Antoine's body. A few were already trying to edge toward the tent exits, only to find Deputy Tyler Lang blocking their way.

Eliza stayed crouched beside Antoine, not touching him but cataloging everything she could see. The foam at his mouth. The distinctive blue tinge to his lips. That bitter almond smell that anyone who'd worked homicide would recognize—cyanide.

Wade was beside her now, having finished his call. "Poison?"

"Cyanide," she said quietly. "In the cake, most likely. Maybe his fork."

"You're sure?"

"The smell. The symptoms. The speed." She stood, knees protesting slightly. "This was murder, Wade."

He nodded grimly, then turned to address the tent. "Everyone who touched food, served food, or was near the judging table—I need you to stay. Everyone else, Deputy Lang will take your names and contact information before you leave."

"You can't keep us here!" Jasper protested, his face still flushed from Antoine's harsh critique. "We have rights!"

"You have the right to be questioned as witnesses to a potential homicide," Wade said evenly. "Or I can arrest you for obstruction. Your choice."

Jasper shut up.

"Everyone stays where they are," Wade said, his voice carrying across the sudden silence. "Nobody leaves this tent until I say so."

The crowd that had been pressing forward now pressed back, as if death might be contagious. Someone—it sounded like young Daisy—let out a hiccupping sob in the summer heat. Patsy Doyle stood frozen with both hands pressed to her mouth, her earlier complaints about fancy chocolate forgotten. Jasper Price had gone pale beneath his careful tan, his hand gripping the edge of the display table hard enough to leave marks.

"Harold," Wade said to Mayor Doyle, who stood blinking like a man who'd walked into bright light. "Call Doc Brennan. Tell him to come quick and quiet. No sirens."

The mayor fumbled for his phone, nearly dropping it twice before managing to dial.

Wade turned to Deputy Lang, who'd materialized at his elbow looking green around the edges. "Tyler, I need you to close the festival. Now. Tell people there's been a medical emergency. Keep it calm, but clear everyone out except essential personnel."

"Yes, sir," Tyler managed, though his voice cracked on the 'sir.'

Millie stepped forward, ever practical even in crisis. "We should cover the cake, Sheriff. Preserve it."

Wade nodded. "Good thinking. But don't touch it directly. Use tongs or—"

"I have serving gloves," Millie said, producing a pair from her apron pocket. She found a clear glass dome on the supplies table and carefully lowered it over the Blackout Velvet cake. The glossy ganache looked almost innocent under glass, like something in a museum display. Beautiful. Deadly.

Eliza stepped closer, Bruno tight at her side. The dog's hackles were raised, his nose working overtime. She studied the scene with eyes that hadn't forgotten how to catalog evidence, even after two years of selling books instead of solving crimes.

"Wade," she said quietly, "look at his plate."

Antoine's final slice of cake sat partially eaten, a fork still resting beside it. The portion was smaller than the others on the judging table—not by much, but enough to notice if you were looking. The knife beside the main cake platter was clean, meticulously so, but there was a smear of darker chocolate on Antoine's fork.

Wade followed her gaze. "You think his portion specifically was poisoned."

"It's too neat," Eliza said. "The rest of the cake looks untouched. Either someone doctored just his slice, or..."

"Or they poisoned his fork," Wade finished. "Targeted. Personal."

Bruno sneezed suddenly, violent enough to shake his whole body. Then again. His eyes watered as he pawed at his nose.

"Easy, boy," Eliza soothed, but she'd caught it too—that bitter almond smell, faint but unmistakable. Cyanide. She'd encountered it twice before—once in Portland years ago, and more recently with Tilda Crane's death right here in Ashford Creek. The memory of finding Tilda at the Teacup Inn was still fresh, barely months old.

"Everyone needs to step back from the table," she said, louder. "Now."

Wade reinforced the order with a gesture. The bakers shuffled backward, some more reluctantly than others. Jasper actually took three steps forward before catching himself.

"I need to see—" he started.

"You need to stand exactly where I tell you," Wade cut him off. "This is a crime scene."

"Crime scene?" George Whitman's voice went up an octave. "It could be an allergy. Or a heart attack. The man was over fifty, high-stress job—"

"Mr. Whitman," Wade said with the kind of patience that wasn't patient at all, "I need you to be quiet now."

Eliza noticed Colin Greer hadn't moved from his position near the tent wall. The reporter's notebook was out, his pen moving across the page in rapid shorthand. His eyes weren't on his notes though—they tracked every movement, every reaction, filing it all away. When he caught Eliza watching, he gave a small shrug as if to say, 'This is what I do.'

"I need everyone's name," Wade announced, pulling out his own notebook. "Full names, what you made, when you set it on the table, and whether you saw anyone else touch anything." He pointed at Patsy. "You first."

Patsy straightened her spine like she was facing a firing squad. "Patsy Anne Doyle. I made shortbread—traditional shortbread, nothing fancy. I brought my tray in right when the ten o'clock bell rang because that's what the rules said. I set it on the left side of the table because that's where Harold —" she shot the mayor a look, "—told me to put it. I didn't touch anything else. I don't do tricks."

Wade wrote steadily. "Did you see anyone else handle your tray or any other entries?"

"No." Patsy hesitated, then added, "Well, Harold fussed with the name cards. Straightened them about six times. And that reporter took pictures of everything."

Colin raised his hand slightly. "Guilty as charged on the photos. But I never touched the food. You don't mess with the subject before you shoot it."

"We'll get to you," Wade said. "Mr. Price, you're next."

Jasper rolled his shoulders, trying to recapture his earlier swagger and failing. "Jasper Price. Sea salt caramels with Madagascar vanilla. I set them down at 10:03—I checked my watch because timing matters with candy. I placed them center-right, optimal lighting position." He paused, seemed to realize how that sounded, and added, "I didn't see anyone tamper with anything."

"Did you interact with Mr. Duval before the judging?"

Something flickered across Jasper's face. "We all did. He made his grand entrance, walked around like he owned the place."

"That's not what I asked."

Jasper's jaw worked. "He stopped at my farm's booth yesterday. Looked at my setup. Said something about 'ambitious amateurs' and walked away laughing."

Wade made another note. "Miss Langley?"

Daisy had been crying quietly, tears tracking through her light makeup. "Daisy Marie Langley. Orange-dark chocolate truffles. I came early—maybe 9:45? I always come early when I'm nervous. I set my tray down and then stood by it until judging started." She swallowed hard. "I didn't mean to break the rules, I just couldn't leave them alone."

"That's not breaking rules," Wade said, gentler now. "Did Mr. Duval speak to you?"

Daisy's face flushed red. She opened her mouth, closed it, then whispered, "Yes."

Everyone turned to look at her.

"What did he say?" Wade asked.

"He..." Daisy wrapped her arms around herself. "When he was walking around before judging, he stopped at my station. Leaned in close. Said I looked 'sweet enough to eat' and asked if I was entering myself in the competition too." Her voice dropped even lower. "He put his hand on my lower back. I stepped away and told him to stop. He laughed. Said I was 'adorably provincial.'"

Patsy made a disgusted sound. "Dirty old—"

"Mrs. Doyle," Wade warned.

Millie moved to Daisy's side, putting an arm around the younger woman's shoulders. "Why didn't you say anything?"

"To who?" Daisy asked miserably. "He's Antoine Duval. I'm nobody. Who would have believed me? Or cared?"

An uncomfortable silence settled over the tent. Even Colin had stopped writing.

Wade cleared his throat. "Mrs. Hart?"

Millie kept her arm around Daisy as she answered. "Millicent Hart. I made a chocolate raspberry roulade. I placed it at exactly ten o'clock—the church bells were ringing. I set it on the right end of the table, away from the tent opening to avoid any dust or wind. I saw the mayor adjust cards, and Mr. Greer take photos, but nothing else unusual."

"What about the Blackout Velvet cake?" Wade asked. "Who placed that?"

For a moment, no one spoke. Then a voice from the back of the tent said, "That was mine."

Everyone turned. Maeve Nolan stood near the supply table, her red hair pulled back in a baker's bun, her face pale but composed. She'd been so quiet that Eliza had almost forgotten she was there.

"I didn't know we were supposed to stay after placing our entries," Maeve said. "I set the cake down and went back to my shop. I only came back when it was time for the judging."

Wade studied her. "What time did you place the cake?"

"Ten-fifteen, maybe? I wanted to wait until most of the crowd was watching the other judging. The cake needed to be cool, and I didn't want people breathing on it."

"And during the judging?"

"I saw him taste it," Maeve said, voice shaking. "He praised it. Said it told the truth about chocolate. Then he left to cleanse his palate, and I..." She swallowed hard. "I went outside for air. I was so nervous, I felt sick. I was behind the tent when I heard Daisy scream."

"Did you see anyone near your cake after Antoine tasted it?"

"No, I left right after he did. The judging seemed to be on break." She paused. "It was perfect when I presented it. Three layers, each one level, the ganache at exactly the right temperature. I tested it myself this morning."

"You tasted it?" Wade asked sharply.

"A crumb from the trimming. Bakers always taste." Maeve's chin lifted. "And I'm still standing, aren't I?"

Wade made more notes. "I'll need a list of everyone who had access to the tent before and during setup."

Harold, the mayor, had finished his call and now looked like he wanted to sink into the ground. "That would be... extensive. We had volunteers setting up tables, bringing in supplies. The tent's been open since seven this morning."

"Then you'd better start making that list," Wade said.

Eliza had been studying the table while the others talked. Besides Antoine's plate and fork, there were five other forks set at precise intervals, all clean. But at the far end, partially hidden behind a water pitcher, was one fork set slightly apart from the others. Also clean, but wrong somehow—the angle, the placement, as if someone had put it there in a hurry.

She caught Wade's eye and nodded toward it. He followed her gaze and made another note.

"What about before?" Grady's voice came from the tent entrance. He stood just outside the tape line, arms crossed. "You're all focused on this morning, but what about last night? Who had access to the supplies then?"

"Mr. Norton," Wade said, "I'm going to need you to—"

"Antoine came to my shop," Grady interrupted. "Yesterday evening. After dinner. Wanted to buy chocolate for comparison, he said. To 'calibrate his palate' before judging locals." Grady's laugh was bitter as his darkest cocoa. "He insulted everything. Said my tempering was amateur, my flavors pedestrian. Then he recognized my last name."

The tent went very still.

"My brother had a shop in Boston," Grady continued. "Five years ago. Small place, but he made beautiful chocolates. Antoine reviewed it. One paragraph in the Globe, maybe two hundred words. Called it 'aggressively mediocre' and 'an embarrassment to cocoa.' My brother closed within a month. Lost his house. His wife left him." Grady's hands clenched.

"He works at a gas station now. Won't even eat chocolate anymore."

Wade had stopped writing. "Mr. Norton, I'm going to need you to come to the station."

"I didn't kill him," Grady said flatly. "Though God knows I thought about it. But I'm not stupid enough to poison a man at a public festival. Besides," he turned to leave, "looks like someone else got there first."

He walked away, leaving silence in his wake.

Bruno had been sniffing steadily along the base of the table, his training keeping him focused despite the chaos. Suddenly he stopped, his whole body going rigid. He pawed at something under the table, whining urgently.

Eliza crouched beside him. There, caught against the table leg, was a wrapper. Small, gold foil, the kind expensive chocolates came in. But this one had a smear of something white on the inside, barely visible.

"Wade," she called softly.

He joined her, saw what Bruno had found, and carefully picked it up with a pair of tweezers from the supply table. The residue on the wrapper had that same bitter almond smell, stronger now.

"Good boy," Eliza murmured to Bruno, who wagged his tail once but kept his attention on the wrapper.

Wade sealed it in an evidence bag he'd produced from his pocket—old habits from his state police days. "This changes things."

Doc Brennan arrived then, medical bag in hand, face grim. As the county medical examiner, he covered suspicious deaths for all the small towns that couldn't afford their own. He was pushing seventy but moved like a man half his age. He took one look at Antoine's body, knelt beside it, and began his examination.

"Everyone out," Wade ordered. "Except you, Eliza. I might need you."

"I'm not a cop anymore," she reminded him.

"No," Wade agreed, "but Bruno is still a cop at heart, and he just found our first real piece of evidence."

As the tent emptied, Eliza heard the voices rising outside—confusion, fear, anger, all mixing in the humid summer air. The Sweet Festival was over, but something darker had just begun.

She looked at the cake under its glass dome, beautiful and deadly, and wondered who in their small town had decided that Antoine Duval's last review would be written in poison.

CHAPTER 3

SECRETS & SUSPECTS

*a*shford Creek woke the next morning like someone nursing a hangover—slow, reluctant, and deeply regretful about the night before.

The festival tents still stood in the square, but they looked wrong now, like party decorations the morning after, when all the magic had worn off. A few volunteers moved between them, packing up what could be salvaged, but their hearts weren't in it. The crime scene tape across the judging tent fluttered in the morning breeze like a flag of surrender.

Eliza stood at her kitchen window, watching the sun paint the maples gold while her coffee cooled in her hands. She'd slept badly, her dreams full of chocolate and bitter almonds, of Antoine's surprised face and Grady's bitter laugh. Bruno lay at her feet, having refused his usual spot by the fireplace in favor of staying close to her.

"Some guard dog you are," she said softly. "You're supposed to make me feel safe, not worried."

Bruno lifted his head and gave her a look that suggested he knew exactly what his job was, thank you very much, and protecting her from her own thoughts was definitely part of it.

Her phone buzzed. Wade.

"You up?" his text read.

"Unfortunately," she typed back.

"Diner. Twenty minutes. Bring your detective brain."

"I'm retired," she sent, though they both knew that was a fiction she told herself when things got too heavy.

"Tell that to Bruno."

She looked down at her partner, who was already standing by the door, tail wagging slightly. He knew the routine—when Wade called this early, it meant work.

"Alright," she said, grabbing his leash. "But we're getting extra bacon."

Bruno's tail wagging intensified.

Mae's Diner was busier than usual for a Sunday morning. The after-church crowd wouldn't arrive for another hour, but the gossip crowd was already in full swing. Every booth was occupied, coffee cups clinked like telegraph keys, and conversations created a low hum that stopped the moment Eliza walked in.

Everyone stared. Then, as if someone had flipped a switch, they all looked away and resumed talking, though the volume had dropped to whispers.

"Like walking into a saloon in an old Western," Eliza muttered.

She found Wade in the back corner booth, the one with a view of both doors—cop habit that never died. He had his notebook out, a cup of coffee that looked like tar, and the expression of a man who'd been up all night.

"You look terrible," she said, sliding in across from him.

"Charming as always." He signaled Mae for another cup.

"Autopsy's scheduled for this afternoon, but Doc Brennan confirmed what we suspected. Cyanide. Enough to kill him in minutes."

Mae appeared with coffee for Eliza and a knowing look. "The usual?"

"And extra bacon for Bruno," Eliza said.

Mae glanced at the dog, who'd settled under the table with professional dignity. "He's the only one in this town I trust completely," she said, then louder, for the benefit of the eavesdroppers, "Shame what happened yesterday. Bad for business, all this talk."

She bustled away, but not before shooting a meaningful look at the occupied booths.

Wade leaned forward, lowering his voice. "The wrapper Bruno found tested positive for cyanide residue. Lab says it's consistent with potassium cyanide, probably dissolved in water and brushed onto something."

"The fork," Eliza said. "Or the cake itself."

"That's the question." Wade flipped through his notebook. "Here's what we know: Antoine was targeted specifically. Only his portion was poisoned. The killer knew about his judging routine, knew which seat he'd take, possibly knew which fork he'd use."

"Someone familiar with the festival," Eliza said. "Or someone who did their homework."

"Or both." Wade pulled out a folded paper. "The mayor gave me the list of everyone with tent access yesterday morning."

Eliza unfolded it. Twenty-three names, including all the competitors, the mayor, various volunteers, Colin Greer, and half the town council.

"Might as well list the whole phone book," she said.

"Gets better. The tent was unlocked overnight. Anyone could have gone in."

Bruno's head suddenly appeared above the table edge, nose twitching. Mae had arrived with their breakfast and, true to her word, a small plate of extra bacon.

"Don't feed him under the table," Mae said loudly, then winked and set the bacon within easy reach.

As they ate, Eliza noticed the conversations around them. Fragments drifted over:

"—told you bringing in outsiders would cause trouble—"

"—Antoine had it coming, the way he treated—"

"—poor Maeve, her cake was beautiful—"

"—Grady's been bitter for years about his brother—"

"—did you see how Jasper was sweating?—"

"—that sweet Daisy wouldn't hurt a fly—"

Wade noticed her listening. "The town's already running its own investigation."

"They always do." Eliza fed Bruno a piece of bacon, ignoring her own advice about table feeding. "What about Antoine's hotel room?"

"Riverside Motel, room twelve. I sealed it last night, but haven't searched yet." He hesitated. "Want to tag along? Unofficially?"

"I'm a bookseller, remember?"

"Who used to be Portland PD's best detective. And whose dog found our only physical evidence."

Bruno, hearing 'dog' and 'evidence' in the same sentence, sat up straighter.

Eliza sighed. "Fine. But this doesn't mean I'm back. I'm just... consulting."

Wade's smile was grim. "Whatever helps you sleep at night."

The Riverside Motel sat on the edge of town, twelve rooms in a row like teeth in a comb. It had seen better decades, but Margaret Holcomb kept it clean and didn't ask questions, which made it perfect for tourists who couldn't afford the Teacup Inn and locals who needed a room for reasons they'd rather not discuss.

Margaret met them at the office, her face pinched with worry. "This is terrible for business, Sheriff. First a dead guest, now police tape. People will think I run a murder motel."

"Nobody thinks that, Margaret," Wade said, though Eliza could already imagine the Yelp reviews.

Room twelve was at the end, segregated from its neighbors by a broken ice machine and a struggling potted plant. Wade cut the tape and unlocked the door with Margaret's key.

The room was surprisingly neat. The bed was made with military precision, though not by Margaret's housekeeping— the corners were different from her style. Antoine's suitcase stood on the luggage rack, closed but not locked. A laptop sat on the small desk beside a leather journal and an expensive fountain pen.

"Organized," Wade observed.

"Controlled," Eliza corrected. "Everything exactly where he wanted it."

Bruno began his own investigation, nose to the carpet, following invisible trails. He paused at the nightstand, whined softly, then moved to the bathroom.

Eliza pulled on gloves and opened the journal. Antoine's handwriting was as precise as his appearance—neat, slanted, consistent. The recent entries were about the festival:

July 13th - Arrived in Ashford Creek. Quaint in that desperate way small towns have. The Teacup Inn adequate, though their wine list is abysmal. The chocolate shop—Norton's—particularly disappointing. The owner recognized me. Still angry about Marcus. Not my fault his brother couldn't take criticism.

July 14th - Morning. Visited several establishments. The local bakeries are what you'd expect—competent mediocrity with delusions of grandeur. One girl, Langley, shows promise but lacks confidence. Price is all flash, no substance. His desperation is palpable. Doyle makes cookies like it's still 1952.

The mayor is hiding something. Mayor Harold Doyle is hiding financial irregularities? Small-town corruption is so predictable.

That reporter, Greer, keeps fishing for quotes. Might be useful.

Must remember to test the samples before judging. Can't be too careful.

Eliza looked up sharply. "Wade, look at this last line."

Wade read it, frowning. "He was worried about being poisoned?"

"Or allergic reactions. But it suggests caution." She kept reading.

July 14th - Evening. Unpleasant encounter with G. Norton. Threatened me, essentially. 'You destroyed my brother.' As if Marcus Norton's mediocrity was my responsibility. I simply reported what anyone with a palate could taste.

Received another letter. Same as Boston. They're getting creative with their threats now. This one included a recipe for 'revenge, best served cold.' Juvenile but unsettling. Kept it as evidence.

"Another letter?" Wade started searching the room. He found it in the laptop case—a folded paper with words cut from magazines, ransom-note style:

YOU RUINED LIVES. NOW SOMEONE RUINS YOURS. SWEET DREAMS, CHEF.

Below the words was a recipe, handwritten:

- 1 cup of pride
- 2 tablespoons of cruelty
- A dash of cyanide
- Mix well. Serve cold.

"Jesus," Wade muttered.

Bruno had emerged from the bathroom carrying something in his mouth—trained to retrieve without damaging evidence. He deposited a small glass vial at Eliza's feet. The label read "Reserve" in Antoine's handwriting.

"He brought his own evidence kit," Eliza said, examining the vial. "He was collecting evidence of threats against him."

"He was investigating his own death threats," Wade said. "That's why he came here. Not just to judge."

"Or someone wanted him here," Eliza suggested. "Someone local who couldn't get to him in Boston."

They spent another hour searching. Found three more threatening letters, all different styles but similar themes. A printout of Antoine's recent reviews, several circled in red. A list of names in his journal—people he'd given bad reviews. Grady's brother Marcus was on it, circled twice.

But it was Bruno who found the most interesting thing. He'd been pawing at the heating vent, whining insistently. Wade unscrewed the grate and pulled out a small paper bag.

Inside were chocolates. Three of them, gold-dusted and perfect. When Wade carefully sniffed them— "Almonds," he said.

"Not just almonds," Eliza said. "Bitter almonds."

They'd been planted. Recently, judging by the dust disturbance.

"Someone's been in here since his death," Wade said. "Since I sealed it."

"Someone with a key," Eliza said, looking meaningfully at the door. No signs of forced entry.

"Margaret wouldn't—"

"Not Margaret. But she's not the only one with access to keys."

Bruno was staring at the door now, a low growl building in his throat. Footsteps in the hallway, trying to be quiet.

Wade put his hand on his service weapon. "Stay here."

He yanked the door open. Colin Greer stood frozen, hand raised to knock, camera around his neck.

"Sheriff!" Colin's voice went up an octave. "I was just—"

"Breaking into a crime scene?"

"The door was open!" Colin protested. "I saw your car, thought I'd check if you had a statement."

"Try again," Wade said.

Colin's shoulders sagged. "Okay, look. Antoine had something of mine. A memory card. From my camera. He... borrowed it yesterday. Said he wanted to review the photos from the festival setup and the vendors preparing."

"What was on it?" Eliza asked.

Colin flushed. "Pictures. Of the festival. And... some other things."

"What other things?"

"Private things. Look, I do freelance work. Sometimes that includes... surveillance. Divorce cases, insurance fraud. Antoine saw me taking pictures and threatened to expose me unless I gave him the card."

"So you came to steal it back," Wade said.

"I came to retrieve my property," Colin corrected. "I didn't kill him, if that's what you're thinking. He was my meal ticket. Drama sells papers."

Wade cuffed him anyway. "You can explain at the station."

As they led Colin away, Eliza noticed something. His shoes —expensive sneakers that didn't match his rumpled suit—had a distinctive tread pattern with triangles and circles. She filed that detail away, her detective instincts automatically cataloging it.

Back at the station, Wade put Colin in the interview room while Eliza waited in Wade's office. Through the window, she could see Main Street slowly coming to life. The church bells rang noon. Normal Sunday activities, except for the crime scene tape visible in the square.

Bruno lay at her feet, apparently asleep but Eliza knew better. His ears twitched at every sound.

Wade returned looking frustrated. "Colin's story checks out, mostly. He was taking pictures of Jasper meeting with someone from the bank. Jasper's wife hired him, wants evidence for the divorce."

"That's why Jasper was so nervous," Eliza said. "He knew he was being watched."

"Colin says Antoine saw him, figured out what he was doing, and blackmailed him for the photos. Wanted dirt on locals for his article."

"Charming man, our victim."

"Getting less sympathetic by the hour," Wade agreed. "But murder's still murder."

Eliza stood, stretching. "I need to check on the bookstore. But Wade—whoever did this isn't done."

"What makes you say that?"

She gestured to the evidence bags on his desk. "The chocolates at the motel. Someone planted them there after his death. They're still playing. They killed Antoine, but they're not satisfied. There's another shoe waiting to drop."

Wade's jaw tightened. "Whoever did this is still out there. And they're getting bolder, planting evidence after the fact."

"I'll be careful," Eliza said. "Bruno and I both will."

Bruno's tail thumped once in agreement.

As they left the station, Eliza noticed Grady's chocolate shop across the street. Still closed, but she could see movement behind the blinds. She made a mental note to visit later.

"Hey," Wade called after her. "Eliza. Be careful."

She looked back. "When am I not?"

His expression suggested he had a list, but he just waved her off.

As she and Bruno walked home, Eliza couldn't shake the feeling they were being watched. She glanced back once and caught a glimpse of red hair disappearing around a corner. Maeve? Or just paranoia?

Bruno pressed closer to her leg, alert and ready.

The afternoon sun was warm, but Eliza felt cold. Someone in Ashford Creek was a killer. Someone she probably knew, someone she'd smiled at in the street or chatted with at the market.

And they weren't finished yet.

Sunday evening, after dinner, Eliza took Bruno for his last walk of the day. The summer heat had finally broken, leaving the air comfortable for walking. They followed their usual route along the waterfront, where the old pier stretched into the harbor.

Bruno suddenly veered off the path, nose to the ground, following some invisible trail. He led her to a bench near the pier's entrance, then sat—his official alert signal from his police days.

"What did you find, boy?"

Under the bench, half-hidden by a crumpled festival flyer, was a small glass vial. Using a tissue, Eliza picked it up carefully. The label read "Reserve" in what looked like Antoine's precise handwriting.

Her pulse quickened. Antoine had been collecting evidence—this must be part of it. Someone had either dropped it while fleeing, or hidden it here deliberately.

She wrapped the vial carefully in the tissue and pocketed it. First thing tomorrow, she'd take it to Wade.

"Good boy," she told Bruno, who wagged his tail once, professionally satisfied.

As they walked home, Eliza couldn't shake the feeling that this vial was important—another piece of the puzzle that was Antoine Duval's death

CHAPTER 4

THE CHOCOLATE SHOP

*T*he vial felt heavier than glass in Eliza's coat pocket as she walked toward the sheriff's station on a humid Monday morning. Bruno trotted beside her, alert to every movement on Main Street. The town was trying to return to normal—shops opening, people heading to work—but there was a brittleness to it all, like ice over deep water.

Wade Barrett's desk was covered with evidence bags, photographs, and enough coffee cups to suggest he'd been there all night. Again. He looked up when she entered, and she could see the frustration written in the lines around his eyes.

"The lab confirmed it," he said without preamble. "The vial from Antoine's room contained traces of potassium cyanide. Same as what killed him."

"About that." Eliza pulled the tissue-wrapped vial from her pocket. "Bruno found something last night."

Wade's eyebrows rose as she carefully unwrapped the vial marked "Reserve" and set it on his desk.

"Where?"

"Under a bench near the pier. Bruno alerted on it during

our evening walk." She pointed to the handwriting. "That looks like Antoine's writing, same as the vial from his room."

Wade leaned forward, studying it without touching it. "You think he was collecting evidence?"

"He was getting threatening letters. He knew someone wanted him dead. Makes sense he'd try to gather proof."

"Fat lot of good it did him." Wade rubbed his face. "The state police want to take over."

"Of course they do." Eliza sat down, Bruno settling at her feet. "High-profile victim, small-town department. They smell headlines."

"I've got forty-eight hours to show progress before they sweep in." Wade's jaw tightened. "I didn't leave Boston to deal with Boston again."

Eliza understood. Wade had been state police himself once, before something—he'd never said what—sent him looking for a quieter life in Ashford Creek. Just like she'd left Portland after the Brennan case went sideways, after a child died because she'd trusted the wrong witness.

"Then we'd better solve it fast," she said. "What about the chocolates from Antoine's room?"

"Professional quality, no maker's mark. Could have come from any high-end shop between here and Boston."

"Or from someone who knows how to make them." Eliza stood. "I want to talk to Grady again."

Wade checked his watch. "His shop's been closed since Saturday."

"His shop is closed," Eliza corrected. "Doesn't mean he's not there."

Norton's Chocolates sat on Cedar Street like a gothic remnant from Ashford Creek's more prosperous past. The building had been a pharmacy in the 1920s, and still had the original tin ceiling and marble counter. Grady had bought it fifteen years ago with his brother's help, back when they'd dreamed of building a chocolate empire together.

Now the CLOSED sign hung crooked, and dust had already started to gather on the window display.

But Eliza could smell chocolate. Fresh chocolate.

She knocked. No answer. Knocked again, harder.

"Grady, I know you're in there. It's Eliza Prescott."

A long pause, then footsteps. The lock turned with a sound like bones breaking.

Grady Norton looked like he'd aged five years in two days. His gray hair stood at angles, his apron was stained with what looked like caramel, and his hands had a tremor that hadn't been there before.

"We're closed," he said flatly.

"You're working," Eliza observed. "I can smell the chocolate."

Something flickered in his eyes—pride, maybe, or just habit. "Chocolate doesn't care if there's been a murder. Temperature still matters. Timing still matters."

"Can we come in?"

Grady's gaze dropped to Bruno, who was sitting perfectly still, watching him with those intelligent brown eyes.

"The dog too?"

"The dog especially," Eliza said. "He's good at finding things."

Grady stepped back, letting them enter.

The shop was dimmer than usual, only the work lights on in the back. The display cases were empty, but Eliza could see through to the kitchen where chocolate molds lined the counter and a double boiler steamed gently on the stove.

"I'm making Marcus's favorites," Grady said, noticing her

looking. "Hazelnut pralines. He invented the recipe when he was seventeen. Won a junior chef competition." His voice went bitter. "Before Antoine Duval destroyed him."

"Tell me about that," Eliza said, settling onto one of the stools at the counter. Bruno remained standing, nose working.

Grady laughed, sharp and hurt. "What's to tell? Marcus had a shop in Boston's North End. Small, but perfect. Every chocolate made by hand. He used our grandmother's recipes, updated them, made them art." His hands moved as he talked, muscle memory of shaping truffles. "Then Antoine came. Ordered one of everything. Sat at Marcus's only table, made notes. Marcus was thrilled—the great Antoine Duval in his shop."

He turned to the stove, stirring the chocolate with violent precision.

"The review came out two weeks later. 'Aggressively mediocre.' That's what he called my brother's life work. Said the chocolate was 'technically competent but spiritually vacant.' Said Marcus was 'playing at being a chocolatier the way children play house.'"

The spoon clattered against the pot.

"Marcus had investors lined up. They all pulled out after the review. The bank called his loan. His wife—she'd been unhappy anyway—used it as an excuse to leave. Took the kids to California." Grady's shoulders sagged. "He tried to keep going. Cut prices, extended hours. But in a city like Boston, one bad review from Antoine Duval is a death sentence."

"Where is Marcus now?" Eliza asked gently.

"Works at a gas station in Medford. Won't even eat chocolate anymore. Says it tastes like failure."

Bruno had moved toward the back of the kitchen, sniffing

intently at a cabinet. He pawed at it once, then looked back at Eliza.

"What's in there?" she asked.

Grady's face went tight. "Supplies."

"Can I see?"

"You need a warrant for that."

"I'm not a cop, Grady. I'm just someone trying to understand what happened."

They stared at each other for a long moment. Then Grady crossed to the cabinet and yanked it open.

Inside were bottles, jars, extracts. And on the middle shelf, partially hidden behind vanilla bottles, was a tin labeled in French: Essence d'Amande Amère.

Bitter almond essence.

"It's for marzipan," Grady said quickly. "Traditional German Christmas cookies. I make them every year."

"It's July," Eliza pointed out. "Christmas is five months away."

"I practice early."

Bruno sneezed, backing away from the cabinet. The bitter almond smell was strong, even with the tin closed.

"This could mimic cyanide poisoning," Eliza said carefully.

"Could," Grady agreed. "But didn't. I may have hated Antoine, but I'm not stupid. You think I'd poison him with something that leads straight back to my shop?"

It was a good point. Too good, maybe.

"Someone wanted us to think you did it," Eliza said. "The wrapper Bruno found at the festival had almond residue. Who else knows you keep this?"

Grady shrugged. "Anyone who's been in my kitchen. Other bakers borrow supplies sometimes. Jasper was here last week, wanting vanilla. Patsy borrowed cocoa powder for her grandson's birthday cake. Even that reporter was snooping around, asking about 'authentic techniques.'"

"When was Colin here?"

"Thursday. Day before the festival. Said he was writing a piece about traditional candy making. Asked a lot of questions about tempering, about flavoring." Grady's eyes narrowed. "Asked specifically about almond extract, now that I think about it."

Eliza filed that away. Colin was looking more interesting by the hour.

Bruno had moved to another corner of the kitchen, where a trash bin sat partially hidden behind a cart. He nosed at it insistently.

"When did you last empty this?" Eliza asked.

"Saturday morning, before..." Grady trailed off.

She pulled on the gloves she'd started carrying since Saturday and carefully lifted the bin's lid. On top of the usual kitchen waste was a crumpled paper bag with dark stains. She lifted it out carefully.

Inside were chocolate shavings, fine and glossy, but dusted with a white powder that made Bruno sneeze again.

"That's not mine," Grady said immediately. "I don't—that's not how I work."

"Someone put this in your trash," Eliza said. "Recently. Since Saturday."

"Someone's framing me." Grady's voice went up. "First the essence, now this—"

A knock at the front door interrupted him. Through the glass, Eliza could see Jasper Price, hands cupped around his eyes, peering in.

"Don't answer it," Grady said.

But Jasper had seen them. He knocked harder. "Grady! I know you're in there. We need to talk!"

"Go away!" Grady shouted.

"It's about Antoine! About what he knew!"

Eliza and Grady exchanged glances. She nodded toward the door.

Grady unlocked it with obvious reluctance. Jasper burst in like a man being chased, his usual swagger replaced by something close to panic.

"They're saying you did it," he said to Grady. "The whole town thinks—"

"I don't care what the town thinks," Grady snapped.

"You should." Jasper's eyes darted between them, lingering on Bruno with obvious nervousness. "Because whoever killed Antoine isn't done. I got this." He pulled out his phone, showing a text message:

You're next, unless you keep quiet about what you saw.

"When did this come?" Eliza asked.

"This morning. Anonymous number." Jasper was sweating in the humid July heat. "I didn't see anything. I don't know anything. But someone thinks I do."

"Or someone wants us to think you're in danger," Grady said cynically.

"This isn't a joke!" Jasper's voice cracked. "Antoine's dead. Someone poisoned him in front of everyone. And now they're threatening me."

"What did Antoine say to you at the festival?" Eliza asked. "Before the judging."

Jasper's face flushed. "Nothing important."

"Try again."

He looked away. "He said he knew about my debts. Said he'd heard interesting things about my 'business practices.'

Said my caramels better be exceptional or he'd have more to say in his review than just their taste."

"He was blackmailing you," Eliza said.

"He was threatening me," Jasper corrected. "There's a difference."

"Not to a prosecutor," Grady muttered.

Jasper whirled on him. "I didn't kill him! But someone did, and now they're coming after anyone who might know why." His shirt was soaked with nervous sweat.

Bruno suddenly stiffened, a low growl building in his throat. He was facing the back door, every muscle tense.

"Someone's out there," Eliza whispered.

They all froze, listening. A scrape of metal on metal—someone trying the lock.

"That door's been broken for years," Grady whispered back. "One good push—"

The door burst open. A figure in a dark hoodie stood silhouetted against the alley light, something clutched in their hand.

Bruno lunged forward with a bark that seemed too big for his body. The figure stumbled backward, dropped what they were carrying, and ran.

Eliza reached the door in time to see them disappearing around the corner—medium height, athletic build, could have been anyone.

On the ground lay a small box wrapped in gold paper. Just like the ones found in Antoine's room.

"Nobody touch it," she said, pulling out her phone to call Wade.

But Jasper was already backing toward the front door. "I'm not staying here. This is insane."

"Jasper, wait—"

He was gone, the bell above the door clanging discordantly.

Grady stood very still, staring at the golden box. "Three boxes. Three targets?"

"Maybe," Eliza said. "Or three warnings."

Wade arrived in minutes, bringing Deputy Lang and an evidence kit. He looked at the box, at the forced door, at Grady's pale face.

"You okay?" he asked Grady.

"Do I look okay? Someone's trying to frame me for murder, and now they're leaving poisoned presents at my door."

"We don't know they're poisoned," Wade said, though he was putting on gloves as he spoke.

He carefully opened the box. Inside were three chocolates, identical to the others they'd found. But this time there was a note:

Stop looking or join Antoine.

"Subtle," Eliza said dryly.

"Effective," Wade countered. "Whoever tried to break in probably saw the closed sign and thought the shop was empty."

He looked around the shop, then back at Grady. "I need you to come to the station. For your protection," he added quickly.

Grady looked around his shop—at the half-finished pralines, the cooling chocolate, the life he'd built after his brother's dreams died.

"Fine," he said finally. "But I'm innocent."

"I know," Wade said, surprising them all. "You're too smart to be this obvious. But someone wants us to think otherwise."

As they prepared to leave, Eliza noticed something on the

floor near the back door—a few threads of red fabric caught on a nail.

She pointed them out to Wade, who bagged them carefully.

"Red," he mused. "Maeve Nolan has red hair."

"Half the town owns red clothing," Eliza pointed out.

"But not half the town is connected to this case."

They locked up the shop, Wade posting Deputy Lang outside. As they walked to the station, Eliza noticed how empty the streets had become. Word was spreading. The Sweet Festival killer was still active.

Bruno pressed close to her leg, and she was grateful for his warmth. Someone was escalating, getting desperate or getting bold.

Either way, it would end soon. In her experience, killers who started leaving threats always made mistakes. The question was whether they'd catch them before someone else died.

She thought of the three chocolates in each box. Three victims planned? Or three people who knew too much?

The summer wind picked up, sending paper napkins from a nearby café skittering across the empty street like fleeing witnesses.

Behind them, Norton's Chocolates stood dark and quiet, keeping its secrets like bitter almonds in a locked cabinet.

CHAPTER 5

DEATH IN THE KITCHEN

*T*uesday morning arrived wrapped in early morning mist that would burn off by noon, the August humidity already building.

Eliza stood at her kitchen window, watching the mist roll past while Bruno finished his breakfast. The events of yesterday felt surreal—Jasper's panic, the hooded figure at Grady's shop, those three perfect chocolates in their gold box. She'd barely slept, her mind turning over the same questions: Who had Antoine angered enough to kill? Who was desperate enough to kill again to cover it up?

Her phone buzzed. Wade.

"Grady never made it home last night," his text read. "His wife is worried. Meet me at his shop."

Eliza's coffee cup froze halfway to her lips. She set it down carefully, her detective instincts already firing. Grady had left the station at eight o'clock last evening, after two hours of questioning that had gone nowhere. Wade had offered him a ride home, but Grady had insisted on walking, said he needed air.

"Come on, Bruno," she said, grabbing his leash. "Something's wrong."

Bruno abandoned his bowl immediately, reading her tone. His tail, usually wagging at the prospect of a walk, stayed low.

The mist made the familiar streets hazy and dreamlike. Shapes loomed and disappeared—a mailbox becoming a crouching figure, a tree transforming into something watchful. Even Bruno seemed unsettled, staying closer to Eliza than usual.

Norton's Chocolates materialized from the morning haze like a mirage. Wade's cruiser was parked outside, engine still running. The front door stood open.

"Stay close," Eliza murmured to Bruno, though she needn't have bothered. He was already in work mode, nose high, cataloging scents.

They found Wade standing by his cruiser, phone pressed to his ear, face grim. He held up a finger—wait—then ended the call.

"Grady's wife says he called her at 8:30 last night, said he had to stop by the shop to turn off the equipment. She went to bed at eleven, assumed he'd come home and slept in the guest room like he sometimes did when he worked late."

"But he never made it home," Eliza finished.

"His car's still here," Wade said, pointing to the small lot beside the shop. "Keys are probably inside."

They entered the shop. Wade led the way toward the kitchen, hands careful not to touch anything. The lights were on, casting harsh shadows. The smell hit them first—chocolate mixed with something else. That bitter almond scent, stronger than yesterday.

"Oh no," Wade breathed.

Grady was on the kitchen floor, slumped against the

cabinet where he'd kept the bitter almond essence. His face was purple-blue, eyes wide, one hand clutched to his throat. On the marble counter above him sat a tray of chocolates— dark, glossy, professional. One was missing.

Bruno whined, low and distressed. He'd found bodies before in his police work, but it never got easier for him either.

Eliza knelt beside Grady, though she knew it was pointless. He'd been dead for hours. Rigor was already setting in.

"Cyanide again," she said quietly. "Look at his lips."

Wade was already calling it in. "I need the coroner at Norton's Chocolates. Yes, another one. No, I'm not joking."

While he coordinated with the state police—who would definitely take over now—Eliza studied the scene with careful eyes. The tray of chocolates was arranged perfectly, each piece identical except for the missing one. Beside it lay a handwritten recipe card in Grady's careful script: "Marcus's Pralines - Family Recipe."

"He was making his brother's chocolates," she said. "The ones he mentioned yesterday."

A small pot on the stove held the remnants of melted chocolate, now congealed and dull. The double boiler beneath it had boiled dry, leaving a burnt ring. Whatever had happened, it had been quick enough that Grady hadn't turned off the stove.

Bruno was nosing around the base of the counter, pausing at a spot near Grady's feet. He pawed at something, then looked at Eliza expectantly.

She bent closer. There, almost invisible against the dark tile, was a small piece of gold foil. Like the wrapper from the festival, but newer, crisper.

"Wade," she called. "Bruno found something."

Wade bagged the foil carefully. "Same type as the others. Our killer has a signature."

"Or wants us to think they do," Eliza said. Something was bothering her about the scene, something beyond the obvious horror of Grady's death.

She stood, surveying the kitchen again. The window was cracked open, letting in wisps of fog. The back door—the one the hooded figure had tried yesterday—was locked from the inside. The bitter almond essence sat on the counter, cap off, a spoon beside it.

"This is staged," she said suddenly. "All of it. It's too neat, too obvious."

"Grady poisoned himself with his own chocolates?" Wade said skeptically.

"That's what we're supposed to think. Guilty conscience, couldn't live with killing Antoine. But look—" She pointed to Grady's hands. "Defensive wounds. Scratches on his palms, like he was pushing someone away."

Wade looked closer. She was right. Fresh scratches, some with blood.

"And the chocolate pot," Eliza continued. "Grady was obsessive about temperature. He'd never leave chocolate burning. Someone was here with him. Someone he trusted enough to let in after hours."

Doc Brennan arrived then, medical bag in hand, face even grimmer than it had been at the festival. "Two in three days, Wade? What's happening to our town?"

While Doc examined the body, Eliza walked through the shop's front room. Everything looked normal—the empty display cases, the vintage cash register, the small table where customers could sample chocolates. But Bruno was agitated, pulling toward the corner where they kept the gift boxes.

The shelf was disturbed. Several gold boxes had fallen, scattering across the floor. And there, caught on the edge of the shelf, were more red threads.

"Same as yesterday," she told Wade. "Someone in red was here."

Wade's phone rang. He answered, listened, then his face went pale. "When? Is she—okay. I'm on my way." He hung up. "That was Tyler. Maeve Nolan just called 911. Someone broke into her bakery this morning. She's hysterical."

"Go," Eliza said. "I'll stay with the scene until the state police arrive."

Wade hesitated. "Eliza—"

"I know. Be careful. Bruno's with me."

After Wade left, Eliza stood in the quiet shop with only Bruno and Doc Brennan for company. The doctor worked methodically, professionally, but she could see the strain in his shoulders. Ashford Creek hadn't seen violence like this in decades.

"He didn't suffer long," Doc said finally. "The dose was massive. Would have been over in minutes."

"Small comfort," Eliza murmured.

"Sometimes small comforts are all we get." Doc stood, knees creaking. "I'll tell you something, though. This wasn't suicide. The angle's wrong, the chocolate placement. Someone fed this to him."

Eliza nodded. She'd suspected as much.

After Doc left to coordinate with the incoming state police, Eliza found herself alone with Bruno in the shop. The fog pressed against the windows like it was trying to get in. Somewhere in the distance, sirens wailed—the outside world coming to take over their small-town tragedy.

Bruno suddenly stiffened, nose pointing toward the storeroom. A soft thump came from behind the door.

Eliza's hand went to her phone, ready to call for backup. But Bruno wasn't growling. His tail was actually wagging slightly.

She opened the storeroom door carefully. A figure huddled in the corner between boxes of cocoa powder and bags of sugar. Daisy Langley looked up, face streaked with tears and chocolate.

"Daisy?" Eliza kept her voice calm, though her heart was racing. "What are you doing here?"

"I didn't—I found him—I couldn't—" Daisy dissolved into sobs.

Eliza approached slowly, hands visible. Bruno followed, his demeanor gentle now. He could always tell the difference between a threat and someone in distress.

"When did you find him?" Eliza asked.

"Last night. Maybe ten? I came to—" Daisy hiccupped. "Grady was teaching me. Traditional chocolate making. Real techniques, not the modern shortcuts. We had a lesson scheduled."

"You had a key?"

Daisy nodded miserably. "He gave it to me last month. Said I had promise, reminded him of Marcus when he was young."

"What happened when you got here?"

"The lights were on. I called out, but no answer. I found him in the kitchen. He was already—" She couldn't finish. "I panicked. I hid. I've been here all night. I couldn't move, couldn't think."

Eliza believed her. The girl was genuinely traumatized. But it raised questions. "Daisy, did you see anyone else? Hear anything?"

"There was a car," Daisy said slowly. "When I arrived. Pulling away fast. Red sedan, I think. Maybe brown? The streetlight makes everything look weird."

"License plate?"

Daisy shook her head. "But—" She reached into her pocket, pulled out her phone. "I took a picture. Of Grady. To show the police. But then I couldn't call them. I was too scared they'd think—"

She showed Eliza the photo. It was blurry, taken with shaking hands, but it showed something crucial. The time-stamp read 10:07 PM. And in the background, just visible, was the clock on the wall showing 10:05.

More importantly, the tray of chocolates only had two missing pieces, not one.

"Daisy," Eliza said urgently, "this is evidence. Someone else was here after you. They took another chocolate."

The implications hit them both. The killer had returned to the scene.

Sirens grew louder. The state police had arrived.

"Listen to me," Eliza said quickly. "You need to tell them everything. Don't leave anything out. You're a witness, not a suspect."

"But I ran. I hid."

"You were in shock. That's normal. But Daisy—who else knew about your lessons with Grady?"

Daisy thought. "Patsy knew. She said I was wasting my time learning old-fashioned methods. Jasper made fun of me for it. And—" She paused. "Maeve. She asked if Grady ever talked about Antoine during our lessons. Wanted to know if he said anything about the review that ruined his brother."

The state police burst in then, all efficiency and protocol.

Eliza recognized the lead detective—Sarah Costa from Boston. They'd worked a joint task force once, years ago.

"Eliza Prescott," Sarah said with surprise. "Heard you retired."

"I did. I just sell books now."

Sarah looked at Bruno, at Daisy huddled in the corner, at Eliza's protective stance. "Sure you do. We'll need statements from both of you."

As they were led out, Eliza noticed something she'd missed before. On the shelf near the storeroom door was a batch of shipping boxes, ready for mailing. The top one was addressed to Marcus Norton in Medford.

Inside, visible through the clear tape, were chocolates. Hazelnut pralines. The ones Grady had been making when they talked yesterday. The ones meant for his broken brother.

He'd finished them before he died. One last act of love before someone fed him his own poisoned chocolate.

The morning mist was lifting as they emerged from the shop, revealing Ashford Creek in all its summer glory. But the beauty felt hollow now. Two men were dead, killed by the very thing that should have brought joy—chocolate crafted with skill and care, turned into a weapon.

Bruno pressed against her leg as Sarah led them to the patrol car. Not arrested, just needed for questioning. But it felt like defeat anyway. The state was taking over. Ashford Creek's chance to solve its own tragedy was slipping away.

But then she saw Wade's truck speeding back toward them, and his expression told her everything.

Whatever had happened at Maeve's bakery had changed the game entirely.

CHAPTER 6

A RECIPE FOR MURDER

*W*ade's truck skidded to a stop beside the state police cruisers, and he was out before the engine fully died. His face told Eliza everything she needed to know—whatever he'd found at Maeve's bakery had shaken him.

"She's alive," he said first, which made Eliza's stomach drop because it meant they'd expected otherwise. "But barely. Someone locked her in her own walk-in freezer. If she hadn't managed to trigger the emergency alarm..."

Detective Sarah Costa stepped forward, all business. "Sheriff Barrett, this is our scene now."

"The hell it is," Wade shot back. "Maeve Nolan is my constituent. This is still my town."

"With two murders and an attempted third? The state has jurisdiction." Sarah's voice was firm but not unkind. "You can assist, but I'm lead."

Eliza watched the power struggle with professional interest. She'd been on both sides of this territorial dance. But

Bruno's attention was elsewhere—he'd caught a scent on the wind and was pulling toward Wade's truck.

"Wade," she said quietly, "what else did you find?"

He glanced at Sarah, then back to Eliza. "Maeve was trying to tell us something. She'd written in flour on the prep counter before she passed out. One word: 'COPY.'"

"Copy?" Sarah frowned. "Copy what?"

But Eliza understood immediately. "The cake. Someone copied her Blackout Velvet cake. That's why only Antoine's slice was poisoned—it wasn't from her original cake at all."

Sarah's expression sharpened. "Explain."

"The killer made an identical slice, poisoned it, and swapped it with the real one. Maeve must have realized it when she heard about the murder. That's why they tried to silence her."

"But she makes dozens of cakes," Wade said. "How would she notice?"

"Because she's a perfectionist," Eliza replied. "She'd know if someone tampered with her work. The ganache temperature, the crumb structure—tiny details only a professional would catch."

Bruno had given up pulling and was now sitting, staring intently at Wade's truck tires. There was mud on them, but not regular mud—it had a reddish tint.

"Wade, where exactly is Maeve's bakery?"

"Cedar Street, back entrance off the alley that runs behind —" He stopped. "Behind Norton's Chocolates."

They all looked at each other. The killer had been using the alley system, moving between the shops unseen.

Sarah was already on her radio, ordering units to search the alleys. "We need to find where this red mud comes from."

"The construction site," Daisy said suddenly. Everyone

turned to look at her—they'd almost forgotten she was there, wrapped in a shock blanket by the ambulance. "They're building new condos at the end of Cedar. They hit red clay last week. Everyone's been complaining about it tracking everywhere."

Sarah dispatched units immediately, then turned back to the group. "I need full statements from everyone. Now."

The state police had commandeered the town hall, turning the main meeting room into an investigation center. Maps covered the walls, timelines stretched across whiteboards, and evidence photos were pinned in neat rows. It was impressive and efficient and completely wrong for Ashford Creek.

Eliza gave her statement to a young trooper who typed fast and asked no follow-up questions. Bruno lay at her feet, occasionally huffing his displeasure at being sidelined. She knew how he felt.

Through the window, she could see Main Street. The remaining festival booths were being dismantled, two days late. Patsy Doyle stood arguing with a volunteer about her display tables. Jasper Price sat on a bench, head in his hands. The town was coming apart.

"Ms. Prescott?" Sarah Costa stood in the doorway. "Can we talk? Unofficially?"

They walked outside, Bruno between them. Sarah lit a cigarette—a habit she'd had even years ago.

"You were good police," Sarah said. "Portland's loss."

"That's generous, considering how the Brennan case ended."

"The kid's death wasn't your fault. The witness lied."

"I should have known." Eliza kept her voice even, though the old wound still ached. "I was trained to know."

Sarah exhaled smoke. "We all miss things. The difference is, you let it destroy your career. You ran."

"I retired."

"To sell books in a town with two murders in three days." Sarah's smile was wry. "How's that working out?"

Before Eliza could answer, a commotion erupted near the town hall. Jasper Price was backing away from Deputy Tyler Lang, hands raised, voice high with panic.

"I didn't do anything! Why won't anyone believe me?"

Tyler looked overwhelmed. "Mr. Price, you need to come in for questioning."

"I've been questioned three times! I told you everything!"

A small crowd was gathering. Mae from the diner, Colin Greer with his camera, various townspeople drawn by drama.

"What's the problem?" Sarah intervened, badge visible.

Tyler straightened. "Mr. Price's car was seen near Norton's Chocolates last night."

"That's impossible!" Jasper's face was red. "I was home. My neighbor saw me."

"Your neighbor saw you at eight," Tyler corrected. "Grady died around ten."

"I was asleep by ten!"

"Can you prove it?" Sarah asked.

Jasper's mouth opened, closed. "I live alone now. How do I prove I was sleeping?"

It was a fair point, but Sarah wasn't moved. "Then you'll need to come with us."

As Tyler led Jasper away, Eliza noticed Colin Greer raising his camera. But he wasn't photographing Jasper—he was focused on something else. Following his lens, she saw Patsy Doyle slipping into the alley beside the hardware store.

"Bruno, stay with Wade," she said quietly, then followed Patsy.

The alley was narrow, shadowed despite the noon sun. Patsy moved quickly for a woman her age, turning corners with purpose. She stopped at a dumpster behind the old print shop, looked around, then lifted the lid.

Eliza watched from behind a delivery van as Patsy pulled out a garbage bag, heavy with something that clinked. She opened it, checked the contents, then resealed it and tucked it under her arm.

"Found what you were looking for?" Eliza asked, stepping out.

Patsy spun around, clutching the bag. "Eliza! You scared me."

"What's in the bag, Patsy?"

"Nothing. Recyclables. The print shop throws away bottles."

"The print shop closed two years ago."

Patsy's face crumbled in the heat. "It's not what you think."

"Then show me."

With shaking hands, Patsy opened the bag. Inside were mason jars filled with clear liquid. The smell of grain alcohol was unmistakable.

"Moonshine?" Eliza said, surprised.

"My husband's." Patsy's voice was bitter. "He's been selling it illegally for years. Small batches to friends, he said. Harmless, he said. But Antoine found out."

"How?"

"That damned reporter. Colin Greer. He was taking pictures of everything, everyone. Caught Harold—my Harold —making a delivery. Antoine saw the photos, recognized what it was. He came to my booth Friday night, after setup."

Patsy sank onto a crate, suddenly looking every one of her seventy years.

"He said he'd mention it in his review. Not just my cookies —my husband's criminal enterprise. We'd lose everything. Harold's pension, our reputation, maybe even jail time." She looked up at Eliza. "But I didn't kill him. I wanted to, God help me, but I didn't."

"Who else knew?"

"Jasper knew about the moonshine. He's been buying it for years, serving it at his pumpkin farm parties and calling it 'artisanal spirits.'" Patsy's voice turned even more bitter. "And Harold—my Harold—he's been skimming festival funds to keep our bills paid. The moonshine money wasn't enough. Where do you think the festival's extra funding came from? Not just the town budget. He's been moving money around for years."

The web of secrets was getting more tangled. Everyone had something to hide, something Antoine had threatened to expose.

"Patsy, where's Harold now?"

"Home. Sick with worry. He thinks they'll arrest him next."

Eliza helped Patsy to her feet. "Go home. Tell Wade everything. The moonshine, the mayor, all of it. It's going to come out anyway."

Patsy nodded miserably and shuffled away, still clutching her bag of evidence.

Eliza returned to find the town hall in chaos. Jasper had collapsed in the interview room—a panic attack, the EMTs said, but Sarah was suspicious. She'd ordered blood tests.

Meanwhile, Colin Greer had been brought in. His camera's memory card revealed hundreds of photos from the past week, and Sarah's tech specialist was going through them on a laptop.

"There," the specialist said, pointing to the screen. "Friday night, 11:47 PM."

The photo showed the alley behind Norton's Chocolates. A figure in dark clothing was barely visible, but they were carrying something. A box. Gold-wrapped.

"Enhance it," Sarah ordered.

The image grew larger, grainier. The figure's face was hidden, but something else was visible—a distinctive watch on their wrist. Silver, with an unusual square face.

"I've seen that watch," Wade said suddenly. "The mayor wears one just like it. His wife gave it to him for their anniversary."

Sarah sent troopers immediately, but Eliza was thinking about something else. The mayor had touched all the name cards at the festival. He'd been fussing with them, straightening them obsessively.

"He could have marked Antoine's seat," she said. "Made sure the poisoned slice went to the right person."

"But why?" Sarah asked. "What's his motive?"

That's when Millie Hart walked in, face pale but determined. "I need to tell you something," she said. "About the mayor. And Antoine. And what happened fifteen years ago."

Everyone stopped. Millie, steady reliable Millie, looked like she was about to shatter.

"Fifteen years ago, Harold Doyle—Mayor Doyle—had a younger brother. David. He was a pastry chef in Boston. Brilliant, Harold always said. Going to make the family proud." She took a breath. "Antoine Duval destroyed him. Not just a bad review—he accused David of stealing recipes, plagiarism. It wasn't true, but the damage was done. David lost everything. His health collapsed under the shame and stress. He died three months later, broken by what Antoine had done to him."

The room was silent.

"Harold never talked about it," Millie continued. "Moved here, started over, became mayor. But when he heard Antoine was coming to judge our festival..." She shrugged. "I saw his face when it was announced. Just for a second. Pure rage."

Sarah was already on her radio, calling units to the mayor's house. But Eliza was putting pieces together differently.

"Wait," she said. "The watch in the photo—can you zoom in more?"

The tech complied. The image was nearly abstract now, but Eliza could see what she was looking for. The watch had a crack across its face.

"Harold's watch isn't cracked," Wade said. "I saw it this morning."

"Then who—" Sarah started, but she was interrupted by commotion outside.

Maeve Nolan was being brought in on a stretcher, conscious but weak. She was trying to speak, gesturing frantically.

"Let her talk," Eliza said, pushing forward.

Maeve's voice was hoarse from cold and screaming. "Not... copy," she whispered. "Coffee."

"Coffee?" Sarah leaned closer. "What about coffee?"

"Antoine's... coffee. Saw them. With his cup."

"Who?" Eliza asked urgently. "Who had his coffee cup?"

Maeve's eyes found Millie in the crowd. "Her... assistant. Young man. Marcus."

The room froze. Millie went white.

"Marcus?" Eliza said. "Marcus Norton? Grady's brother?"

Millie's hand went to her throat. "He's not my assistant. He's my nephew. My sister's son. He came to stay with me six months ago. Said he needed a fresh start after his shop failed."

"Where is he now?" Sarah demanded.

"I don't...the inn. He was doing inventory."

But Eliza was already moving, Bruno at her heels. Marcus Norton. He'd been there the whole time, hidden in plain sight. Grady's broken brother, working at the inn, serving coffee to the judges.

He had access to everything. The festival setup. The spare keys to every shop in town—Millie kept a set for emergencies. The bitter almond essence from his uncle's shop.

And he had the ultimate motive: Antoine had destroyed his life, and now his brother was dead too, killed to keep the frame-up intact.

They found him at the Teacup Inn, calmly packing a bag. He looked up when they entered, and Eliza saw no surprise in his eyes. Just exhaustion.

"I wondered when you'd figure it out," Marcus said. He looked nothing like the broken man Grady had described. He was thin, yes, but his eyes were clear and cold. "Aunt Millie's tea room. So quaint. So perfect for serving coffee to judges."

"You poisoned Antoine's coffee?" Sarah had her weapon drawn but not raised.

"Just a little insurance," Marcus said. "In case the cake didn't work. But it wasn't needed. The chocolate did its job."

"You killed your own brother," Eliza said.

For the first time, emotion flickered across Marcus's face. "That wasn't supposed to happen. He was supposed to take the blame and disappear. I left him money, a new identity. But he wouldn't run. Said he'd rather die than be thought a murderer."

"So you granted his wish," Wade said grimly.

"He was going to confess to protect me," Marcus said. "Stupid, noble Grady. Still trying to save his little brother." His voice turned bitter. "Antoine took everything from me. My shop, my marriage, my self-respect. Grady sent money, tried to help, but you can't rebuild from those ashes."

"And Maeve?" Sarah asked.

"She knew the cake was wrong. She makes each layer herself, counts every raspberry. She noticed one slice was different. I couldn't let her tell anyone."

"You're under arrest," Sarah said, moving forward.

Marcus laughed. "For what? You have no physical evidence. I wore gloves. Burned the clothes. The poison came from Grady's shop, and he's not alive to say I took it."

"We have Maeve's testimony," Sarah said.

"A hypothermic woman's confused rambling? Good luck with that."

But Eliza smiled. "Bruno?"

The dog had been sitting perfectly still, but at her word he moved to Marcus's bag and sat, tail rigid, nose pointing. His alert signal.

"What's in the bag, Marcus?" Eliza asked.

"Clothes. Personal items."

"And chocolates," she said. "The same ones you've been leaving around town. Bruno can smell the bitter almonds. You couldn't resist keeping trophies."

Marcus went still. Sarah moved in, cuffing him while he stared at the dog who'd undone him.

"Grady always said you were good with dogs," Marcus said to Eliza. "Said Bruno was the best cop in town."

As they led him away, Millie stood frozen in the doorway, tears streaming down her face. "I brought him here," she whispered. "After he lost the gas station job too. After everything fell apart. I gave him work at the inn. I gave him access to everything."

You gave him a second chance," Eliza said gently. "What he did with it was his choice."

The state police spent the rest of the day unraveling Marcus's plan. He'd been planning it for months, ever since he'd learned Antoine would be judging the festival. The threatening letters had been sent from Boston before he'd even arrived in Ashford Creek, establishing the narrative of a threatened celebrity chef.

He'd made the duplicate cake slice in the inn's kitchen after hours, using Maeve's exact recipe—which she'd practiced there the week before. The poisoned coffee had been backup, delivered with a smile and a compliment about Antoine's discerning palate.

The chocolates left around town had been misdirection, keeping suspicion on Grady and creating panic. Marcus had counted on the investigation focusing on his brother, the man with the obvious motive and the bitter almonds in his shop.

He hadn't counted on Grady's stubborn refusal to run. Or Maeve's professional pride noticing the substitution. Or a retired police dog who could smell cyanide through three layers of packaging.

By evening, the town hall was quiet. Sarah Costa and her team had packed up their mobile command center, leaving Wade to handle the cleanup. The mayor had been arrested for embezzlement—the festival funds he'd skimmed over the years. Harold Doyle faced charges for the moonshine operation. Colin Greer was negotiating with three different papers for exclusive rights to his story.

Eliza sat on the steps of the town hall, Bruno's head in her lap, watching the last of the festival come down. The lanterns were packed away, the booths dismantled, the sweet smell of chocolate and sugar finally fading from the air.

"Hell of a week," Wade said, sitting beside her.

"Three days," she corrected. "It's only been three days."

"Feels longer."

They sat in comfortable silence, watching Main Street return to normal. Or as normal as it could be after two murders and a town's worth of secrets exposed.

"The state police offered me a consultant position," Eliza said finally. "Sarah thinks I'm wasted selling books."

"You considering it?"

She scratched Bruno's ears, thinking. "No. I left that life for a reason. But this—helping you, helping the town—that felt right."

"Good," Wade said. "Because I'm going to need help rebuilding trust here. People are scared, angry. They need to know we can protect them."

"We couldn't protect Antoine or Grady."

"No," Wade agreed. "But we caught their killer. And we'll do better next time."

"You think there'll be a next time?"

Wade looked at the quiet streets of Ashford Creek, at the shadows lengthening between buildings where secrets had hidden for so long.

"There's always a next time," he said.

Bruno whined softly, and Eliza knew he was right. Small towns were full of secrets, and secrets had a way of turning deadly when threatened with exposure.

But for now, the immediate danger was over. Marcus Norton would face justice for the murders he'd committed in the name of revenge. The town would heal, slowly. And next year, there would probably even be another Sweet Festival, though nothing would ever taste quite as innocent again.

The church bells rang seven o'clock. Somewhere, Millie was preparing dinner service at the inn, trying to maintain normalcy. Patsy was home with Harold, deciding whether their marriage could survive his crimes. Daisy was probably still in shock, processing the trauma of finding Grady's body. Jasper was with his lawyer, preparing to declare bankruptcy and start over.

And Maeve—Maeve was alive, thanks to an emergency alarm and her own determination to reveal the truth even while freezing to death.

"Come on, Bruno," Eliza said, standing. "Let's go home."

The dog rose immediately, tail wagging slightly. He knew the word "home" and approved.

As they walked through the town square, Eliza noticed something. Where the judging tent had stood, someone had left flowers. Not a formal memorial, just a simple bunch of grocery store carnations. The card read: "For Antoine. You were cruel, but you didn't deserve this."

It was unsigned, but Eliza recognized Daisy's handwriting.

Even in a town full of people Antoine had hurt, someone mourned him. That was Ashford Creek's true character—not the secrets or the grudges, but the fundamental decency that let them grieve even an enemy.

Tomorrow, Wade would start the long process of rebuilding. The state police would file their reports. The media would move on to other tragedies.

But tonight, Eliza walked home with her dog through

streets that smelled of October rain instead of chocolate, and let herself believe that the worst was over.

CHAPTER 7

SWEET ENDINGS

*T*wo days after Marcus Norton's arrest, the Teacup Inn reopened its doors. Millie Hart had called them all—not for drama or tears, but for tea and normalcy. The dining room filled slowly with familiar faces: Wade, Eliza and Bruno, Patsy and Harold (out on bail with an ankle monitor that he kept trying to hide under his trouser leg), Daisy, Maeve still using her cane, even Jasper Price. Colin Greer sat in the corner with his notebook, having promised not to publish photos of anyone crying in exchange for exclusive quotes.

"Before we start," Colin said, raising his hand like a school-boy, "I need to apologize. I've been treating this like a story instead of your lives. That was wrong."

"You're a reporter," Patsy said, though not unkindly. "It's what you do."

"Still," Colin said. "I could have been less... ghoulish about it."

"Ghoulish," Jasper repeated. "That's rich coming from someone who tried to photograph the body."

"I did not—"

"You absolutely did. I saw you with your camera."

Wade cleared his throat. "Gentlemen. We're here to move forward, not backward."

Millie emerged from the kitchen carrying a silver tray. "I made chocolate," she announced simply, setting it on the center table. "Not poisoned. Not bitter. Just chocolate."

The tray held an array of simple treats—nothing fancy, nothing like the elaborate festival entries. Just honest chocolates, the kind she used to make before everything went wrong.

For a moment, nobody moved.

"Oh, for heaven's sake," Patsy said, reaching for one. "If Millie wanted to poison us, she wouldn't do it in front of the sheriff."

"That's... weirdly comforting," Daisy said.

Then Bruno stood, sniffed the tray professionally, and sat back down in his official "all clear" posture from his police days.

"Well, if Bruno says they're safe," Wade said, reaching for one.

"That dog's been right about everything else," Harold added, trying to reach the tray but being pulled up short by his ankle monitor's cord. "Patsy, could you—"

"I'm not your servant just because you're under house arrest," Patsy said, but she handed him a chocolate anyway.

"Technically, I'm not under house arrest yet," Harold corrected. "This is just monitoring while—"

"Harold," Patsy said sweetly, "would you like me to tell everyone about the time you tried to hide moonshine in the church organ?"

Harold became very interested in his chocolate.

"We'll need a special election," Wade said, looking at Harold. "For mayor."

Harold nodded, looking older than his years. "I know. The town council meets Thursday. I'll officially resign then. Though I still say moving funds between accounts isn't technically embezzlement if it all stays in town—"

"Harold," Patsy warned.

"Resigning. Thursday. Got it."

"Ellen Fairbanks from the library wants to run," Wade continued. "She's got good ideas. Transparent budgeting, for one."

"Transparent budgeting," Harold muttered. "Where's the fun in that?"

"The fun is in not going to prison," Patsy said.

"I'm not going to prison. Probably. My lawyer says community service is more likely."

"Your lawyer also said making moonshine was a gray area," Patsy reminded him.

"It is gray! It's for personal consumption—"

"That you sold—"

"Shared. For a small donation to cover costs—"

Wade rubbed his temples. "Can we please focus?"

"And Jasper," Wade continued, turning to him, "I heard you're filing for bankruptcy?"

Jasper nodded, looking down at his hands. "Monday. Meeting with the court." He paused, then took a breath. "My ex-wife's coming back to help. We're going to try again. Run a vegetable stand. No more pretending to be something I'm not."

"A vegetable stand?" Patsy asked. "What happened to your gourmet truffle empire?"

"It was never an empire. It was barely a shed. And the truffles were never gourmet. The chocolate was bulk chocolate from the wholesale store."

Everyone turned to stare.

"The wholesale store?" Maeve said faintly. "You told us it was Belgian!"

"Belgium is a state of mind," Jasper said defensively.

"No," Daisy said, "Belgium is a country. A country where they make actual chocolate."

"The caramels were real!" Jasper protested. "The salt really was from France! I ordered it online!"

"Amazon?" Colin guessed.

Jasper's silence was answer enough.

"Well," Millie said after a moment, "at least you're being honest now."

"Speaking of honesty," Daisy said, voice stronger than it had been in days, "I'm keeping my bakery open. Grady taught me things before he died. Real techniques. Not wholesale store techniques," she added, looking at Jasper. "I won't let that knowledge die with him."

"Good for you," Maeve said. "I'm starting teaching in the fall. Just one class a week at the Portland culinary school. They want me to do a unit on traditional French pastry techniques."

"The ones Antoine taught you?" Millie asked carefully.

"Among others. I figure... knowledge is knowledge. It doesn't become evil just because an evil person shared it."

"Antoine wasn't evil," Wade said. "He was just—"

"Mean," Patsy supplied.

"Cruel," Jasper added.

"Pompous," Harold contributed.

"A bully," Daisy said quietly.

"Okay, he wasn't great," Wade conceded. "But Marcus was the evil one."

"Marcus was broken," Millie said softly. It was the first time she'd spoken his name since the arrest. "My sister called this morning. She doesn't blame me. She says Marcus broke a long time ago, when Antoine destroyed his shop. Everything after was just him falling apart in slow motion."

"That's very poetic," Colin said, scribbling in his notebook.

"Don't you dare put that in your article," Millie warned.

"I'm not writing an article anymore," Colin said. "I'm writing a book. 'Death by Chocolate: A True Crime Story.' My editor loves it."

"Oh good," Patsy said dryly. "We'll be famous."

"I'll change your names if you want."

"Don't you dare," Harold said. "If I'm going to be in a book about crime, I want full credit."

"You want credit for crime?" Wade asked.

"For surviving it," Harold corrected. "Also, maybe it'll help with the judge. Show remorse and whatnot."

"I don't think being in a true crime book shows remorse," Eliza pointed out.

"It does if Colin writes it right. You will write it right, won't you, Colin?"

Colin looked uncomfortable. "I'll write the truth."

"The truth is that I'm very remorseful," Harold said firmly. "Extremely remorseful. The most remorseful person in Ashford Creek."

"You literally just said moonshine was a gray area," Patsy reminded him.

"I can be remorseful about gray areas!"

Bruno suddenly stood and walked to the window, tail

wagging. Through the glass, they could see a delivery truck pulling up.

"That'll be my chocolate order," Millie said. "First one since... since everything."

"You're going to keep making chocolates for the inn?" Jasper asked.

"Someone has to. The town can't survive on wholesale store truffles."

"They weren't that bad," Jasper protested.

"Yes, they were," everyone said in unison.

As Millie went to sign for the delivery, Daisy spoke up. "What about the festival? Do we cancel it next year?"

"Absolutely not," Wade said firmly. "We keep the Sweet Festival. We're not giving Marcus the satisfaction of changing our traditions because of what he did. The Sweet Festival has been running for thirty years. It'll keep running."

"But no outside judges," Patsy added quickly. "We judge our own."

"Blind tasting," Maeve suggested. "Numbers instead of names."

"Triple-locked ballot box," Harold added. Everyone looked at him. "What? I know about election security. I rigged three of them."

"Harold!" Patsy gasped.

"Kidding! I'm kidding!" He paused. "Mostly kidding."

"And we should add a memorial," Daisy said. "For Grady. Maybe a scholarship for young bakers."

"The Grady Norton Excellence in Chocolate Award," Millie said, returning from the door. "He would have hated that. Too fancy. He'd have wanted it called the 'Just Make Good Chocolate' award."

"That's actually better," Eliza said.

They spent the next hour planning, eating chocolate, and slowly stitching their community back together. No dramatic speeches, no tears, just neighbors figuring out how to move forward. Harold tried to sneak three more chocolates despite Patsy's watchful eye. Colin filled six pages with notes that were supposedly off the record. Bruno fell asleep under the table, occasionally woofing softly at whatever retired police dogs dream about.

As they prepared to leave, the Henderson sisters burst through the door, their matching Pomeranians yapping in their arms.

"We just heard!" Mrs. Henderson exclaimed while her sister nodded vigorously. "Is it true Marcus Norton was living here the whole time? And he poisoned Antoine? And Grady? And tried to frame poor Jasper?"

"He didn't try to frame me," Jasper said. "He tried to frame Grady. I was the backup patsy."

"Backup patsy," Mrs. Henderson repeated. "How thrilling! Wait until the garden club hears about this. We were going to discuss mulch varieties at tomorrow's meeting, but this is much better."

"Please don't gossip about our tragedy," Millie said tiredly.

"It's not gossip if it's true," Mrs. Henderson said. "Besides, the whole town needs to process this together. We're having an emergency meeting tomorrow. Two o'clock. You're all invited."

"To process?" Wade asked skeptically.

"To plan the memorial service. For Antoine and Grady both. The Reverend says we need closure."

"Antoine tried to destroy half the people in this room," Harold pointed out.

"And yet he's still dead," Mrs. Henderson said practically.

"The dead deserve remembrance, even the unpleasant ones. Besides, his chocolate shop is sending a donation for the service. Guilt money, probably, but it spends just the same."

She swept out as dramatically as she'd entered, Pomeranians still yapping.

"Is it wrong that I don't want to memorialize Antoine?" Jasper asked.

"No," Wade said. "But we'll do it anyway. That's what makes us better than him."

As they filed out, Eliza stopped beside Millie. "You okay?"

"I will be," Millie said. "The inn needs me. The town needs normal. And I need..." she paused. "I need to stop feeling guilty for something that wasn't my fault."

"That's a good need," Eliza said.

Outside, the summer sun was shining, and Main Street looked almost normal. The crime scene tape was gone. Shops were opening. Kids were playing in the square, their laughter carrying on the breeze.

"Come on, partner," Eliza said to Bruno. "Let's go home."

The Sweet Festival was over, but Ashford Creek would survive. It always did. Even if some of its truffles came from the wholesale store.

EPILOGUE

THREE WEEKS LATER

$\mathcal{L}$ate August brought a different kind of sweetness to Ashford Creek—the lazy, golden kind that made people sit a little longer on benches and smile a little easier at neighbors.

Eliza stood outside Bookmark & Brew with Bruno, watching Main Street return to its rhythm. The Sweet Festival booths were long gone, but the town square bustled with the weekly farmers' market. No chocolate vendors this time—that would come later, when the memories weren't quite so fresh.

"Morning," Wade called, crossing from the sheriff's station with two cups of coffee. "Heard from Sarah Costa yesterday. Marcus took the plea deal. Life without parole."

"Good," Eliza said simply, accepting the coffee.

The Blessed Bean coffee shop had opened where Norton's Chocolates once stood, the young couple from Vermont treating the space with appropriate respect. They'd kept a small plaque by the door: "In memory of Grady Norton, Chocolatier."

Daisy Langley waved from her bakery, where a line of

customers waited for her orange-chocolate truffles—now her signature item. She'd hired an assistant and started teaching what Grady had taught her, keeping his knowledge alive.

"How's Millie?" Eliza asked.

"Better. The inn's busy again. Her sister visits weekly." Wade paused. "Harold's under house arrest. Trial's set for October."

"And Patsy?"

"Standing by him. Says forty years of marriage is worth more than his stupidity about money."

Bruno's tail wagged as Maeve Nolan walked past with just a slight limp now, no cane needed. She'd start teaching at the Portland culinary school come fall—one class a week to begin.

"Town council met last night," Wade said. "Ellen Fairbanks from the library is running for mayor. She'll probably win."

"She'd be good."

"And," Wade said carefully, "they approved that community liaison position. Part-time. Flexible hours. Comes with an official badge for Bruno."

Eliza smiled. "Still trying to recruit me?"

"Just saying the option's there."

A car with Massachusetts plates drove slowly past, passengers craning to see the town where the "Sweet Festival Murders" had happened. It happened less often now, but enough to be a reminder.

"Next year's festival," Wade said. "You going to enter something?"

"I don't bake."

"You could learn."

"Bruno could enter a dog biscuit contest," Eliza suggested.

Bruno's ears perked at "biscuit," and they both laughed.

The church bells rang nine o'clock. Shops opened. Life continued.

"I should go," Eliza said. "First customer's due any minute."

"Think about the position," Wade said.

"I will."

Inside her bookstore, Eliza straightened the mystery section, particularly the cozies with their cheerful covers hiding fictional murders. Real murder was messier, sadder, harder to solve. But it could be solved. Justice could be found. Communities could heal.

Bruno settled on his usual rug by the counter, watchful but relaxed.

Three weeks wasn't long enough to heal completely. The Sweet Festival would return next summer, but it would be different—local judges only, complete transparency, the town celebrating itself rather than seeking outside approval. They'd learned that lesson the hard way.

But Ashford Creek would survive. It had weathered worse storms than Marcus Norton's revenge.

The bell above the door chimed as her first customer entered. Mrs. Henderson, looking for a "nice mystery, but not too violent, dear."

Eliza smiled and led her to the cozies. In books, at least, murder could be cozy. In real life, Ashford Creek had learned, it never was.

But that didn't mean you stopped living. It just meant you appreciated the quiet mornings more, held your loved ones closer, and maybe—just maybe—you kept a retired police dog close by.

Just in case.

DAISY'S ORANGE-DARK CHOCOLATE TRUFFLES

THE RECIPE THAT EARNED PRAISE EVEN IN TRAGEDY

Makes approximately 24 truffles

Ingredients:

- 8 ounces dark chocolate (70% cacao), finely chopped
- ½ cup heavy cream
- 2 tablespoons unsalted butter
- Zest of 1 large orange (about 1 tablespoon)
- 1 tablespoon orange liqueur (optional)
- Pinch of salt
- Unsweetened cocoa powder for rolling

Instructions:

1. Place chopped chocolate in a heatproof bowl.
2. In a small saucepan, heat cream and orange zest over medium heat until it just begins to simmer. Remove from heat and let steep for 5 minutes.

3. Pour the hot cream through a fine-mesh strainer over the chocolate, pressing the zest to extract flavor. Discard zest.
4. Let sit for 2 minutes, then stir gently from the center outward until smooth and glossy. Add butter, orange liqueur (if using), and salt. Stir until combined.
5. Cover and refrigerate for 2 hours until firm enough to shape.
6. Using a teaspoon or melon baller, scoop small portions and roll between palms to form balls.
7. Roll in cocoa powder and place on a parchment-lined tray.
8. Store in an airtight container in the refrigerator for up to 2 weeks.

Daisy's tip: "The secret is confidence. Don't overwork the chocolate—trust that it knows what to do."

MILLIE'S HEALING HOT CHOCOLATE

SOMETIMES THE SIMPLEST COMFORTS ARE THE BEST

Serves 4

Ingredients:

- 4 cups whole milk
- 6 ounces dark chocolate (60-70% cacao), chopped
- 2 ounces milk chocolate, chopped
- ¼ cup sugar (adjust to taste)
- 1 teaspoon vanilla extract
- Pinch of salt
- Whipped cream for topping
- Chocolate shavings for garnish

Instructions:

1. In a medium saucepan, heat milk over medium-low heat until steaming but not boiling.
2. Add both chocolates and sugar, whisking constantly until completely melted and smooth.

3. Remove from heat and stir in vanilla and salt.
4. Pour into mugs and top with whipped cream and chocolate shavings.
5. Serve immediately with shortbread cookies if desired.

Millie's note: "This is what I served at the inn after everything happened. Sometimes you need something warm and sweet to remind you that not everything bitter lasts forever."

* * *

A Note from the Author: These recipes are inspired by the resilient bakers of Ashford Creek. While the Sweet Festival brought tragedy, it also revealed the strength of a community that chose to continue creating beauty and sweetness despite their loss. Please enjoy these treats with friends and family—and perhaps keep a good dog nearby, just in case.

DEATH AT THE TASTING TENT

PROLOGUE

ONE WEEK BEFORE THE MURDER

*T*he morning started the way Eliza Prescott liked best—with the smell of dark roast coffee and the particular satisfaction of a bookstore preparing to open. She stood behind the counter of Bookmark & Brew, watching autumn sunlight filter through the front windows. Bruno dozed on his bed near the door, one ear twitching occasionally toward the street sounds outside.

At forty-two, Eliza had built herself a life of pleasant routines in Ashford Creek. Morning inventory, afternoon customers, evening walks with Bruno past the harbor where the fishing boats rocked gently in their slips. It was everything Portland hadn't been—quiet, predictable, safe. The mystery section along the north wall stood perfectly organized by subgenre, spines aligned like soldiers, each book exactly where it should be. Order. Control. Peace.

The bell above the door chimed, and the Henderson sisters bustled in with their matching Pomeranians, Bitsy and Mitsy, both women pink-cheeked from the November chill.

"Eliza, dear, tell me you have the new Louise Penny,"

Eleanor Henderson said, unwinding her scarf with urgent hands while Bitsy strained at her leash toward Bruno's bed.

"Came in Friday." Eliza produced the book from behind the counter where she'd been saving it. "First copy is yours, as always."

"This is why we adore you." Eleanor clutched the book like treasure. "Don't tell Edith I said that."

"I heard you," Edith said mildly, already browsing the new releases table while Mitsy sniffed delicately at the baseboards.

Bruno lifted his head as the sisters settled into the reading nook, his gray muzzle tracking their movement with the professional assessment of a dog who'd spent eight years evaluating threats. The Pomeranians he ignored with the dignity of a retired police dog who'd dealt with far more serious concerns. Two years into retirement hadn't dulled his instincts. Eliza sometimes thought he missed the work—the clear purpose of police duty, the satisfaction of a case closed. She understood the feeling.

Her phone buzzed with a news alert. She glanced at it, then stopped, reading more carefully.

Local Author Margot Sterling Announces Book Tour - Returns to Ashford Creek Roots

The article included a photo: a woman in her early fifties, expensively dressed, holding up her latest cookbook with the kind of smile that suggested she knew exactly how photogenic she was. The book's cover featured an artful arrangement of autumn vegetables and the title *Autumn Harvest: New England's Secret Recipes.*

"Oh, how exciting!" Eleanor had noticed over Eliza's shoulder. "Margot Sterling is from here originally, you know. Left years ago, before you arrived. Made quite a name for herself with those cookbooks."

"I didn't realize she was local."

"Moved away twenty-five years ago, something of a scandal at the time though I can't quite remember what." Eleanor's eyes gleamed with the pleasure of half-remembered gossip. "But she's done wonderfully for herself. We should absolutely have her do a signing here!"

Eliza pulled up the publisher's website on her computer, already calculating how many copies to order. A local author returning home—that would draw customers from neighboring towns, maybe even Boston tourists doing the fall foliage circuit. She clicked through to the book's description, skimming the praise quotes and recipe highlights.

Her finger paused on the trackpad. One of the recipes listed was "Traditional New England Lemon Scones with Signature Glaze."

The description made her frown: *A secret family recipe perfected over generations, these delicate scones capture the essence of coastal New England baking traditions.*

That sounded remarkably like—

The bell chimed again, and Millie Hart entered in a flutter of movement, her signature pink scarf bright against the gray morning. But her usual cheerful energy was absent. She moved to the counter with jerky steps, her hands twisting the strap of her purse.

"Eliza, have you seen—" She stopped, noticing the computer screen. Her face went pale, the color draining so quickly Eliza half-rose from her stool in concern.

"Millie?"

"That woman." Millie's voice was barely above a whisper. "She's coming back?"

"You know Margot Sterling?"

"Know her?" Millie's laugh was harsh, so unlike her usual

warm chuckle that Bruno's ears pricked forward. "Look at page forty-seven."

Eliza clicked through the preview pages the publisher had made available. Page forty-seven featured the lemon scone recipe in elegant layout, with a photo of golden scones arranged on vintage china. The headnote read: *These scones were inspired by the coastal inns of my childhood, where baking was an art form passed from grandmother to granddaughter.*

The recipe that followed was nearly identical to the one Millie guarded like a state secret—her grandmother's formula, the one that made the Teacup Inn famous, the one she kept in her safety deposit box at the bank.

"That's—" Eliza started.

"My grandmother's recipe. Changed just enough to avoid copyright issues, but it's hers. The ratios, the technique, even the signature glaze." Millie's hands had gone from nervous to shaking. "She took it. She actually took it and published it."

"Can you prove it's yours?"

"I have grandmother's original recipe card, dated 1952. Handwritten, with her notes in the margins." Millie's voice cracked slightly. "But recipes can't be copyrighted, everyone knows that. Unless the exact wording is copied, there's nothing illegal about what she did. Just... wrong."

The Henderson sisters had gone quiet in their corner, pretending to read but obviously listening. Even the Pomeranians had settled, as if sensing the tension. In a town the size of Ashford Creek, privacy was a polite fiction everyone maintained.

Eliza looked back at the announcement. The book tour schedule showed Margot would be in Ashford Creek in exactly one week—Friday for a signing, Saturday for the Harvest Festival's tasting event.

"Maybe it's a coincidence," Eliza offered, though she didn't believe it. Eight years as a detective had taught her the difference between coincidence and theft.

"It's not." Millie's jaw set with uncharacteristic hardness. "And it's not just me. Look at page seventy-three."

Apple cider donuts. The recipe featured a photo of golden-brown donuts dusted with cinnamon sugar, credited as "adapted from a traditional New England bakery." The technique described was specific, unusual—exactly the method that made Morrison's Morning Goods special.

Diane Morrison had been making those donuts the same way for fifteen years, following her grandmother's formula. They were what kept her small bakery afloat in a town that couldn't quite support two bakeries but managed because everyone loved Diane's donuts.

"She's been stealing recipes," Eliza said quietly.

"For years, apparently. I looked through her other books last night after I saw the announcement. There are at least six recipes I recognize from local establishments, all claimed as 'family traditions' or 'New England heritage.'" Millie's composure finally cracked completely. "She's built a career on other people's work, Eliza. And now she's coming back here like a conquering hero."

"What are you going to do?"

"What can I do? Sue her with what money? Take on her publishers' legal team?" Millie shook her head. "I'll do what I always do. Smile, serve tea, and pretend it doesn't hurt that she stole seventy years of my family's work and got rich from it."

She left before Eliza could respond, the bell's cheerful chime mocking the heavy silence she left behind.

Eleanor spoke first, her voice unusually subdued. "Well. That's rather awful, isn't it?"

"Rather," Edith agreed, and both Pomeranians whined softly.

Eliza looked back at Margot Sterling's publicity photo— that confident smile, those expensive clothes, the casual way she held a book filled with other people's recipes. Something cold settled in her stomach, the old detective's instinct that recognized trouble brewing.

She placed the order anyway. Thirty copies, returnable if they didn't sell. This was business, and whatever personal drama existed between Margot and the town, people would want to meet a celebrity author.

The rest of Monday passed in normal rhythms. Eliza helped customers find books, recommended mysteries to tourists, restocked the local authors section. But her mind kept returning to Millie's stricken face and those stolen recipes.

* * *

TUESDAY MORNING BROUGHT rain and Diane Morrison.

The baker looked like she hadn't slept, dark circles under her eyes and flour still dusting her sleeve from the pre-dawn baking shift. She clutched a coffee from the café next door instead of her usual tea from Millie's inn.

"I assume you've heard," Diane said without preamble.

"About Margot Sterling? Yes."

"My grandmother gave her that recipe." Diane's voice was flat, exhausted. "Twenty-five years ago, Margot was in high school, doing some kind of project about local food traditions. She interviewed grandmother, who was thrilled someone young was interested in preserving recipes. She shared the family donut recipe on the condition it was for educational purposes only."

"And Margot published it."

"In her second book, five years ago. Suddenly tourists were coming to my bakery asking if my donuts were 'like Margot Sterling's recipe from her book.' Like I was copying her." Diane's laugh was bitter. "Do you know what that did to business? People assumed I was riding her coattails. Sales dropped forty percent that year. I had to lay off my assistant. I almost lost everything."

"Did you confront her?"

"Sent a letter to her publisher with proof of the recipe's origin—grandmother's handwritten card, photos from our bakery in the eighties showing the donuts. They sent back a form letter saying recipes couldn't be copyrighted and thanked me for my interest." Diane's hands tightened around her coffee cup. "I couldn't afford a lawyer. Margot could. So I did nothing and watched her get rich off my grandmother's work."

Bruno had padded over, sensing distress the way he always did. He leaned against Diane's leg with his solid warmth, and her hand automatically went to scratch his ears.

"Why are you telling me this?" Eliza asked gently.

"Because you're smart. Because you notice things. Because —" Diane stopped, struggling with something. "When she comes back for that book signing, I don't trust myself. I'm so angry, Eliza. Twenty-five years of rage just sitting in my chest, and she's going to walk into town like she's done nothing wrong."

"Diane—"

"I'm not going to do anything stupid. I'm not. But I needed

to tell someone that I'm angry enough to want to." She set down her coffee cup with careful precision. "There. I've said it. Now you know, and maybe that's enough to keep me honest."

She left, and Eliza stood in the quiet bookstore wondering if she'd just heard a confession or a warning.

* * *

WEDNESDAY AFTERNOON BROUGHT AN UNEXPECTED VISITOR.

The woman who entered Bookmark & Brew moved with careful grace, her dark hair pulled into a neat bun, her camera bag worn but expensive. She browsed the photography section for ten minutes before approaching the counter, her smile professional and slightly distant.

"I'm Claire Hartwick. I'm covering the Harvest Festival for the Ashford Creek Gazette—freelance photography." She pulled out a business card with elegant simplicity. "I understand Margot Sterling will be doing a signing here Friday?"

"That's right."

"I'd like to photograph it, if you don't mind. Local author returns home, that sort of thing." Claire's voice was carefully neutral, but something in her posture suggested tension held in check. "I'm relatively new to town—moved here about five years ago. Still building my portfolio."

"Of course. Friday at two o'clock."

"Perfect." Claire started to leave, then paused. "I've read her books. They're very popular."

"Have you tried any of the recipes?"

Something flickered across Claire's face—pain, quickly masked. "Once. A long time ago." She adjusted her camera bag. "See you Friday."

After she left, Eliza found herself studying the business card. Claire Hartwick, Food & Lifestyle Photography. The website listed was professional, the portfolio impressive. But something about the woman's carefully controlled demeanor reminded Eliza of herself in the early Portland days— someone working very hard to keep old pain buried.

Bruno woofed softly from his bed, a questioning sound.

"I don't know, boy," Eliza said. "But I think next week is going to be interesting."

* * *

THURSDAY EVENING, Eliza walked Bruno past the Town Square where volunteers were setting up for the Harvest Festival. Orange and black bunting hung from the Victorian lamp-posts, and someone was testing the sound system with bursts of static and apology. The square would be transformed by Saturday—food vendors, craft booths, the annual costume contest, and the tasting event that would showcase local cuisine.

Wade Colton stood near the gazebo, supervising the setup with the patient authority of someone who'd done this for fifteen years. His gray eyes tracked the controlled chaos, making mental notes about traffic flow and emergency access.

"Sheriff," Eliza greeted him.

"Eliza. Bruno." Wade bent to scratch the dog's ears, his knees popping audibly. "Getting too old for this."

"The festival or the job?"

"Both, probably." He straightened, watching a volunteer nearly drop a speaker. "You're hosting Margot Sterling's book signing."

"News travels."

"It does." Wade's expression was carefully neutral. "You should know there's been some... tension. Millie's upset, Diane Morrison's upset, and I got a call from Richard Pemberton—you know, Dr. Pemberton's nephew, the food blogger—complaining that Margot used one of his recipes without credit."

"How many people has she stolen from?"

"In this town? At least four that I know of. Probably more who haven't realized it yet." Wade sighed. "I can't do anything about it. Recipe theft isn't illegal, and she's technically not breaking any laws. But keep an eye on things Friday, will you? Emotions are running high."

"You think someone might cause trouble?"

"I think Margot Sterling has a talent for making enemies, and she's walking back into a town full of people she's wronged." Wade's hand moved to his belt where his latex gloves sat in their usual pouch—a habit from thirty years of law enforcement. "Just be careful. When people feel powerless, they do stupid things."

That night, Eliza lay in bed in her apartment above the bookstore, listening to Bruno's gentle snoring and thinking about recipes and theft and the particular kind of violation that came from having your work stolen and credited to someone else.

She'd left Portland to escape that feeling—the case that had carved too deep, the sense that something essential had been taken from her. She understood, perhaps better than Wade realized, what it felt like to have someone take something you'd built and claim it as their own.

Below her, Bookmark & Brew sat quiet and orderly, every book in its place, every mystery properly shelved. But next week, Margot Sterling would arrive with her stolen recipes and celebrity smile, and Eliza had a feeling the careful order of Ashford Creek was about to be disturbed.

* * *

FRIDAY MORNING, one week before the murder, Margot Sterling posted on social media:

Can't wait to return to my hometown of Ashford Creek! Book signing at the charming Bookmark & Brew today at 2 PM, then celebrating local cuisine at Saturday's Harvest Festival. There's nothing quite like coming home. #AutumnHarvest #NewEngland-Cooking #LocalFlavors

The post included a photo of her holding the book, backlit by autumn sunshine, looking every inch the successful author returning in triumph.

In her small apartment above Morrison's Morning Goods, Diane Morrison saw the post and felt rage burn hot enough to make her hands shake.

In the Teacup Inn's private office, Millie Hart looked at the photo and carefully, deliberately, closed her laptop.

In her modest rental house on Elm Street, Claire Hartwick stared at Margot's smile for a full minute before deleting the notification and returning to editing photographs that had nothing to do with cookbook authors or stolen recipes or the life she'd lost ten years ago.

And in Bookmark & Brew, Eliza Prescott prepared for a book signing, unaware that in exactly one week, Margot Sterling would be dead, and Ashford Creek would learn that some debts could never be repaid—only avenged.

CHAPTER 1

THE BOOK SIGNING

*T*he Friday afternoon crowd at Bookmark & Brew exceeded Eliza's expectations. She'd arranged thirty folding chairs in rows facing the reading nook where Margot Sterling would hold court, and by one-forty-five, every seat was filled with more people standing along the walls. The smell of fresh coffee mingled with autumn rain—the weather had turned sometime after lunch, the sky going gray and heavy.

Bruno lay behind the counter on his bed, watching the crowd with the patience of a retired professional who'd seen far more chaotic gatherings than this. But his ears swiveled constantly, tracking voices and movement, cataloging each new arrival.

Eliza had pushed the new releases table against the wall to make room, stacking Margot's books in an artful pyramid that would make unpacking later a nightmare but photographed beautifully. Thirty copies of *Autumn Harvest*, their autumn-leaf covers bright against the dark wood shelves.

The Henderson sisters had claimed front-row seats, Bitsy

and Mitsy tucked into their carrying bags and peering out with bright black eyes. Dr. Pemberton hid behind his newspaper in the back corner, though Eliza noticed he hadn't turned a page in ten minutes. Tom Garrett from the pharmacy stood near the mystery section, pretending to browse thrillers while actually watching the door.

Millie arrived at one-fifty, her pink scarf knotted with unusual tightness around her neck. She didn't sit, just stood near the cooking section with her arms crossed, her face carefully neutral.

Diane Morrison entered moments later, still wearing her bakery apron with flour dusting one shoulder. She caught Millie's eye across the room, and something passed between them—solidarity in stolen recipes, perhaps, or mutual recognition of rage held barely in check.

Claire Hartwick moved through the crowd like water, her camera already raised, capturing candid shots of the assembled townspeople. She worked with professional efficiency, checking her settings, adjusting her position for better light. Every movement spoke of someone who knew her craft.

Wade appeared in the doorway at one-fifty-five, not in uniform but in civilian clothes—jeans and a button-down that made him look less like a sheriff and more like a concerned neighbor. Which, Eliza supposed, was probably the point. He caught her eye and gave a slight nod: *I'm here. Just in case.*

At precisely two o'clock, Margot Sterling swept through the door like she owned not just the bookstore but the entire town.

She wore what Eliza's detective eye priced at roughly two thousand dollars—designer jeans, a cashmere sweater in deep burgundy, and leather boots that clicked against the wooden floor with confident authority. Her hair was professionally styled, her makeup camera-ready, and she carried herself with the ease of someone accustomed to being the most important person in any room.

"Eliza Prescott?" Her smile was brilliant, practiced. "Thank you so much for hosting me. What a charming little shop."

Little. The word landed like a dismissal wrapped in compliment.

"Welcome to Bookmark & Brew." Eliza kept her voice professionally warm. "We're excited to have you."

"The pleasure is mine, returning to my roots." Margot's gaze swept the assembled crowd with the precision of someone calculating book sales and publicity value. Her smile widened as she spotted Claire with her camera. "Wonderful, we'll have professional photos. I'll make sure to tag you when I post them."

Claire's expression didn't change, but something in her posture stiffened, like a person bracing for impact.

Margot settled into the reading chair Eliza had positioned, arranging herself with the ease of someone who'd done hundreds of these events. She placed her designer handbag—Eliza recognized it as Prada, another thousand dollars at least—on the small side table within easy reach.

"Before we begin," Margot said, her voice carrying effortlessly to the back of the room, "I should mention I'm severely allergic to walnuts. Deathly allergic, actually." She lifted her wrist to show a medical alert bracelet, silver and discrete. "I always carry an EpiPen, of course—can't be too careful. But I wanted to mention it in case anyone brought treats to share."

Several people glanced at the refreshment table Eliza had set up—coffee, tea, and some cookies from the general store. No walnuts in sight.

"Now then." Margot picked up a copy of her book from

the stack beside her chair. "Let me tell you about *Autumn Harvest* and my journey back to New England's culinary traditions."

The presentation was polished, professional, and subtly condescending. Margot spoke about "rediscovering authentic flavors" and "preserving heritage recipes before they were lost to time." She described her research process—traveling to small towns, interviewing "local characters," testing and refining recipes until they met her standards.

"Of course," she said with a modest laugh, "many of these recipes came from family oral traditions. Written down for the first time in my books. It's important work, really, preserving this culinary history."

In the cooking section, Millie's knuckles went white where she gripped her arms.

Margot read a passage about autumn entertaining, her voice warm and engaging. She was good at this, Eliza had to admit. Whatever else Margot Sterling was, she knew how to work a crowd.

"The lemon scones, for instance," Margot said, flipping to a bookmarked page, "are based on techniques I learned from old New England inns. The secret is in the glaze—that perfect balance of tart and sweet that makes them irresistible."

She didn't look at Millie, but somehow the words felt aimed like an arrow.

When Margot opened the floor for questions, Richard Pemberton stood immediately. Dr. Pemberton's nephew was in his late twenties, thin and intense, with the nervous energy of someone who'd been waiting for this moment.

"Ms. Sterling, I'm Richard Pemberton. I write a food blog —New England Table. I noticed one of your recipes, the maple-glazed Brussels sprouts on page eighty-nine, is remarkably similar to one I posted three years ago. Same proportions, same technique, even the same finishing touch with pomegranate seeds."

The room went very quiet.

Margot's smile didn't waver. "Recipes evolve, Mr. Pemberton. Brussels sprouts with maple is hardly a novel concept. Great minds think alike, as they say."

"But the pomegranate seeds—that's a very specific choice. I developed that combination over months of testing."

"And I'm sure many other cooks have arrived at the same conclusion independently." Her tone remained pleasant but something in her eyes had gone hard. "The joy of cooking is that there are only so many ingredients. Convergent evolution, if you will."

"That's not—"

"I appreciate your passion for food," Margot cut him off smoothly, "but I'm afraid we don't have time to debate every recipe origin. These things happen in the culinary world. Ideas travel. Perhaps you should be flattered that professionals arrive at similar conclusions."

Richard's face flushed red. "I'm not flattered. I'm—"

"Next question?" Margot turned away from him with dismissive finality.

Claire's camera clicked, capturing Richard's humiliated expression, Margot's imperious profile, the tension written across every face in the room.

Wade had shifted position, Eliza noticed, moving closer to Richard in case the young man's anger boiled over. But Richard just sat down hard, his jaw clenched tight enough to crack teeth.

The Henderson sisters asked about her favorite autumn ingredients—a soft question that let Margot recover her charming persona. Dr. Pemberton asked about her writing process. A tourist from Connecticut wanted to know her tips for entertaining.

Then Diane Morrison stood.

"Ms. Sterling, my name is Diane Morrison. I own Morrison's Morning Goods, the bakery on Main Street."

"How lovely." Margot's smile was automatic.

"Your apple cider donut recipe on page seventy-three—that's my grandmother's recipe. She gave it to you twenty-five years ago for a school project. You published it without permission or credit."

The room went silent again, but this time the quality of the silence was different. Everyone leaned forward.

Margot's expression shifted through several emotions too quickly to fully catalog—surprise, calculation, then a careful settling into concerned sympathy. "I'm afraid you're mistaken. That recipe has been in my family for generations."

"No." Diane's voice shook slightly but held firm. "It hasn't. I have proof—my grandmother's original recipe card, photographs from our bakery in the eighties. You stole it."

"Recipes can't be copyrighted, Ms. Morrison. I'm sorry if you feel some sort of ownership, but culinary traditions belong to everyone." Margot's tone had gone from sympathetic to patronizing. "Perhaps your grandmother shared a recipe that had been passed to her. These things have complex histories."

"She developed that recipe herself. The technique, the spice ratios, everything. And after your book came out, my business nearly failed because people thought I was copying you."

"I can hardly be responsible for your business challenges." The sympathy had evaporated entirely now, replaced by cool disdain. "If you're struggling, perhaps you should focus on innovation rather than accusations."

Diane opened her mouth, closed it, opened it again. No words came. She looked like someone who'd been slapped and couldn't quite process the shock of it.

"I think we're done here," Wade said quietly, standing. His voice carried the weight of authority despite the civilian clothes. "Ms. Morrison, why don't we step outside for some air?"

"I'm fine," Diane said, but her voice cracked on the word.

Margot had already moved on, gesturing to the stack of books beside her. "Well, that was unfortunate. Shall we begin the signing? I'd love to personalize copies for each of you."

The crowd stirred uneasily, but people began forming a line. The pull of celebrity, Eliza thought cynically, was stronger than solidarity with their neighbors. Or perhaps they just wanted their books signed before the situation deteriorated further.

She found herself watching Margot work the line with professional charm. Each person received a smile, a brief personal comment, a flourished signature. Margot seemed to have an instinct for what each person wanted to hear—compliments for the elderly tourists, enthusiasm for the young mothers with their cookbook collections, knowing sophistication for the Henderson sisters.

When Eleanor reached the front of the line, Margot's smile was particularly bright. "Oh, these antiques are extraordinary. Tell me, do you have any vintage kitchenware? I collect Depression-era mixing bowls."

"We do!" Eleanor practically glowed under the attention. "Beautiful pieces, some quite rare."

"I'd love to visit your shop tomorrow after the festival. Perhaps we could discuss a few pieces I might purchase?"

"Of course! We open at nine."

Eliza watched Eleanor return to her seat, clutching her signed book and beaming. Margot had made a friend, neutralized a potential ally of Diane and Millie, and set up a future transaction—all in ninety seconds. Whatever else she was, the woman was skilled at manipulation.

The line moved steadily. Margot signed books, charmed tourists, and carefully avoided eye contact with anyone who'd challenged her. Richard Pemberton didn't join the line, just stood with his arms crossed, glowering. Diane had finally left with Wade, who returned alone and positioned himself where he could watch both Margot and the remaining crowd.

Millie hadn't moved from her spot near the cooking section. When the line finally thinned, she walked forward with deliberate steps.

"I don't need you to sign my book," Millie said quietly. "I just want you to know that I recognize my grandmother's lemon scone recipe on page forty-seven. You changed a few words, adjusted one ratio slightly, but it's hers. You stole seventy years of my family's work."

Margot looked up, and for just a moment, something cold flashed in her eyes. Then the professional mask slid back into place. "Millie Hart. Of course. The Teacup Inn. Such a charming little establishment."

Little again.

"Your grandmother's scones were legendary, I remember them from my childhood. It's possible my family recipe has similar elements—after all, New England baking traditions share common roots. But I assure you, my recipe is my own."

"It's not."

"Can you prove that?" Margot's smile was sharp now, predatory. "In court, I mean. Because my publisher has excellent lawyers, and they take accusations of plagiarism very seriously. Very seriously indeed."

The threat hung in the air, crystal clear despite the pleasant tone.

Millie's face went white, then red. "You're—"

"Successful, yes. And I've worked very hard for that success. I'd hate to see unfounded accusations damage the reputation I've built." Margot's gaze was steady, challenging. "These little misunderstandings can become quite costly for everyone involved."

Millie turned and walked out, her pink scarf trailing behind her like a banner of retreat.

The remaining customers finished getting their books signed in uncomfortable silence. Claire had stopped photographing, her camera lowered, her expression unreadable. She stood near the mystery section, close enough to hear everything but far enough to seem separate from the confrontation.

When the last customer left, Margot stood and stretched like a cat, seemingly unbothered by the tension she'd created. "Well, that was eventful. Small towns do have their dramas, don't they?"

Eliza kept her voice professionally neutral. "Will you need anything else?"

Margot pulled out her phone, checking something. "I have a dinner reservation at seven, so I should get back to my hotel. The Harborview Inn, do you know it?"

"I do."

"Charming place, though the shower pressure leaves something to be desired." She gathered her things, slipping her phone into her expensive bag. "Tomorrow's tasting event should be interesting. I'm looking forward to evaluating the local cuisine. It's been so long since I've had authentic Ashford Creek cooking."

The way she said *authentic* made it sound like an insult.

Eliza observed when Margot suddenly frowned and began digging through her bag with increasing urgency.

"Is everything all right?" Eliza asked.

"My EpiPen. I always keep it in the side pocket, but..." Margot pulled items out of her bag—wallet, lipstick, phone charger, keys. "That's odd. I could have sworn—"

She dumped the entire contents onto the counter. Makeup, receipts, breath mints, a small notebook. No EpiPen.

"I must have left it at the hotel," Margot said, though she didn't sound convinced. "How careless of me. Well, I have a backup there. Still, I should be more careful."

She repacked her bag quickly, her professional composure slightly ruffled. "Thank you for hosting me, Eliza. See you tomorrow at the festival."

After she left, Eliza stood in the suddenly quiet bookstore, looking at the empty chair where Margot had held court, the depleted stack of signed books, the folding chairs that would need to be put away.

Bruno padded over and sat at her feet, looking up with dark eyes that seemed to hold a question.

"I know, boy," Eliza said quietly. "Something's wrong."

She thought about the missing EpiPen, Margot's certainty that it should have been there, the way she'd dumped her entire bag out. It hadn't been left at the hotel. Someone had taken it.

The signing had been chaos—people crowding around, bumping into each other, the confusion of thirty people in a space meant for browsing. Anyone could have gotten close to Margot's bag while she was distracted signing books.

Eliza looked around the bookstore. The crowd had created disorder—chairs pushed askew, books slightly out of place on the shelves, coffee cups abandoned on the refreshment table. She began straightening automatically, her mind working through the afternoon's events.

Diane Morrison, humiliated and furious, had left halfway through. Richard Pemberton had stood in the back, watching with visible anger. Millie had been threatened in front of everyone. Claire Hartwick had documented it all with her camera, her face carefully blank.

And now Margot's EpiPen was missing.

Wade appeared in the doorway as Eliza was folding the last chair. "Some signing."

"You could say that."

"I followed up with Diane. She's upset but calm. Not going to do anything rash." He moved to help with the chairs, stacking them against the wall with practiced efficiency. "Margot Sterling has a talent for making enemies."

"She's missing her EpiPen."

Wade's hands stilled. "Missing how?"

"It was in her bag at the start of the event. She mentioned it specifically, said she always carries it because of her walnut allergy. When she was leaving, she realized it was gone."

"Could she have left it at her hotel?"

"She said she always keeps it in the same pocket. She was certain it should have been there." Eliza met his eyes. "Someone took it, Wade. During the signing, when everyone was crowded around."

"Why would someone—" He stopped, understanding crossing his face. "That's premeditation."

"That's what I'm worried about."

They stood in the quiet bookstore, surrounded by mysteries whose solutions were always in the final chapter, always neat and clear. Real life was messier, Eliza thought. Real life was missing EpiPens and angry bakers and threats wrapped in pleasant smiles.

"Keep an eye on things tomorrow," Wade said finally. "The festival, the tasting event. If someone took that EpiPen..."

"They're planning to use it," Eliza finished. "Or planning to make sure Margot can't."

After Wade left, Eliza finished cleaning up. She flipped the sign to closed, locked the door, and stood looking out at Main Street where rain had started falling in earnest. The cobblestones gleamed like oil under the old-fashioned lampposts the town council had fought to preserve.

Somewhere out there, someone had Margot Sterling's EpiPen. Someone who'd been humiliated or threatened or robbed of their life's work. Someone who'd decided that Margot's return to Ashford Creek would be more than just unpleasant.

CHAPTER 2

THE HARVEST FESTIVAL

*S*aturday arrived with the kind of autumn perfection that made tourists drive hours for a glimpse of New England at its finest. The rain had cleared overnight, leaving the air crisp and clean, and the morning sun painted Main Street in shades of amber and gold. By ten o'clock, the Town Square was transformed into a harvest wonderland.

Orange and black bunting draped between the Victorian lampposts. Hay bales lined the walkways, topped with arrangements of pumpkins, gourds, and late-season chrysanthemums. The gazebo had been converted into a small stage where a bluegrass band would perform in the afternoon. Food vendors lined the perimeter, their tents bright against the autumn foliage, and the smell of cider donuts, kettle corn, and roasted nuts filled the air.

Eliza had left Bookmark & Brew in the capable hands of her part-time assistant and arrived with Bruno at eleven. The festival was already crowded—families with children, elderly couples holding hands, tourists with cameras, locals who'd been coming to this event for decades. The costume contest wouldn't start until two, but already she could see pirates and princesses, superheroes and ghosts wandering through the crowd.

Bruno walked at her heel, his professional training evident in how he navigated the chaos without pulling or getting distracted. But his ears swiveled constantly, cataloging sounds, and his nose worked overtime processing the riot of festival smells.

The food displays were set up throughout the square, each local establishment showcasing their specialties. Millie had arranged the Teacup Inn's offerings at a prominent booth— her famous lemon scones displayed on vintage china plates. Diane's apple cider donuts from Morrison's Morning Goods drew a steady line of customers. The Henderson sisters had contributed their pumpkin cookies, and several other local businesses had added their own harvest specialties.

At the center of the square, a large tent housed the main food displays, including Diane's award-winning pumpkin soup—the recipe that had won the regional competition three years running. The soup was kept warm in an elegant tureen, garnished with roasted pumpkin seeds and sage-brown butter.

Millie moved between the displays with mechanical efficiency, arranging serving items and adjusting flower arrangements. She wore her inn uniform—crisp white blouse and black skirt—but her signature pink scarf was absent. Her face was carefully composed, but Eliza noticed how her hands trembled slightly when she thought no one was watching.

"How are you holding up?" Eliza asked quietly, approaching the table where Millie was fussing with the scone display.

"Fine." The word came out too quickly, too bright. "Just

fine. Professional hospitality, that's what grandmother always said. Kill them with kindness."

She realized what she'd said and her face went pale. "I didn't mean—that's just an expression—"

"I know." Eliza touched her arm gently. "Millie, if you need to leave, no one would blame you."

"And let her win? Let her walk around sampling my grandmother's recipe—or her version of it—while everyone watches?" Millie's jaw set with determination. "No. I'll be here. I'll serve refreshments. I'll smile. And I'll watch her choke on every bite."

She walked away before Eliza could respond, disappearing behind her display booth with quick, angry steps.

Bruno woofed softly, a questioning sound.

"I'm worried too, boy," Eliza murmured.

Wade appeared at her elbow, dressed in full uniform today, his presence a visible reminder that law enforcement was watching. "Situation report?"

"Tense. Millie's barely holding it together. Have you seen Diane?"

"Her booth is on the north side, selling fresh donuts. She looks exhausted but stable." Wade's gaze swept the crowd with practiced efficiency. "Richard Pemberton is here too, doing some kind of live blog coverage. Claire Hartwick is photographing everything, as usual."

"And Margot?"

"Not here yet. She's supposed to arrive at noon for the publicity walk-through." He checked his watch—a sturdy Timex that had survived three decades of police work. "Fifteen minutes."

They didn't have to wait that long. At eleven fifty-three, a black town car pulled up as close to the square as traffic allowed, and Margot Sterling emerged like visiting royalty.

She'd dressed for the occasion—designer jeans, cashmere sweater in deep plum, and a silk scarf that looked like it might be Hermès. Her hair and makeup were camera-ready, and she carried the same expensive Prada bag from yesterday.

A small camera crew followed her—local TV station, by the look of their equipment. Margot had clearly arranged for coverage. She paused for a sound bite, smiling brilliantly for the camera.

"It's wonderful to be home in Ashford Creek, celebrating the harvest traditions that shaped my approach to cooking. These local flavors, these heritage recipes—this is what *Autumn Harvest* is all about. Preserving our culinary past for future generations."

Eliza watched Millie's face go rigid with barely suppressed fury.

Tom Garrett, pressed into service as festival coordinator, approached with a clipboard and nervous energy. "Ms. Sterling, welcome back to Ashford Creek. We're honored to have you here. I thought we'd start with the heritage food displays, then work our way through the craft booths?"

"Perfect," Margot said, adjusting her scarf against the autumn breeze. "I'm looking forward to sampling authentic Ashford Creek cuisine. It's been so long since I've tasted the real thing."

The emphasis on *real* made several nearby vendors shift uncomfortably.

The impromptu tour began with appetizers. Tom guided Margot to the Henderson sisters' booth, where Eleanor and Edith stood with their matching Pomeranians tucked into carrier bags.

"These are our grandmother's pumpkin cookies," Eleanor said proudly, offering a small plate. "The recipe's been in our family since 1923."

Margot took a delicate bite, chewed thoughtfully, and smiled for the camera. "Charming! Good spice balance, though perhaps a touch heavy on the ginger for my taste. But family traditions are so important, aren't they? Even when they might benefit from a professional's refinement."

Eleanor's smile faltered slightly, but she rallied with New England politeness.

They moved to Tom Garrett's pharmacy booth, where he was selling locally-sourced honey and maple syrup. Then to a savory tart display from the general store deli. Each stop was accompanied by Margot's commentary—sometimes praise, more often criticism wrapped in compliments, always with the subtle suggestion that she could do better.

The camera crew followed it all, capturing both Margot's performance and the increasingly uncomfortable faces of the local vendors.

Finally, they reached Diane's booth. Morrison's Morning Goods had the prime corner location, with fresh donuts displayed in glass cases and the famous pumpkin soup featured prominently in an elegant serving station.

Diane stood beside her display, her bakery apron crisp and white, her face carefully blank as Tom introduced her.

"This is Diane Morrison of Morrison's Morning Goods. Diane, would you tell Ms. Sterling about your apple cider donuts?"

"They're my grandmother's recipe," Diane said quietly, her voice steady despite the tension. "Three generations of Morrison bakers. We won a ribbon at the state fair in 1987."

Margot examined a donut like a scientist studying a specimen, then took a bite. She chewed slowly, her expression thoughtful.

"Interesting," she said finally. "The spice blend is quite good. Very similar to the apple cider donut recipe in my book, actually. Great minds thinking alike, as I mentioned yesterday."

The crowd around the booth went silent.

"Though I think my version has a touch more depth," Margot continued, oblivious—or deliberately blind—to the tension. "Perhaps a longer proof time? Or different apple cider reduction technique? But these are certainly serviceable."

Serviceable. The word hung in the air like an insult.

Diane's face flushed dark red, but she said nothing. Her hands clenched at her sides, knuckles going white, but she maintained her position behind her booth with rigid dignity.

Claire Hartwick's camera clicked steadily, capturing Margot's casual cruelty, Diane's barely restrained rage, the uncomfortable faces of the crowd.

"And this must be your famous pumpkin soup," Tom said quickly, trying to move past the awkward moment. "Award-winning recipe, I understand?"

"Three years running at regionals," Diane said, pride creeping into her voice despite everything. "It's been in the family for four generations. My great-grandmother's creation."

The soup was served in small ceramic bowls, garnished with roasted pumpkin seeds and a drizzle of sage-brown butter. It smelled divine—earthy and sweet and savory all at once.

Margot lifted her bowl, inhaled deeply, and smiled. "This looks absolutely divine. The presentation is lovely."

She took a spoonful, tasting carefully. Her expression shifted through several stages—pleasure, surprise, then something calculating.

"Oh my," she said. "This is extraordinary. The depth of flavor, the complexity—"

She took another spoonful, then another, apparently lost in the experience. "The subtle nuttiness, the way it balances the sweetness of the pumpkin—this is really quite special."

For a moment, Diane's face showed something like hope. Perhaps Margot would acknowledge the quality without claiming to do better. Perhaps, just this once—

"I'll have to get this recipe," Margot said, setting down her bowl. "This would be perfect for my next book. With a few refinements, of course. Perhaps a different garnish, maybe some modifications to the spice blend—but the base is excellent. Really excellent work."

The hope in Diane's face curdled into something darker.

"The recipe isn't for sale," Diane said quietly.

"Oh, I'm sure we can work something out. A credit in the book, perhaps? 'Inspired by Diane Morrison of Ashford Creek.'" Margot's smile was brilliant, oblivious. "It would be wonderful publicity for your bakery."

"I said it's not for sale."

"Don't be silly. Recipes are meant to be shared. And with my platform, I could introduce this soup to thousands of people. Think of it as honoring your great-grandmother's legacy on a much larger scale."

"By stealing it? Like you stole everything else?" Diane's voice had gone flat, dangerous.

The square had gone absolutely silent. Even the camera crew seemed frozen, unsure whether to keep filming.

Margot's smile finally faltered. "I don't appreciate that

accusation. As I've explained repeatedly, recipes cannot be copyrighted. If you're upset that I've achieved success with traditional New England cooking, perhaps you should examine your own career choices rather than attacking mine."

"Get out." Diane's voice shook, but with rage now, not fear. "Get away from my booth before I—"

Wade moved forward, his presence commanding without being threatening. "Ladies, let's take a breath."

But Diane wasn't finished. "You're a thief. A liar and a thief. You've built your entire career on stolen work, and you have the audacity to come back here and insult us while eating our food. You're—"

"I'm successful," Margot said coldly, the pleasant mask dropping completely. "And you're a bitter baker in a failing shop in a nothing town. That's the difference between us. I took these recipes and made something of them. You just... kept making the same donuts year after year, expecting the world to notice."

The cruelty in her voice was breathtaking.

Diane lunged forward, and only Wade's quick reflexes prevented her from reaching Margot. He caught her arm, held her back with the practiced ease of someone who'd broken up countless confrontations.

"Diane, don't," he said quietly. "She's not worth it."

"She's worth going to jail for," Diane spat, tears streaming down her face now. "She's worth—"

"Let's get some air." Wade was already guiding her away from the booth, leaving Deputy Morris to watch the crowd. "Come on. Walk with me."

They disappeared into the festival crowd, Diane's shoulders shaking with sobs she'd held back for years.

The square erupted in whispered conversation. The

camera crew exchanged glances, clearly wondering if they should have recorded that. Claire Hartwick lowered her camera, her face thoughtful.

Margot dabbed at her mouth with a napkin, composure already returning. "Well. That was unfortunate. Emotions do run high at these events, don't they?" She glanced at her watch. "I believe I have time for one more stop before my interview?"

Tom Garrett nodded mutely, still processing what he'd witnessed.

"Wonderful." Margot stood, gathering her things. "Perhaps we could visit the craft booths? I'd love to see what other local traditions are being preserved."

She walked away from the food displays with her head high, apparently unbothered by the confrontation. The camera crew followed her, still hoping for usable footage.

Eliza found herself standing near Diane's soup station, looking at the half-empty bowl Margot had left behind. Bruno pressed against her leg, and she absently scratched his ears while her mind worked through what she'd just witnessed.

Diane had been physically restrained from attacking Margot. Richard Pemberton had watched from the back of the crowd, his face dark with satisfaction at Margot's public cruelty being exposed. Millie had disappeared behind her booth, probably hiding her own tears. Claire had documented it all with her camera, her expression unreadable.

And somewhere out there, someone had Margot's EpiPen. Someone who knew about her deadly walnut allergy. Someone who'd just watched her taste pumpkin soup and comment on its "subtle nuttiness."

Eliza's blood ran cold.

She looked at the soup bowl again, then at the serving

tureen on the display table. The garnish on top was roasted pumpkin seeds and brown butter—she'd watched Diane prepare it this morning. But the soup itself, the base that had been made yesterday and reheated this morning...

"Wade," she said urgently into her phone. "You need to get back here. Now."

She knelt beside the table, Bruno sitting at attention beside her. She could smell the soup—pumpkin, sage, cream, butter. And underneath, barely detectable, something else. Something that might be nutmeg or might be...

Bruno's nose twitched. He leaned forward, sniffing the bowl Margot had used, and then he sat. His alert posture. His evidence signal.

"Good boy," Eliza whispered, her heart pounding. "What did you find?"

She looked around the square. Millie was still behind her booth. Claire had set down her camera and was checking something on her phone. The Henderson sisters were whispering urgently. Tom Garrett was trying to manage the aftermath of the confrontation.

No one was paying attention to Eliza and Bruno at the soup station.

She pulled out her phone and took a photo of the bowl, the serving tureen, the setup. Then she carefully moved the bowl away from the edge of the table, making sure no one else would accidentally consume any.

Wade returned five minutes later, slightly out of breath. "What is it?"

"The soup. Bruno alerted to something in Margot's bowl."

Wade's face went grim. He pulled on latex gloves from his belt—he always carried them, a habit from thirty years of law enforcement—and carefully lifted the bowl. He sniffed it cautiously, the way she'd taught herself in Portland, wafting the scent rather than breathing directly.

His eyes met hers. "Bitter almonds."

"Walnut oil?"

"Or something worse. We need to—"

A scream cut through the festival noise, sharp and terrified.

They ran toward the sound, Bruno at their heels. People scattered, pointing toward the craft booth area near the edge of the square.

Margot Sterling lay on the ground beside a display of handmade quilts, her body convulsing. Her expensive bag had spilled its contents across the grass—phone, wallet, makeup, keys. Her hands clawed at her throat, her face already turning an alarming shade of blue.

"Where's her EpiPen?" someone shouted.

"She doesn't have it—it's missing—"

"Someone call 911!"

Eliza pushed through the crowd, her detective training overriding civilian instinct. Wade was already there, checking for a pulse, looking for the missing medication that might save Margot's life.

"Her purse," he barked. "Check her purse!"

Three people emptied the bag completely. No EpiPen. No emergency medication. Nothing that could stop the allergic reaction that was killing Margot Sterling in front of dozens of witnesses.

"My car," Wade said, already moving. "I have an emergency kit—"

But the parking area was three blocks away, through festival crowds too thick to run through easily. Even at a full sprint, it would take him minutes he didn't have.

Margot's convulsions were getting weaker. Her lips had gone from blue to purple. Her eyes rolled back, and the horrible gasping sounds she'd been making stopped.

Claire Hartwick was suddenly there, her camera forgotten, pulling something from her own bag. "I have one," she said. "I'm allergic to bees, I always carry—"

She jammed the EpiPen into Margot's thigh with practiced efficiency. The auto-injector clicked, delivering its dose of epinephrine.

For a moment, nothing happened. Then Margot gasped, her body jerking. Her chest heaved, pulling in air. The blue tinge to her lips began to fade, slowly, too slowly, but fading.

"Ambulance is two minutes out," Deputy Morris announced, phone pressed to his ear.

Eliza looked at Margot's scattered belongings, then at the crowd that had gathered. Her mind cataloged faces, positions, who was where when the scream came. The detective's instinct she'd tried to leave behind in Portland was fully awake now, recording every detail.

Wade knelt beside Margot, keeping her airway clear, talking to her in low, steady tones. She was breathing now, gasping and weak, but breathing. Her eyes fluttered open, unfocused and terrified.

"You're okay," Wade said. "Help is coming. Stay with me."

The ambulance arrived in a controlled chaos of flashing lights and urgent voices. EMTs took over, loading Margot onto a stretcher, starting an IV, administering oxygen. She was conscious but barely, her hand weakly grasping at the oxygen mask as they loaded her into the ambulance.

As the ambulance pulled away, siren wailing, Wade turned to the assembled crowd. His face was grim, his cop voice steady and commanding.

"Everyone stays here. Nobody leaves this area until I've taken statements. This wasn't an accident—this was attempted murder."

The crowd murmured, shocked voices overlapping. Eliza watched their faces—surprise, fear, calculation. Someone in this crowd had known about the walnut oil in the soup. Someone had made sure Margot's EpiPen was missing when she needed it.

Someone had just tried to kill Margot Sterling, and they'd nearly succeeded.

Eliza felt Bruno press against her leg, his solid presence grounding her. The autumn sunshine suddenly felt too bright, the festival atmosphere grotesque. Somewhere in this crowd of costumed children and elderly couples, of local business owners and innocent tourists, was someone who'd committed attempted murder in broad daylight.

And if Margot died—when she died, Eliza's detective instincts corrected grimly—this would become a homicide investigation. In a town of barely three thousand people, where everyone knew everyone's business, someone had decided that Margot Sterling's theft of recipes was worth killing for.

The question was: who?

CHAPTER 3

MISSING MEDICINE

*T*he Ashford Creek Community Center had never been used for a police investigation before. Wade commandeered the main meeting room, sending Deputy Morris to cordon off the tasting tent as a crime scene and Deputy Lang to the hospital to guard Margot Sterling—if she survived.

By two o'clock, the room was filled with uncomfortable townspeople sitting in folding chairs that squeaked every time someone shifted position. The costume contest had been cancelled. The bluegrass band had packed up without playing a note. Parents hurried children home, away from whatever darkness had invaded their festival.

Eliza sat near the back with Bruno at her feet, observing. She'd given her statement first—what she'd seen, what Bruno had alerted to, the timeline of events. Wade had asked her to stay, and she understood why. She knew these people. She'd hear things in their statements that he might miss.

Claire Hartwick sat alone near the windows, her camera bag at her feet. She'd been separated immediately and questioned first—the woman who'd saved Margot's life was also a person of interest. Her EpiPen had been confiscated as evidence, photographed, documented. She'd submitted to the questions with quiet cooperation, her face revealing nothing.

Millie Hart sat with the Henderson sisters, all three women looking shaken. Millie's hands twisted a tissue into shreds, over and over, a nervous gesture that spoke volumes about her state of mind.

Diane Morrison sat apart from everyone, her bakery apron removed, her arms wrapped around herself like she was holding something fragile inside. Tom Garrett sat beside her—whether for support or surveillance, Eliza couldn't tell.

Richard Pemberton paced near the refreshment table, too agitated to sit. Every few minutes he'd pull out his phone, check it, put it away again. His blog post about the tasting event had gone viral in the past hour—local drama captured and broadcast to thousands of readers before the ambulance had even left.

Wade worked methodically, interviewing witnesses one at a time in the small office off the main room. Deputy Morris took notes, his neat handwriting filling page after page of his notebook.

Eliza's phone buzzed. A text from the hospital contact she'd cultivated during her Portland days—a nurse who understood that sometimes information saved lives.

Critical but stable. Severe anaphylactic shock. Lucky someone had epinephrine. Another 2 minutes and she'd be gone. Asking for police protection.

Eliza showed Wade the text during a break between interviews. His jaw tightened.

"She knows someone tried to kill her," he said quietly. "Question is whether she knows who."

"When can you interview her?"

"Doctors say tomorrow at the earliest. She's sedated, being monitored." Wade rubbed his face with both hands, suddenly looking every one of his fifty-plus years. "This is Ashford Creek. We don't do attempted murders. We do drunk and disorderly, occasional theft, teenagers being stupid. Not this."

"You can handle it."

"Can I?" He looked around the room at his neighbors, his community, people he'd known for decades. "One of them did this, Eliza. One of these people I've had coffee with, whose kids I've watched grow up, who waves at me on Main Street— one of them tried to commit murder."

Before Eliza could respond, Wade's phone rang. He answered, listened, his expression darkening. "Understood. Thank you."

He stood, commanding the room's attention without raising his voice. "I just got preliminary results from the state lab. The pumpkin soup contained walnut oil—enough to trigger a severe allergic reaction. Someone deliberately contaminated it, knowing Margot Sterling would taste it."

The room erupted in shocked voices. Wade waited for quiet, then continued.

"Both of Margot's EpiPens are still missing. One was stolen from her purse yesterday at the book signing. The other—her backup—was taken from her hotel room sometime Friday night or early Saturday morning."

"Hotel room?" Eleanor Henderson's voice was shrill. "Someone broke into her hotel room?"

"The lock wasn't forced. Either someone had a key or picked it. The hotel's security footage is being reviewed." Wade's gaze swept the room. "This was premeditated. Someone planned this carefully. They knew about the allergy, stole the medication, contaminated the food, and ensured the victim couldn't save herself."

Millie made a small sound, quickly stifled. Her face had gone white.

"I need to know who had access to the soup," Wade continued. "Who prepared it, who handled it, who was near it. Deputy Morris?"

Morris stood, consulting his notes. "The soup was made by Diane Morrison yesterday afternoon at her bakery. She transported it to the festival site this morning at seven AM in an insulated container. It was placed in the warming station by —" he checked his notes, "—Millie Hart at seven-thirty. The warming station was in the catering tent, which was secured overnight."

"Who had keys to the catering tent?" Wade asked.

"Three people," Morris read. "Millie Hart, Tom Garrett as festival coordinator, and Owen Kraft from the Teacup Inn— he was helping with setup."

Eliza made a mental note. Owen wasn't here—he'd been working at the inn during the festival, serving lunch to tourists. But he'd had access.

"The soup stayed in the warming station until service at noon," Morris continued. "Multiple people were in and out of the catering tent during that time. Volunteers, vendors, the Henderson sisters delivered their cookies around ten, Richard Pemberton was there taking photos for his blog around eleven—"

"I didn't touch anything," Richard interrupted. "I was just documenting the setup."

"—and Claire Hartwick was photographing the tent setup around nine-thirty."

Claire's voice was quiet but steady. "I took exterior shots

only. I didn't enter the catering area."

Wade turned to Diane. "When did you add the walnut oil?"

"I didn't." Diane's voice was raw from earlier crying. "I would never. That soup is my grandmother's recipe—pure pumpkin, cream, sage, butter. No nuts. Never any nuts. I know half the town has allergies."

"Then someone else did it. Someone who had access between seven-thirty AM and noon." Wade pulled out an evidence bag containing a small glass bottle. "We found this in the trash behind the catering tent. Walnut oil, nearly empty. No fingerprints—wiped clean."

The room fell silent, everyone staring at the small bottle that had nearly killed someone.

"I want to know everyone's movements this morning," Wade said. "Everyone who was near that tent, near that soup. And I want to know where you were Friday afternoon during the book signing, and Friday night between eleven PM and two AM."

He started calling people one by one into the office. The Henderson sisters went first, twittering nervously about their early arrival to deliver cookies, their brief chat with Millie, their return home by eight-thirty to open their antique shop.

Richard Pemberton went next, defensive and angry. "I was at the signing, yes. I was angry, yes. But I didn't poison anyone. I was documenting her cruelty for my blog, exposing her for what she is. That's all."

Tom Garrett's interview was shorter—he'd been coordinating setup all morning, visible to dozens of volunteers. His movements were accounted for.

When Millie's turn came, she stood with visible effort, her legs shaking. Bruno's ears pricked forward, tracking her movement. He could sense her distress, and Eliza saw his professional interest sharpen—victims and perpetrators often showed the same nervous behaviors.

Millie was in the office for twenty minutes. When she emerged, her face was streaked with tears and her hands trembled so badly she could barely hold her purse.

"I didn't do it," she said to the room, her voice breaking. "I wanted to. God help me, I wanted to hurt her for what she did to my family. But I didn't. I couldn't."

She fled before anyone could respond, the door closing behind her with a hollow thud.

Wade called Diane next. Her interview lasted longer—thirty minutes. Through the office's small window, Eliza could see Wade's careful body language, the way he leaned forward when asking questions, the patient waiting for answers. Diane's body language was defensive, arms crossed, shoulders hunched, but she answered every question.

When Diane finally emerged, she looked exhausted beyond measure. She caught Eliza's eye across the room, and something in her expression was desperate, pleading.

"I didn't do it," Diane said quietly, seemingly to everyone and no one. "The soup was clean when I made it. I swear on my grandmother's memory, I didn't put anything in it that wasn't supposed to be there."

"But you wanted to," someone muttered from the back. Eliza couldn't identify the voice.

"Of course I wanted to," Diane said, turning toward the speaker. "She destroyed my business, mocked my grandmother's work, and had the nerve to steal again. Yes, I wanted her to pay. But wanting and doing are different things."

She left then, walking out with what little dignity she had remaining.

Claire was called last among the primary suspects. Her

interview took the longest—forty-five minutes. When she finally emerged, her controlled composure had fractured slightly. Her eyes were red, though she hadn't been crying. She looked like someone who'd been forced to open old wounds and examine them under harsh light.

Wade appeared in the doorway, looking grim. "I'm releasing everyone for now, but nobody leaves town. I'll have more questions tomorrow." His gaze found Eliza. "Can I speak with you?"

She followed him into the office, Bruno padding beside her. Deputy Morris excused himself, leaving them alone.

"Tell me what you're thinking," Wade said, closing the door.

"Claire saved Margot's life."

"I know. Doesn't mean she didn't try to kill her first."

"Why would she carry an EpiPen if she'd planned the murder? That's either incredibly stupid or incredibly clever."

"Or she panicked when it was actually happening. Realized she couldn't go through with it." Wade sat heavily in the desk chair. "Her story checks out for the most part. She was at the book signing, photographing. She was at the festival this morning, photographing. She admits she was near the catering tent but says she only took exterior shots."

"What about her access to Margot's hotel room?"

"She's a photographer—she carries lock picks in her equipment bag. Says she uses them for location shoots, accessing locked buildings for architectural photography. I confiscated them."

Eliza thought about Claire's controlled demeanor, her careful invisibility despite being everywhere with her camera. "There's something else going on with her. Something personal."

"I know. She finally told me." Wade pulled out his notes. "Claire Hartwick isn't her birth name. She changed it legally five years ago, when she moved here. Her birth name was Claire Brennan."

"Why change it?"

"She wouldn't say directly, but I got the impression she was running from something. Or someone." Wade flipped through his notes. "I did a background check. Clean record, no red flags. But ten years ago, she was involved in a lawsuit—she sued a publisher for plagiarism. Lost the case, paid court costs and lawyer fees that bankrupted her."

Eliza's detective instincts sharpened. "Who did she sue?"

"That's the interesting part. She sued claiming someone stole her cookbook manuscript. The defendant's publisher was the same company that publishes Margot Sterling."

The pieces clicked together with sickening clarity. "Margot stole Claire's work."

"If the lawsuit allegations are true, yes. Claire claims she shared a manuscript with a friend for feedback. That friend allegedly stole it and published it under their own name. Claire couldn't prove the manuscript was hers first—no registration, no formal copyright filing. Just her word against theirs."

"And Margot's publisher buried her in legal fees."

"Exactly." Wade rubbed his eyes. "So we have a woman whose life was destroyed by recipe theft, living quietly in the same town where the thief has returned to steal again. That's motive."

"It's also means," Eliza said quietly. "If she wanted revenge, she had the skills—lock picking, knowledge of Margot's routines from photographing her. She could have stolen the

EpiPens, contaminated the soup, and set the whole thing in motion."

"But?"

"But she saved Margot's life. With her own EpiPen, which she'd lose if Margot died and it became evidence. That doesn't fit the profile of a careful killer."

Wade was quiet for a moment. "Unless she's building reasonable doubt. Save the victim, look like a hero, deflect suspicion."

They sat in silence, turning over possibilities. Outside, the community center was emptying as people were released to go home, taking their fear and suspicion with them.

"What about the hotel break-in?" Eliza asked. "Any security footage?"

"The Harborview has cameras at the main entrance but not in the hallways. Someone entered at eleven forty-seven PM Friday, wearing a baseball cap and keeping their head down. Could be any of our suspects—the build could be male or female, the face isn't visible."

"That's calculated."

"Everything about this is calculated." Wade stood, moving to the window that overlooked the festival site. The tent was surrounded by police tape now, evidence markers where the soup had been, where Margot had collapsed. "Whoever did this planned carefully. The timing, the method, the disposal of evidence—it's not amateur work."

"You're thinking someone with police training?"

"Or detective experience." He glanced at her. "Present company excluded, of course."

Eliza felt the old familiar weight of suspicion, the occupational hazard of being an ex-cop. "I was at the bookstore all Friday afternoon. You saw me. And I was home Friday night—Bruno can confirm, though I know that's not admissible."

"I'm not suspecting you, Eliza. I'm just noting that this was done by someone who understands police procedure. Who knew to wipe the bottle, avoid cameras, plan escape routes." He paused. "Though I suppose anyone who watches crime TV could figure that out."

Bruno woofed softly from his position by the door. Eliza checked—Deputy Morris had returned and was hovering outside, clearly needing Wade for something.

"We're not done," Wade said as they left the office. "I'll need formal statements from everyone tomorrow. And I want you to—" He stopped himself.

"You want me to help investigate."

"Unofficially. Just... keep your eyes open. These people trust you. They'll say things to the bookstore owner they won't tell the sheriff."

"Wade—"

"I know. You left Portland to get away from this. But right now, I need someone who knows how to investigate a murder—"

"Attempted murder," Eliza corrected.

Wade's phone rang. He answered, listened, and his face went still. "When?" A pause. "Understood. Thank you."

He lowered the phone slowly, and Eliza knew before he spoke what he was going to say.

"Margot Sterling died ten minutes ago. Her heart couldn't handle the strain. Multiple organ failure from the shock." Wade's voice was flat, professional, but his eyes were haunted. "This is officially a homicide investigation now."

The words hung in the air between them, transforming everything. Attempted murder became murder. Suspects became potential killers. A town festival became a crime scene where someone had committed premeditated homicide.

"I need to call the state police," Wade said. "This is beyond our—"

"You can handle it," Eliza said firmly. "You have the skills, you know the town. The state police will treat everyone like strangers. You know these people."

"That's the problem. I know them too well." Wade looked out at the empty festival site, the abandoned tents, the decorations that suddenly seemed grotesque. "Somewhere in this town of three thousand people, someone committed murder. And I probably had coffee with them this morning."

Bruno pressed against Eliza's leg, solid and real. She scratched his ears absently, her mind already working through suspects, timelines, evidence. The detective she'd tried to leave in Portland was fully awake now, and she knew with grim certainty that she couldn't ignore this.

Someone in Ashford Creek had committed murder. Someone she'd probably sold books to, smiled at on Main Street, served coffee to in her shop.

And she was going to help find them.

CHAPTER 4

RECIPES AND REVENGE

*S*unday morning arrived with fog thick enough to muffle sound and turn Main Street's lampposts into pale ghosts. Eliza opened Bookmark & Brew at eight, two hours earlier than usual, unable to sleep. Bruno followed her downstairs, his nails clicking against the wooden steps, his presence a comfort in the gray morning.

The news had spread through Ashford Creek with the speed that only small towns could manage. By the time Eliza unlocked the front door, her phone had accumulated seventeen text messages, three voicemails, and a missed call from a Boston reporter who'd somehow gotten her number.

She made coffee, strong and black, and sat in the reading nook where Margot Sterling had held court just two days ago. The folding chairs were gone, the book display dismantled, but the memory lingered like smoke.

Murder had returned to Ashford Creek.

Wade arrived at eight-thirty, looking like he hadn't slept. His uniform was slightly rumpled, and his gray eyes had dark circles beneath them that spoke of a long night reviewing evidence and making calls to the state police.

"Coffee?" Eliza offered.

"Please." He sank into the chair across from her, Bruno immediately padding over to lean against his leg. Wade's hand automatically went to scratch the dog's ears. "State police are sending a detective up from Boston. Should arrive by noon. They're treating it as suspicious death pending autopsy results, but we all know what those will show."

"Anaphylactic shock from walnut oil poisoning."

"Exactly." Wade accepted the coffee mug gratefully. "Medical examiner confirmed no EpiPen was administered at the scene except Claire's, which was too late. If Margot had had her own medication immediately available, she might have survived."

"So the theft of the EpiPens is murder, not just assault."

"Felony murder at minimum. Premeditated if the prosecutor's ambitious." Wade sipped his coffee, grimacing at the temperature. "I spent half the night going through security footage from businesses around the square. Got nothing useful. Whoever contaminated that soup knew where the cameras were."

"Tell me about the soup's timeline again."

Wade pulled out his notebook, flipping to a page dense with neat handwriting. "Diane Morrison made the soup Friday afternoon at her bakery. She has a small commercial kitchen in the back—health department approved, up to code. She makes soups for the general store deli program."

"Who was there when she made it?"

"Just her. Her assistant had the day off. Diane says she made the soup between two and four PM, using ingredients she'd purchased that morning from the farmer's market."

Wade consulted his notes. "Pure pumpkin puree, heavy cream, vegetable stock, butter, sage, salt, pepper. She's very specific about the recipe—no nuts, no nut oils, nothing that could trigger allergies."

"And after it was made?"

"She let it cool, then transferred it to an insulated container around five PM. Locked the bakery at five-thirty. The container stayed in her walk-in cooler overnight—she has security footage from her own camera showing no one entered the bakery after she left."

"So it was clean when it left her possession."

"According to the footage, yes. She transported it to the festival site at seven AM Saturday morning. Handed it directly to Millie Hart, who placed it in the warming station in the catering tent."

Eliza pictured the timeline. "That's when it became vulnerable."

"Exactly. Between seven-thirty AM and noon, when it was served, multiple people had access to the catering tent. We found the walnut oil bottle in the trash, wiped clean. Whoever did it was in and out quickly, knew exactly when they'd have privacy."

"Who had keys to the catering tent?"

"Millie Hart, Tom Garrett, and Owen Kraft. But it wasn't locked during setup—too many volunteers coming and going. Anyone could have slipped in during a quiet moment."

The bell above the door chimed. Diane Morrison entered, still wearing yesterday's clothes, looking like she'd been awake all night.

"I heard Wade was here," she said without preamble. "I need to talk to you. Both of you."

Wade gestured to a chair. Diane sat, her hands trembling as she clutched a worn folder to her chest.

"I didn't kill her," Diane said. "But I wanted to. I need you to understand that. I spent five years wanting her dead, fantasizing about it, imagining her choking on one of my grandmother's recipes. So when it actually happened..." She stopped, tears streaming down her face. "Part of me was glad. Part of me is still glad. Does that make me a monster?"

"It makes you human," Eliza said quietly.

"The police will think I did it. They'll say I had motive, means, opportunity—all of it. My soup, my kitchen, my hatred." Diane opened the folder with shaking hands. "But I need you to see this. I need someone to understand what she took from me."

Inside the folder were photographs—old ones, faded with age. A young woman in an apron, flour dusting her cheek, standing behind a bakery counter. The sign above her head read "Morrison's Morning Goods - Est. 1952."

"My grandmother," Diane said. "She started the bakery when she was twenty-three. Built it from nothing, one recipe at a time. This was her life."

More photographs: the grandmother with a young girl, teaching her to roll dough. Birthday cakes, wedding cakes, rows of golden donuts cooling on wire racks. A life built on baking, on feeding people, on the particular magic of turning flour and sugar into something that brought joy.

"These are her recipe cards." Diane pulled out a small metal box, opened it to reveal dozens of index cards covered in faded handwriting. "Every recipe she ever created. Some worked, some didn't. But they were hers. Her creativity, her experiments, her legacy."

She pulled out one card, handling it like it was made of glass. The recipe for apple cider donuts, written in careful cursive, with notes in the margins: "Add extra cinnamon in October. Reduce sugar slightly for tourists—locals like it sweeter."

"Margot interviewed my grandmother in 1995," Diane said. "She was doing a college project about local food traditions. Grandmother was thrilled—finally, someone young cared about preserving these recipes. She shared everything. The techniques, the stories, the family history behind each dish."

Wade was taking notes, but his expression was sympathetic.

"Five years later, Margot's second cookbook came out. 'Heritage New England.' And there it was—the donut recipe, barely changed. No credit, no acknowledgment. Just Margot Sterling claiming it as her family's tradition." Diane's voice broke. "Grandmother died that same year. She never knew. That's the only mercy in this story."

"Did you confront Margot at the time?" Wade asked.

"I sent a letter to her publisher. They sent back a form response saying recipes couldn't be copyrighted and wishing me well. I couldn't afford a lawyer—I'd just taken over the bakery, I had loans, expenses, no savings. So I did nothing and watched her get famous on my grandmother's work."

"And when she came back to town?"

"I wanted to hurt her. Publicly, legally, I didn't care how. I wanted everyone to know what she'd done." Diane closed the folder carefully. "But I didn't poison her. I wouldn't dishonor my grandmother's recipes that way. Every dish we make is about nourishment, about care. I couldn't turn that into a weapon."

After Diane left, Wade and Eliza sat in silence for a long moment.

"Do you believe her?" Wade asked finally.

"I believe she wanted Margot dead. I believe she's capable of rage. But poisoning the soup?" Eliza thought about it. "That's intimate, personal. It uses food as a weapon, which violates everything a baker stands for."

"People do things that violate their principles when pushed far enough."

"True. But there's something else." Eliza pulled out her phone, scrolling through the photos she'd taken at the festival. "Look at the soup station setup. The serving tureen was large, ornate, meant to be visible. Anyone adding something to it would be obvious."

"Unless they did it in the catering tent before it was brought out for display."

"Which brings us back to access. Who was in that tent between seven-thirty and noon?" Eliza had been thinking about this all night. "We need a complete timeline."

Wade's phone buzzed. He read the text, his face tightening. "State police detective is here early. I need to brief him, then we're interviewing everyone again. Formal statements this time."

"What do you need from me?"

"Keep your ears open. People will talk to you—the friendly bookstore owner—in ways they won't talk to cops." Wade stood, Bruno moving with him. "And Eliza? Be careful. Someone in this town committed premeditated murder. They won't hesitate to protect themselves."

After Wade left, Eliza found herself staring at the spot where Margot had sat, signing books and dismissing people's pain with casual cruelty. The woman had been awful, there was no denying it. A thief, a bully, someone who'd built her success on stolen work.

But murder?

The bell chimed again. Claire Hartwick entered, her camera bag absent for the first time. She looked exhausted, wrung out, like someone who'd spent the night crying or thinking or both.

"I need to tell you something," Claire said. "Something I should have said yesterday."

Eliza gestured to the reading nook. Claire sat, her hands folded tightly in her lap.

"My name wasn't always Claire Hartwick. Ten years ago, I was Claire Brennan. I went to culinary school with Margot Sterling—we were roommates, best friends. I was writing a cookbook, my life's work. Stories about my grandmother's recipes, my family's history, everything I'd learned about food and love and memory."

Eliza waited, letting Claire find her words.

"I showed Margot the manuscript. I trusted her. We'd spent three years learning together, competing together, supporting each other. I thought we were friends." Claire's voice hardened. "She stole it. The entire manuscript. Changed just enough to avoid copyright issues, but it was mine. Every word, every recipe, every story."

"You sued her."

"Wade told you." Claire nodded. "I couldn't prove it was mine first. She'd been smart—taken my manuscript, rewritten it slightly, then registered it for copyright before I could. She published it as 'Margot Sterling's Family Table.' It became a bestseller. My publisher dropped me, saying I'd plagiarized her. My reputation was destroyed."

"And you moved here."

"Five years ago. Changed my name, started over as a photographer. Ashford Creek seemed safe—small enough to disappear in, far enough from the food world that no one would connect me to the lawsuit." Claire's hands tightened. "Then she came back. Announced she was returning home for the book tour. And I realized she was doing it again—stealing from Millie, from Diane, from everyone. She couldn't help herself."

"Did you poison her?"

The question hung in the air, direct and unavoidable.

"I wanted to," Claire said quietly. "God help me, I wanted to watch her suffer the way she made me suffer. But no. I didn't. I'm not a killer, Ms. Prescott. I'm just someone whose life was stolen, trying to build a new one."

"Then why did you save her? You could have let her die, claimed you didn't have your EpiPen with you."

"Because watching someone die in front of you isn't the same as wishing them dead in the abstract. When I saw her on the ground, convulsing, turning blue—" Claire stopped, swallowing hard. "I couldn't let her die. Not like that. Not in front of everyone."

"Even though she destroyed your life?"

"Even though." Claire stood, moving to the window. "I'm a suspect, I know. Motive, opportunity, the skills to break into her hotel room. Wade confiscated my lock picks. But I didn't do it. I just wanted her to leave town, to stop stealing, to face consequences for once in her privileged life."

After Claire left, Eliza made more coffee and thought about revenge. How far would someone go to avenge stolen work? To reclaim a legacy? To punish years of theft and mockery?

Far enough to steal EpiPens and contaminate soup?

Her phone rang. An unknown number.

"Ms. Prescott? This is Detective Sarah Martinez, Massachusetts State Police. Sheriff Colton said you might be able to help with some background on the victim and potential suspects. Could we meet?"

An hour later, Eliza sat in Wade's office at the sheriff's station with Detective Martinez—a sharp-eyed woman in her late thirties who radiated competence and skepticism in equal measure.

"Walk me through what you observed," Martinez said, her recorder running.

Eliza described the book signing, Margot's casual cruelty, the missing EpiPen. The festival, the tasting event, Diane's public humiliation. Bruno's alert to the contaminated soup. Margot's collapse. Claire's intervention.

"You're former law enforcement," Martinez said. It wasn't a question.

"Portland PD. Eight years as a detective. Retired two years ago."

"Why'd you leave?"

"Personal reasons." Eliza kept her voice neutral. The case that carved too deep wasn't relevant here.

Martinez studied her for a moment, then nodded. "Sheriff Colton speaks highly of you. Says you know this town, these people. I need that local knowledge."

"What do you want to know?"

"The victim had a pattern of recipe theft spanning decades. How many people in Ashford Creek had motive?"

"At least four that I know of personally. Probably more who haven't come forward."

"Give me names."

"Millie Hart—grandmother's lemon scone recipe stolen.

Diane Morrison—grandmother's donut recipe stolen. Richard Pemberton—blog recipe stolen. And Claire Hartwick, though that's more complicated."

Martinez wrote quickly. "Tell me about Hartwick."

Eliza explained the lawsuit, the name change, the five years of hiding. Martinez's expression didn't change, but her pen moved faster.

"She saved the victim's life but also had the means to end it. That's interesting." Martinez flipped through her notes. "What about the innkeeper—Millie Hart? Her recipe was in the victim's bestselling book. That's significant financial loss."

"Millie's entire identity is hospitality. She feeds people, nurtures them. The Teacup Inn is about creating comfort and safety."

"And yet she had access to the soup, had keys to the catering tent, and was witnessed polishing things nervously all morning—classic stress behavior."

Eliza couldn't argue. Millie had been visibly distressed, had access, had motive. On paper, she looked guilty.

"The baker, Morrison. Her soup was the weapon. Convenient."

"Also incredibly obvious. If Diane wanted to poison someone, why use her own recipe as the delivery method? Why not contaminate someone else's dish?"

"Maybe that's exactly what she wants us to think." Martinez closed her notebook. "In my experience, the obvious answer is usually correct. Someone with access, motive, and opportunity. Usually, that's your killer."

"This is Ashford Creek," Eliza said quietly. "People here have known each other for decades. They're neighbors, friends, family. Whoever did this had to live with that guilt every day, see these people on Main Street, serve them in their shops."

"Which makes it more likely, not less. Familiarity breeds contempt, Ms. Prescott. Long-held grudges, festering resentments—those are what lead to murder in small towns."

After the interview, Eliza walked Bruno through the fog-shrouded streets. The town felt different now—the comfortable familiarity replaced by suspicion. She found herself watching people differently, wondering. The Henderson sisters hurrying into their antique shop—had they known about Claire's lawsuit? Tom Garrett locking up the pharmacy —had he secretly resented Margot enough to act?

Bruno stopped suddenly, his ears pricking forward. His nose pointed toward an alley between buildings, and he gave a soft woof—his alert sound, but questioning.

Eliza followed his gaze. In the alley, partially hidden by morning fog, someone was moving. Not walking, exactly— more like pacing. Back and forth, back and forth.

As they got closer, Eliza recognized Millie. She was talking to herself, her hands gesturing, her pink scarf wrapped so tightly around her neck it looked painful.

"Millie?"

Millie jumped, spinning around. Her face was blotchy from crying, her eyes wild.

"I can't stop thinking about it," Millie said, words tumbling out in a rush. "The soup sitting there, unguarded. Anyone could have done it. Anyone. But they'll think it was me because I was there all morning, because I had access, because I wanted her dead—"

"Millie, slow down—"

"Did I do it? Could I have done it and not remembered? Sometimes when I'm upset I do things automatically, and I was so angry Friday night, I couldn't sleep, I kept thinking about her stealing grandmother's recipe, about all those years of lies, and when I got to the festival Saturday morning I was in such a state—"

"Millie, stop." Eliza took her gently by the shoulders. "Look at me. Did you put walnut oil in that soup?"

"I don't know!" The confession came out as a wail. "I don't think so. I wouldn't. But I was so angry, and I had opportunity, and what if I did something in a moment of rage and can't remember?"

Bruno pressed against Millie's legs, offering his solid comfort. She collapsed onto a nearby bench, sobbing.

"I wanted her dead," Millie whispered. "Is that the same as killing her? If you want something badly enough, and it happens, are you responsible?"

"No," Eliza said firmly. "Wanting and doing are completely different things. Thoughts aren't actions."

"Then why do I feel so guilty?"

Because the guilty and the innocent often wore the same face, Eliza thought. Because in a small town, everyone carried secrets, and murder threw harsh light on all of them.

"Go home," Eliza said gently. "Rest. You didn't do this, Millie. I know you didn't."

But as she watched Millie walk away, still sobbing, Eliza wondered if she really knew anything at all.

CHAPTER 5

THE MANUSCRIPT

*M*onday morning brought Detective Martinez to Bookmark & Brew with a warrant and two state police technicians carrying evidence collection kits.

"We need to process the scene from Friday's book signing," Martinez said, showing Eliza the paperwork. "Specifically, we need to document where the victim's purse was positioned and collect any potential evidence from that area."

Eliza stepped aside, watching the technicians photograph the reading nook, dust for fingerprints on the side table where Margot's bag had sat, collect fiber samples from the chair. Bruno observed from behind the counter, his professional interest evident in his alert posture.

"We're also executing a search warrant on the victim's hotel room," Martinez continued. "And we need to interview you formally about what you observed during the EpiPen theft."

"I didn't see it happen. Just the confusion afterward when Margot realized it was missing."

"But you noticed something. Sheriff Colton says you have good instincts."

Eliza thought back to Friday afternoon. The signing line, people crowding around, books being passed back and forth. Someone had bumped into Margot's chair—she remembered that. The bag had fallen, items spilling out. Several people had helped pick things up.

"Claire Hartwick helped pick up the bag," Eliza said slowly, the memory clarifying. "When it fell. She was there, crouched down, gathering items."

"So she had physical access to the bag's contents."

"So did three other people. It was chaos—everyone reaching, helping. I remember thinking it was kind of Margot to let people be so close to her expensive things."

Martinez made notes. "Who else was close enough?"

"Diane Morrison was in line. Richard Pemberton was standing near the back. The Henderson sisters were in their seats but Eleanor stood up when the bag fell—she's the helpful type." Eliza tried to visualize it. "Tom Garrett was browsing nearby. Millie was in the cooking section. Wade was by the door."

"So half the town had access."

"Welcome to small-town events. Personal space isn't really a thing."

After the evidence team finished, Eliza found herself staring at the reading nook, trying to see it as a crime scene. Someone had stood here, bumped that chair, caused the bag to fall, and in the confusion, stolen medication that would later save or fail to save a life.

Premeditated. Calculated. Cold.

Her phone buzzed with a text from Wade: *Martinez*

searching Margot's hotel room. Found something interesting. Come to Harborview Inn?

Twenty minutes later, Eliza stood in Margot Sterling's hotel room—a suite with harbor views that probably cost four hundred dollars a night. The state police had turned it into an evidence collection site, every surface tagged and photographed.

"Look at this," Wade said, gesturing to the desk where Margot had been working.

Laptop, phone charger, makeup bag. And a stack of printed pages—a manuscript, by the look of it. The title page read: *A Life in Recipes: Stories from My Grandmother's Kitchen* by Claire Brennan.

Eliza's blood ran cold.

"It's Claire's original manuscript," Martinez said, pulling on gloves to handle the pages carefully. "Or part of it. Approximately sixty pages, printed from digital files. The copyright registration shows this was filed ten years ago in Claire Brennan's name."

"What was Margot doing with it?"

"That's the question." Martinez flipped through the pages, each one marked with handwritten notes in Margot's distinctive script. *Good story—use for intro. Recipe needs tweaking but base is solid. Change protagonist's name.*

"She was stealing from it again," Eliza breathed. "Even after the lawsuit, after everything—she kept a copy and was planning to use more of it."

Wade pointed to a sticky note on page fifteen: *Perfect for next book. Adapt for coastal setting.*

"This gives Claire renewed motive," Martinez said. "She thought the theft was over, that she'd moved past it. Then

Margot comes back to town with evidence that she was planning to steal again. That's a fresh wound, not an old one."

"Or it gives her a reason to confront Margot, not kill her," Eliza countered. "If Claire wanted revenge, she had ten years to act. Why now?"

"Because now she could prove it. Look—" Martinez indicated the laptop. "Margot's computer has digital files of Claire's manuscript, dated from ten years ago. That's evidence that could reopen the plagiarism case. Claire didn't have this before—the lawsuit failed because she couldn't prove she wrote it first. But these files, with their timestamps, could prove Margot had her work all along."

The implications settled like weights. Claire could have confronted Margot with this evidence. Could have demanded justice, threatened to expose her, maybe even blackmailed her.

Or she could have decided that justice through the legal system wasn't enough. That Margot Sterling needed to pay with her life.

"We're bringing her in for questioning," Martinez said. "Formal interview under caution. She's our primary suspect."

After they left, Eliza wandered the hotel room, Bruno at her side. The space felt sterile now, picked clean by evidence technicians. But it still held traces of Margot—expensive perfume lingering in the bathroom, designer clothes hanging in the closet, the particular kind of disorder that came from someone accustomed to having others clean up after her.

On the nightstand, Eliza found a leather-bound journal. The evidence team had photographed it but left it behind—personal writings weren't relevant to the murder investigation.

She shouldn't read it. It was private, possibly protected.

She opened it anyway.

The entries were sporadic, self-congratulatory. Notes about book sales, TV appearances, fan letters. Margot had documented her success with the narcissism of someone who believed their own publicity.

But then, three weeks ago: *Returning to Ashford Creek for the book tour. Mother thinks it's a mistake, but I need to go back. Need to see the faces of all those people who thought they were better than me. Show them what I became.*

A week later: *The look on that innkeeper's face when she sees her grandmother's recipe in my book will be priceless. She always looked down on me in high school—the scholarship kid who didn't belong. Now I'm a bestselling author and she's still serving tea in a small-town inn.*

And most damningly, dated Friday night: *The signing went perfectly. Saw the anger, the helplessness. They know I took their recipes and they can't do anything about it. Legal, profitable, and deeply satisfying. Tomorrow's tasting event will be even better.*

Eliza closed the journal, feeling sick. Margot hadn't just stolen recipes for profit. She'd done it for revenge, for the satisfaction of hurting people who she believed had slighted her.

"She was awful," Eliza said to Bruno. "Truly, comprehensively awful."

Bruno woofed agreement.

But awful people didn't deserve to be murdered. That was the line between justice and vengeance, between law and chaos.

Her phone rang. Wade.

"Claire's not at home," he said without preamble. "Her car is gone. Martinez has issued a BOLO—be on the lookout. She's officially a fugitive."

"She ran."

"Or she's protecting herself. Or she's innocent and scared." Wade's voice carried the weight of too many possibilities. "Either way, we need to find her."

Eliza ended the call and stood looking out the hotel window at Ashford Creek spread below. Somewhere in those streets, Claire Hartwick was hiding or running. Somewhere in this town, the truth waited to be uncovered.

And somewhere, in the back of Eliza's detective mind, a piece didn't fit. Something about the timeline, the method, the evidence. Something that nagged at her with the persistence of a loose thread.

She pulled out her phone and reviewed the photos she'd taken at the festival. The soup station, the catering tent, the crowd. She zoomed in on faces, looking for—what? Guilt? Satisfaction? Fear?

Then she saw it. A detail so small she'd missed it the first dozen times she'd looked. In the background of one photo, barely visible through the catering tent's mesh siding, a figure in dark clothes. The timestamp was 10:47 AM—over an hour before the soup was served.

The figure's build was wrong for Claire... too broad in the shoulders. Wrong for Millie...too tall. Wrong for Diane...the posture was different, more rigid.

Military bearing, Eliza thought suddenly. That particular way of holding oneself that came from training.

Owen Kraft.

She'd forgotten about Owen. The inn's cook, Millie's loyal employee for three years. The man with a dishonorable discharge, a mysterious past, and keys to the catering tent.

Eliza texted Wade: *Need to talk. About Owen Kraft.*

The response came immediately: *On my way.*

* * *

THEY MET at the sheriff's station, in Wade's office with the door closed. Martinez was still coordinating the search for Claire, which gave them privacy.

"Owen Kraft," Wade said, pulling up his file. "Age 34. Dishonorable discharge from Fort Bragg four years ago. Came to Ashford Creek three years ago, hired by Millie Hart when no one else would give him a chance."

"What was the discharge for?"

"File's sealed—military records, classified. But I made some calls when I first vetted him for Millie." Wade's expression was grim. "Unofficially, I heard it involved a command dispute. Something about refusing an order, possible assault on a superior officer."

"So he has a history of violence."

"Or a history of standing up for what he believed was right. Depends on who you ask." Wade pulled out more documents. "He's been a model employee at the inn. Quiet, professional, never any trouble. Millie swears by him."

"But he had access to the catering tent. And look—" Eliza showed Wade the photo. "That's him, I'm almost certain. In the tent at ten forty-seven."

Wade studied the image, then pulled up Owen's driver's license photo for comparison. The build matched, the bearing matched.

"He could have contaminated the soup," Wade said slowly. "But what's his motive? He didn't know Margot Sterling. His connection to this is tangential at best."

"Unless it's not about Margot. What if it's about protecting Millie?"

The idea hung between them, growing more solid as they

examined it. Owen, the loyal employee who'd been given a chance when everyone else had rejected him. Millie, the kind innkeeper whose grandmother's recipe had been stolen and mocked. The intense loyalty that came from gratitude mixed with isolation.

"He could have seen Millie's distress," Eliza continued, thinking it through. "Heard her talk about the theft, seen her cry, watched her struggle with rage and helplessness. And he decided to fix it."

"By committing murder on her behalf."

"By eliminating the threat. That's how soldiers think—identify the threat, neutralize it. The military trains you to solve problems with decisive action."

Wade was already typing, pulling up Owen's work schedule. "He was at the inn Sunday, Monday, Tuesday, Wednesday. Off Thursday and Friday. Back Saturday morning for the festival prep."

"So he was off during the book signing. Could have been there, seen the EpiPen theft, maybe even committed it himself."

"And Friday night—the hotel break-in happened at eleven forty-seven PM. Owen would have the skills—lock picking isn't complicated for someone with military training."

They sat in silence, the pieces rearranging themselves into a new pattern. Not Claire's revenge, not Diane's rage, not Millie's desperation. But Owen's cold calculation, a soldier solving a problem with lethal efficiency.

"We need to talk to him," Wade said. "Carefully. If he's got military training and PTSD, confronting him wrong could be dangerous."

They found Owen at the Teacup Inn, working the Monday lunch service. The inn was quiet. The murder had kept tourists away, and locals were avoiding it out of respect or discomfort. Only a few tables were occupied.

Owen worked in the kitchen with his usual efficiency, plating sandwiches and soups with precise movements. When Wade appeared in the kitchen doorway, Owen's hands stilled for just a moment before continuing their work.

"Sheriff. Ms. Prescott." His voice was even, professional. "Can I help you?"

"We need to ask you some questions. About Saturday morning."

"Of course. Let me just finish these orders." Owen completed the plates, handed them through the service window, then wiped his hands on his apron. "Shall we use Millie's office?"

In the small office behind the kitchen, Owen sat with military posture—back straight, hands on knees, eyes forward. The position of someone accustomed to being interrogated.

"Where were you Saturday morning between seven and noon?" Wade asked.

"I arrived at the festival site at six-thirty to help with setup. Worked on the catering tent—arranging equipment, setting up warming stations. I left around seven-thirty to return here for the breakfast service. Came back to the festival around eleven to check on Millie."

"Did you enter the catering tent after seven-thirty?"

"No. Why?"

Wade showed him the photo. "This looks like you. In the tent at ten forty-seven."

Owen studied the image, his expression unreadable. "That's not me. I was here at the inn during that time. Millie can confirm—I served breakfast from eight until ten-thirty without break."

"Can anyone else confirm that?"

"The breakfast guests. Check the reservation book—we had six tables that morning. They all interacted with me."

The alibi was solid, verifiable. But something in Owen's stillness bothered Eliza. The way he held himself, the careful control of his expression.

"What's your relationship with Millie Hart?" she asked.

"She's my employer. She gave me a job when I needed one. I'm grateful."

"Just grateful?"

"She's a good person who runs an honest business. That's rare." Owen's jaw tightened slightly. "When I got discharged, no one would hire me. Military record follows you. She took a chance. I respect that."

"Enough to kill for her?"

The question landed like a stone in still water. Owen's expression didn't change, but something shifted in his eyes—calculation, assessment.

"I didn't kill anyone," he said evenly. "But if I had, it would have been cleaner than poison. More efficient. Less chance of failure."

The statement hung in the air, neither confession nor denial.

"That's an interesting answer," Wade said.

"It's an honest one. Sheriff, I've killed people. In combat, under orders, following rules of engagement. I know how to end a life efficiently when necessary. What happened to Ms. Sterling was sloppy—contaminated soup, missing medication, public venue. If I wanted someone dead, I wouldn't rely on allergies and timing. I'd use methods that work."

The cold professionalism in his voice was chilling.

"So you're saying you didn't do it because you would have done it better?"

"I'm saying I didn't do it, period. But I understand why you're asking." Owen stood. "If there's nothing else, I have work to finish."

After he left, Wade and Eliza sat in Millie's office, processing the interview.

"He's either innocent or a very good liar," Wade said finally.

"Or both. The best liars tell the truth in ways that mislead." Eliza thought about Owen's controlled demeanor, his careful words. "But that alibi—if the breakfast guests confirm it, he couldn't have been in the catering tent."

"Unless someone helped him. Unless this was a conspiracy."

The word hung heavy between them. Not one killer, but two. Not individual rage, but coordinated revenge.

Eliza's phone buzzed. A text from an unknown number: *I know what you're looking for. Meet me at the covered bridge. Come alone. - C*

Claire.

"She wants to meet," Eliza showed Wade the text.

"It's a trap."

"Or she has information. Or she's ready to confess. Or she's innocent and terrified." Eliza stood. "I'm going."

"Not alone you're not."

"She said alone. If she sees police, she'll run."

Wade's hand moved to his service weapon. "She's the primary suspect in a murder investigation. I can't let you meet her unsupervised."

"Then stay hidden. But let me talk to her first. Wade, if she did this, I need to understand why. And if she didn't—if someone's setting her up—she might only trust someone outside law enforcement."

After a long moment, Wade nodded. "Fifteen minutes. If I don't hear from you, I'm coming in."

The covered bridge sat at the edge of town, spanning Ashford Creek where it widened before flowing to the harbor. The old wooden structure was picturesque in daylight, tourist-photo perfect. In the gray afternoon, it looked ominous.

Claire stood in the center of the bridge, her back to the water. No camera bag, no props. Just a woman who looked like she'd been running for days.

"You came," Claire said as Eliza approached.

"You asked." Eliza kept her distance, aware of Bruno's tension, his professional assessment of threat level. "Claire, you need to turn yourself in."

"I didn't do it."

"Then prove it. Come back, give a formal statement, let them clear you."

"They won't clear me. I had motive, means, opportunity—everything points to me. Even I can see it." Claire's laugh was bitter. "I'm the perfect suspect. The woman whose life was destroyed, who came back for revenge. It's a good story. Probably true."

"Is it?"

"I wanted her dead. I'll admit that. When I saw her at the book signing, so smug, so certain she'd gotten away with it—I wanted to hurt her the way she hurt me." Claire pulled something from her pocket—a small USB drive. "But I didn't. Because I found something better than revenge."

She held up the drive. "This was on Margot's laptop. I went to her hotel room Friday night—yes, I broke in, yes, that's illegal. I was looking for my manuscript, proof that she'd kept it. I found this. Her entire hard drive, backed up. Every file, every email, every document."

"You could have taken that to the police, used it to reopen your case."

"I could have. I should have. But I was angry and I wanted to confront her first, make her admit what she'd done. I was going to find her Sunday morning, show her the evidence, force her to confess." Claire's voice cracked. "But then she was dead. And suddenly I'm a murder suspect with a USB drive full of stolen evidence from the victim's computer."

Eliza's mind worked through the implications. If Claire had broken into the hotel Friday night to copy files, she would have seen the backup EpiPen. Would have had opportunity to steal it.

"Did you take her medication?"

"No. I swear. I went in, copied the files, left. I never touched her things except the laptop." Claire thrust the drive at Eliza. "Take it. Give it to the police. Let them see what she really was—the emails to her publisher discussing how to 'adapt' other people's recipes, the files full of stolen work, the whole ugly truth."

Eliza took the drive carefully. "This doesn't prove you're innocent."

"I know. But it proves she was guilty. And maybe that matters." Claire turned toward the water, her shoulders slumping. "I didn't kill her, Ms. Prescott. I wanted to. I planned to destroy her reputation instead. But someone else decided death was better than exposure."

"Who?"

"I don't know. But whoever it was, they did what I couldn't. They made her pay." Claire looked back at Eliza, her eyes red-rimmed. "And part of me is grateful. Does that make me a monster?"

Before Eliza could answer, headlights cut through the gray afternoon. Wade's cruiser, pulling up to the bridge entrance. He'd given her the fifteen minutes.

"You need to come in," Eliza said gently.

Claire nodded, exhausted beyond resistance. "I know."

As Wade approached to make the arrest, Eliza clutched the USB drive and thought about justice and revenge, about the thin line between wanting something and doing it, about how many people in Ashford Creek had crossed that line.

And about the question that still nagged at her: if not Claire, then who?

CHAPTER 6

PATTERNS AND PROOF

*C*laire's arrest made the evening news—not just local, but Boston stations too. "Local Photographer Arrested in Cookbook Author Murder" played on every channel. Eliza watched from her apartment above the bookstore, Bruno pressed against her leg, both of them troubled by how neat the story seemed.

Too neat.

She couldn't sleep. At two AM, she was downstairs in the bookstore, the USB drive Claire had given her sitting on the counter like an accusation. Wade had it catalogued as evidence, but he'd let her keep a copy—unofficial, probably not admissible in court, but useful for understanding.

She plugged it into her laptop.

Margot's files were organized with obsessive precision. Folders labeled by book title, each containing recipes, research notes, and correspondence. Eliza clicked through them, her detective instincts recognizing patterns.

The lemon scone recipe appeared in three different folders —first as "Hart family recipe - interviewed grandmother

1999," then as "Adapted coastal scone - needs refinement," finally as "Traditional New England Lemon Scones" in the published cookbook files.

Diane's donut recipe had similar progression: "Morrison grandmother interview notes" became "Apple cider donut variation" became published content.

But it was the emails that made Eliza's blood run cold.

From: Margot Sterling To: Editorial Team Subject: Recipe sources

Don't worry about attribution. These small-town bakers won't sue—they can't afford lawyers. Even if they try, recipes aren't copyrightable. We're legally protected. Just change enough details to avoid obvious copying.

Another email, dated six months ago:

The Ashford Creek book tour is perfect timing. I can gather more material—these people love to share their "secret" recipes if you show enough interest. Small-town hospitality is wonderfully naive.

Eliza felt sick. Margot hadn't just stolen recipes—she'd planned it, documented it, celebrated it. The cruelty was systematic, calculated.

But murder?

She pulled up her festival photos again, studying them with fresh eyes. The timeline bothered her. The soup had been contaminated between 7:30 AM and noon. Claire had an alibi—witnesses placed her photographing the square's setup from 8:00 to 11:00 AM, never near the catering tent.

Owen claimed to be at the inn serving breakfast, verifiable through guest interactions.

Diane had been at her bakery until 10:00 AM, then at her festival booth—dozens of witnesses.

Millie had been everywhere, fluttering between the

catering tent and the main square, but always visible to volunteers.

So who had the private moment needed to contaminate the soup?

Eliza zoomed in on background details in her photos. In one shot, taken at 9:15 AM, she could see through the catering tent's mesh walls. Someone was inside, moving between the warming stations. The figure was blurred, but the pink scarf was visible.

Millie.

But that didn't prove anything—Millie was supposed to be there, managing the catering.

Eliza clicked to the next photo, taken at 9:47 AM. The tent was empty, the soup station unattended. Anyone could have slipped in during that window.

Her phone rang. Wade, also awake at two AM.

"Can't sleep either?" he said.

"Looking through the files Claire copied. Wade, Margot documented everything—the theft, the planning, the deliberate targeting of vulnerable people."

"I know. Martinez has the full drive. It's damning character evidence but doesn't help us find the killer." He paused. "Though it gives about twenty more people motive. Every baker she interviewed, every recipe she adapted, every small-town cook she exploited."

"Too many suspects is the same as no suspects."

"Exactly. We're missing something, Eliza. Some connection we're not seeing."

She thought about connections, about the web of relationships in small towns. "Wade, what if it's not about the recipes? What if that's just the surface?"

"What do you mean?"

"Margot wrote in her journal that she was getting revenge on people who looked down on her in high school. The scholarship kid who didn't belong. What if someone else had a similar grudge? Something older, deeper than recipe theft?"

"I'll pull high school records tomorrow. See who else was in Margot's class, who might have had conflicts with her." Wade sighed heavily. "Martinez wants to charge Claire. The evidence is circumstantial but compelling—motive, means, the hotel break-in. She thinks we have our killer."

"But you don't."

"I think we have someone who wanted Margot dead but didn't act on it. And I think the real killer is smart enough to let Claire take the fall."

After Wade hung up, Eliza sat in the dark bookstore, thinking about intelligence and planning. Whoever did this understood police procedure, knew how to avoid cameras, how to create reasonable doubt. They'd stolen the EpiPens when chaos provided cover, contaminated the soup during a brief window of privacy, and let the obvious suspect—Claire —draw all the attention.

Bruno woofed softly, his alert sound. Eliza followed his gaze to the window.

Outside, in the pre-dawn darkness, someone was walking past the bookstore. A figure in a hooded jacket, moving with purpose toward the harbor.

Eliza recognized the gait—the particular way of moving that came from carrying heavy things, from years of physical work.

Diane Morrison.

At 2:30 AM, walking toward the water.

Eliza grabbed her jacket, clipped Bruno's leash, and followed.

The harbor was empty at this hour, the fishing boats rocking gently in their slips. Diane stood at the end of the pier, looking out at dark water. She held something in her hands—a small box, wooden, worn with age.

"Diane?" Eliza called softly, not wanting to startle her.

Diane turned, her face streaked with tears. "I can't keep it anymore. The guilt is eating me alive."

"Keep what?"

"The truth." Diane opened the box. Inside were papers—old, yellowed, carefully preserved. "My grandmother's original recipe cards. The ones Margot saw when she interviewed her. But there's something else here too. Something I found after grandmother died."

She pulled out a letter, the paper brittle with age. "It's from Margot's mother to my grandmother, dated 2000. Right after Margot published her first cookbook."

Eliza took the letter carefully, reading by the pier's security light:

Dear Margaret,

I must apologize for my daughter. I know she used the recipes you shared for her school project. I confronted her, and she admitted she'd kept copies, used them in her cookbook without permission. I'm so ashamed. We raised her better than this.

I'm enclosing a check for $5,000—it's not enough, I know, but it's what I can afford. Please accept it as partial compensation for what she stole. If you want to take legal action, I'll support you. My daughter needs to face consequences.

With deepest regrets, Patricia Sterling

"This proves Margot's mother knew," Eliza said, stunned. "Knew and tried to make it right."

"Grandmother never cashed the check. She kept the letter but told no one. I only found it after she died, hidden in this box with the recipe cards." Diane's voice broke. "She wanted to protect me, I think. Didn't want me to know how badly we'd been wronged. But I found out anyway when Margot's second book came out."

"Why didn't you show this to anyone?"

"Because it proves my grandmother knew about the theft before she died. That she chose silence over justice. And I couldn't bear for anyone to think less of her for that choice." Diane looked at the dark water. "But now someone's dead, and Claire might go to prison for something she didn't do, and I can't stay silent anymore."

"Diane, did you poison Margot?"

"No. I swear on my grandmother's memory, I didn't. But I understand why someone did. And part of me is glad they did it." She handed Eliza the box. "Give this to the police. Let them know the full story. Maybe it will help somehow."

After Diane left, Eliza stood on the pier with the box of evidence, thinking about secrets and silence. How many people in Ashford Creek had pieces of this story? How many had stayed quiet, protecting themselves or their loved ones, while the truth scattered into fragments?

Dawn was breaking when she returned to the bookstore. Wade arrived at seven, looking as exhausted as she felt.

"Diane brought me this last night," Eliza showed him the letter. "Margot's mother knew about the theft, tried to compensate. This proves pattern, knowledge, intent."

Wade read it carefully. "This changes things. Margot wasn't just casually stealing—she was deliberately continuing theft her own mother tried to stop. That's calculation, not inspiration."

"It also means someone might have known about this

letter. Might have felt that Margot had been given chances to stop and refused them all."

"Someone who decided she'd had enough opportunities for redemption." Wade pulled out his notes. "I got the high school records. Margot's graduating class, 1991. Forty-three students. I cross-referenced with current Ashford Creek residents."

He showed Eliza the list. Most names were familiar—people who'd left and never returned, or who'd moved away for college and stayed away. But two names jumped out:

Tom Garrett (class of '91) Patricia Morrison (Diane's mother, class of '91)

"They were all in school with her," Eliza said slowly.

"And according to yearbook records, Patricia Morrison and Margot Sterling were best friends freshman year. Something happened sophomore year—they stopped appearing in photos together. By senior year, Margot was isolated, no friend group."

The pieces were rearranging again, forming a new pattern. Not recipe theft in the present, but old wounds from high school, festering for twenty-five years.

"We need to talk to Patricia Morrison," Wade said. "Diane's mother. She's been conspicuously absent through all of this."

"Because she's been protecting her daughter. Just like her mother before her protected Diane." Eliza felt the truth hovering just out of reach, like a word on the tip of her tongue. "Generational protection. Generational secrets."

Her phone buzzed. A text from an unknown number: *You're looking in the wrong place. The answer is in the recipes themselves. Check the scone glaze formula. - A friend*

"Wade, look at this."

He read the text, frowning. "Who sent it?"

"Unknown number. But they're pointing us to something specific—Millie's grandmother's lemon scone glaze."

They drove to the Teacup Inn, the morning sun burning away the last of the fog. Millie was preparing for lunch service, moving through the dining room with mechanical efficiency. Owen worked in the kitchen, his usual precise movements shadowed by exhaustion.

"Millie, we need to see your grandmother's original recipe," Wade said gently.

Millie's hands stilled on the teacup she was polishing. "Why?"

"Because someone suggested the answer might be there. In the glaze formula specifically."

"That's ridiculous. It's just sugar, lemon juice, and—" She stopped, her face going pale. "No. No, that's not possible."

"Millie?"

She fled to her office, returning with a worn recipe box. Her hands shook as she pulled out a yellowed index card covered in careful handwriting.

Grandmother's Lemon Scone Glaze: 1 cup powdered sugar, 3 tablespoons fresh lemon juice, 1 tablespoon heavy cream, pinch of salt. For special occasions, add ¼ teaspoon almond extract—the good kind, never imitation.

"Almond extract," Eliza said softly. "That's where the bitter almond smell comes from."

"But I never use it," Millie said desperately. "Never. Too many people are allergic. I left it out decades ago, just use the basic glaze now."

"Does Owen know the original recipe?"

"I showed him all of grandmother's cards when he started working here. He wanted to understand the inn's history, the traditions." Millie's voice rose. "But he wouldn't—he couldn't—"

They found Owen in the kitchen, calmly preparing soup for lunch service. When he saw their faces, he set down his knife with careful precision.

"You're looking for who knew about the almond extract," he said quietly. "I knew. Millie showed me all the original recipes when I started. But I didn't kill anyone, Sheriff."

"Then who did?"

"I don't know. But I can tell you who else saw those recipe cards." Owen wiped his hands on his towel. "Patricia Morrison. Diane's mother. She came in about three weeks ago, asked Millie if she could see her grandmother's original recipes. Said she was helping Diane research family baking history, trying to document the Morrison-Hart connection through their grandmothers' friendship."

Millie's face went white. "I showed her everything. The whole collection. We spent an hour going through them, and she took photos of several cards for Diane's records. Including the lemon scone glaze with the almond extract note."

"Where is Patricia now?" Wade asked.

"She's been staying with Diane since the festival. Helping her cope with everything." Millie's hands twisted her pink scarf. "You don't think—she couldn't have—"

But Eliza was already remembering. Patricia Morrison, class of '91. Margot's former best friend. And Diane had said her mother knew about the recipe theft, had been quietly furious about it for years.

Generational protection. Generational revenge.

"We need to talk to Patricia Morrison," Wade said. "Now."

CHAPTER 7

THE BREAKING POINT

They found Patricia Morrison at Diane's apartment above the bakery, calmly washing dishes from breakfast. A small woman in her early fifties, neat and contained, with the kind of careful composure that came from years of holding things together.

"Mrs. Morrison," Wade said from the doorway. "We need to talk."

Patricia dried her hands methodically on a kitchen towel. "I wondered when you'd figure it out. Come in, Sheriff. No need to make a scene on Main Street."

Diane emerged from her bedroom, confusion crossing her face. "Mom? What's going on?"

"It's all right, sweetheart. Why don't you go downstairs and start the afternoon prep?" Patricia's voice was steady, maternal. "I'll be down in a bit."

"Mom—"

"Go on now."

After Diane reluctantly left, Patricia gestured to the small kitchen table. "Would you like coffee? I just made a fresh pot."

The domesticity of the offer in the context of a murder investigation was surreal. Wade declined. Eliza and Bruno took positions near the door—protocol for a potential arrest, though Patricia showed no signs of fleeing.

"You were Margot Sterling's best friend in high school," Wade began.

"Freshman year, yes. Before I knew who she really was." Patricia poured herself coffee with steady hands. "We met in home economics class—ironic, isn't it? Both loved cooking, both dreamed of doing something with food someday. She was the scholarship kid, brilliant but hungry in a way that went beyond food. Hungry for status, for recognition, for proof she was better than where she came from."

"What happened between you?"

"Sophomore year, we entered a regional baking competition together. My grandmother Morrison's apple cider donut recipe—the one that's been in my family for generations. We were going to share credit if we won." Patricia's jaw tightened. "We won. And Margot accepted the award alone, told the judges it was her family recipe, her creation. When I confronted her, she said I should be grateful for the association with a winner. That my family name didn't mean anything, but hers would."

"So you stopped being friends."

"I stopped trusting anyone after that. Learned that some people will take everything if you let them—your work, your credit, your dreams." Patricia sipped her coffee. "Years later, Margot interviewed my mother-in-law for that college project. I warned Margaret not to share the recipes, told her what Margot had done to me. She shared them anyway. Said everyone deserved a second chance, that people change."

"But Margot didn't change," Eliza said quietly.

"No. She published those recipes, got rich and famous on work she stole. And my mother-in-law died never knowing she'd been betrayed again. That stayed with me— the waste of trust, the cruelty of theft disguised as inspiration." Patricia set down her cup with careful precision. "When Margot announced she was coming back to town, I knew she'd do it again. Steal more, hurt more people, walk away richer while we stayed here counting our losses."

"So you decided to stop her."

Patricia was quiet for a long moment, looking out the window at Main Street below. "I decided my daughter wouldn't suffer what I suffered. Wouldn't watch her life's work stolen, her grandmother's memory desecrated. I decided enough people had been hurt."

"Walk me through what you did," Wade said, pulling out his notebook.

"I went to Millie three weeks ago, asked to see her grandmother's recipe collection. Told her I was helping Diane document the Morrison-Hart family baking connection— which was true, actually. We really were researching." Patricia's voice remained steady, almost clinical. "I saw the lemon scone glaze recipe with the almond extract notation. And I remembered Margot's allergy from high school. She'd gone into anaphylaxis once when someone brought walnut brownies to a potluck. Nearly died. Had to carry an EpiPen everywhere after that."

"So you knew the walnut allergy was severe."

"I knew." Patricia pulled a small notebook from her pocket —the kind used for grocery lists and daily tasks. She flipped it open to reveal neat handwriting: dates, times, observations. "I planned it carefully. I'm not impulsive, Sheriff. I'm methodical. It's how you survive running a household on limited means while raising a daughter alone."

She showed them the notebook. Every detail documented: Margot's book signing schedule, the festival layout, the catering tent's security gaps, the timing of volunteer rotations.

"Friday afternoon, I attended the book signing. Stood in line like everyone else, got my book signed. When someone bumped Margot's chair and her bag fell, I helped pick things up. The EpiPen was in the side pocket, exactly where she'd always kept it in high school. I palmed it while pretending to gather scattered items. Simple sleight of hand—years of managing a bakery's till taught me quick fingers."

"And Friday night?" Wade asked.

"I went to her hotel. I learned lock picking from YouTube videos—it's remarkably easy if you practice. Entered at eleven forty-seven, found her backup EpiPen in her toiletry bag, and left. Eight minutes total. She was at dinner, never knew I was there." Patricia turned the notebook page. "Saturday morning, I arrived at the festival at six-thirty as a volunteer. Helped set up the catering tent. At nine forty-five, during the volunteer rotation gap, I was alone in the tent for approximately four minutes. I added walnut oil to the soup—one tablespoon, enough for a severe reaction. Wiped the bottle clean, disposed of it in the trash."

The confession was delivered with the calm efficiency of someone reciting a recipe. Eliza felt chilled by the lack of emotion, the practical detailing of premeditated murder.

"You knew she'd die without her medication," Wade said.

"I knew she'd have minutes to find help, to borrow someone else's EpiPen, to get to a hospital. I knew she'd suffer, realize she was dying, understand that someone had finally made her pay." Patricia's composure finally cracked slightly. "I didn't enjoy it, Sheriff. I'm not a monster. But I couldn't let her hurt my daughter the way she hurt me, the way she hurt so many others. Someone had to stop her."

"So you became judge, jury, and executioner."

"I became a mother protecting her child." Patricia's voice hardened. "What would you have done, Sheriff? Watched her steal again? Sued her with money we don't have, knowing she'd bury us in legal fees like she did Claire Hartwick? Written angry blog posts like young Richard Pemberton, achieving nothing but catharsis? Or would you have done what needed to be done?"

"I would have trusted the system," Wade said.

"The system that failed Claire? That failed Diane when she tried to prove the donut recipe was stolen? That failed every small-town baker Margot exploited because recipes can't be copyrighted?" Patricia laughed bitterly. "The system protected her, Sheriff. Someone had to protect us."

Bruno had been sitting quietly at Eliza's feet, but now he shifted position slightly—not threatening, but alert. He recognized the change in atmosphere, the shift from interview to arrest.

"Patricia Morrison, you're under arrest for the murder of Margot Sterling." Wade stood, pulling handcuffs from his belt. "You have the right to remain silent—"

"I understand my rights." Patricia stood as well, extending her wrists with the calm acceptance of someone who'd planned for this moment. "I'm ready."

"Mom?" Diane's voice came from the stairs. She must have heard, must have realized. "Mom, no. No, please tell me you didn't—"

"I did it for you, sweetheart. For your grandmother's memory. For all of us she hurt." Patricia's composure finally shattered as she saw her daughter's face. "I couldn't let her take anything else from you."

"But I didn't want this!" Diane was crying now, her voice breaking. "I wanted justice, not murder. Not you in prison. Not this!"

"Sometimes protecting someone means they hate you for it." Patricia's voice gentled even as Wade secured the handcuffs. "But I'd do it again. I'd do anything to keep you safe."

As Wade led Patricia out, Diane collapsed against the doorframe, sobbing. Eliza stayed with her, offering the silent comfort of presence while Bruno pressed his solid warmth against Diane's legs.

"She did it for me," Diane whispered. "All of it. And now she's going to prison and it's my fault. If I hadn't been so angry about the recipe, if I hadn't talked about it constantly—"

"This isn't your fault," Eliza said firmly. "Your mother made her own choice. A wrong choice, but hers to make."

"She's a good person. She's my mother. How can a good person do something like this?"

Eliza thought about all the murders she'd investigated in Portland, all the seemingly ordinary people who'd committed extraordinary violence. "Good people can do terrible things when they feel powerless. When they love someone and see them hurting. That doesn't make it right. But it makes it human."

* * *

LATER, at the sheriff's station, Patricia gave a full confession. Every detail, every step of planning, every moment of execution. She showed no remorse for killing Margot Sterling, only regret that Diane would suffer for her actions.

"Will Claire be released?" Patricia asked Wade.

"Yes. The charges will be dropped."

"Good. She didn't deserve to pay for what I did." Patricia looked at Eliza through the bars of the holding cell. "You understand, don't you? You're a mother's age. If you had a child, and someone kept hurting them, kept stealing from them—wouldn't you stop it however you could?"

Eliza thought about the case in Portland that had carved too deep, about the choices people made when systems failed and desperation set in. "I understand the impulse. But I would have found another way."

"There wasn't another way. Not one that would have worked."

As Eliza left the station with Bruno, the afternoon sun was breaking through clouds, painting Main Street in warm autumn light. The town looked peaceful, picturesque, exactly like a postcard of small-town New England.

But Ashford Creek had learned what she already knew from Portland: violence lived everywhere, even in pretty places. Murder could be committed by good people with understandable motives. And sometimes the only thing separating the person who killed from the person who thought about it was the willingness to cross a line that could never be uncrossed.

Patricia Morrison had crossed that line for love of her daughter. And now both of them would live with the consequences—one in prison, one with guilt.

Justice had been served. But nobody had won.

EPILOGUE

*T*hree weeks later, Eliza stood in the doorway of Bookmark & Brew watching November rain wash Main Street clean. The cobblestones gleamed under the old-fashioned lampposts, and fallen leaves swirled in small eddies near the storm drains. Inside, the bookstore smelled of coffee and paper and the particular comfort of stories waiting to be discovered.

Bruno dozed on his bed behind the counter, occasionally twitching in dreams that probably involved chasing rabbits or alerting to evidence.

The bell chimed. Claire Hartwick entered, her camera bag over her shoulder, looking more solid than she had in weeks. The charges had been dropped, her name cleared, but the town's whispers would take longer to fade.

"I wanted to thank you," Claire said. "For believing I didn't do it."

"I knew you didn't." Eliza poured two cups of coffee without asking. "What will you do now?"

"Stay. Ashford Creek is home, strange as that sounds."

Claire accepted the coffee gratefully. "And I'm publishing my cookbook. The original manuscript, under my own name. A small press in Vermont wants it—they specialize in books about food and memory. It won't be a bestseller, but it'll be mine."

"That's good."

"Patricia Morrison's lawyer contacted me. She wanted me to know she's glad I'm getting my work published properly. Said that was part of why she did it—so people like us could finally have justice." Claire's voice was complicated. "I don't know how to feel about that."

"You don't have to feel any particular way. Murder isn't justified by good intentions."

After Claire left, the Henderson sisters arrived with Bitsy and Mitsy, both Pomeranians wearing tiny raincoats that matched their owners' scarves. They needed book recommendations for their niece's birthday, and the familiar routine of helping customers select mysteries was comforting in its normalcy.

Diane came in around noon, looking exhausted but functional. She'd kept the bakery running despite everything, her morning donuts still drawing customers who understood that a daughter wasn't responsible for her mother's crimes.

"How are you holding up?" Eliza asked.

"Day by day." Diane's hands twisted around her coffee cup. "I visited her yesterday. She doesn't regret it, Eliza. She says she'd do it again to protect me. How am I supposed to process that?"

"One conversation at a time. One day at a time."

"The lawyer says she'll plead guilty, probably get twenty years with possibility of parole in fifteen. I'll be almost sixty when she gets out." Diane's voice broke. "And part of me is still angry at Margot Sterling for creating this situation. Is that wrong?"

"It's human."

Wade stopped by mid-afternoon, looking more rested than he had during the investigation. Detective Martinez had returned to Boston, satisfied with the resolution even if she'd initially arrested the wrong person.

"Town council wants to give you a commendation," Wade said, accepting coffee. "For helping solve the case."

"Pass."

"That's what I told them you'd say." He scratched Bruno's ears, earning a contented grumble from the dog. "Patricia Morrison's case goes to the grand jury next week. Her lawyer's arguing diminished capacity due to protective maternal instinct, but the premeditation is well-documented. She'll be convicted."

"Small towns are good at rallying around their own," Wade continued. "People are supporting Diane—buying extra donuts, leaving anonymous donations, that sort of thing. But the gossip will never completely stop."

"No. It won't."

After Wade left, Eliza found herself in the mystery section, straightening spines that didn't need straightening. The familiar titles looked back at her—stories where justice always prevailed, where the detective solved the case and order was restored. Real life was messier. Real murders left scars on entire communities.

But Ashford Creek would heal. It always did. Small towns were resilient that way, absorbing tragedy and transforming it into shared history, into stories told carefully around new people.

Bruno stirred from his bed, stretched with a jaw-cracking

yawn, and padded over to lean against her leg. His solid warmth was grounding, real, a connection to the work they'd done together and the life they'd built here.

Outside, the rain was letting up. Through the window, Main Street looked clean and fresh, the autumn colors deeper for the washing. Tomorrow the sun would return, tourists would wander the shops, and life in Ashford Creek would continue its comfortable rhythms.

For now, Eliza locked the door, flipped the sign to CLOSED, and headed upstairs with Bruno. She had tea to make and the particular comfort of knowing that mysteries could be solved, even if the solutions weren't always satisfying.

Justice had been served. Lives had been changed. And in the small bookstore on Main Street, order had been restored —one properly shelved mystery at a time.

WANT to know when the next Ashford Creek Mystery releases? Join my newsletter at https://ellaandrew.com/

DIANE MORRISON'S AWARD-WINNING PUMPKIN SOUP

THREE YEARS REGIONAL CHAMPION— A RECIPE BUILT ON LOVE, NOT THEFT

Serves 6-8

"This soup is four generations of Morrison women perfecting a recipe through trial, error, and love. Every spoonful carries their stories, their kitchen wisdom, their care. It was my great-grandmother's creation, and no one— not even someone with a bestselling cookbook—can steal what this really means to our family." —Diane Morrison

Ingredients:

- 3 tablespoons unsalted butter
- 1 large yellow onion, diced
- 3 cloves garlic, minced
- 1 tablespoon fresh sage, finely chopped (plus extra for garnish)
- 4 cups pure pumpkin puree (fresh roasted or canned— never pie filling)
- 4 cups vegetable stock
- 1½ cups heavy cream
- 2 tablespoons pure maple syrup
- 1 teaspoon salt (adjust to taste)

- ½ teaspoon black pepper
- ¼ teaspoon ground nutmeg

For Sage Brown Butter (Garnish):

- 3 tablespoons butter
- 6-8 fresh sage leaves
- Roasted pumpkin seeds

Instructions:

1. **Start with aromatics:** Melt butter in a large pot over medium heat. Add onion and cook until softened and translucent, about 8 minutes. Add garlic and chopped sage, cooking for another 2 minutes until fragrant.

2. **Build the base:** Add pumpkin puree and vegetable stock. Stir well to combine. Bring to a gentle simmer and cook for 15 minutes, stirring occasionally, to let flavors meld.

3. **Add richness:** Stir in heavy cream and maple syrup. Season with salt, pepper, and nutmeg. Simmer for another 5 minutes.

4. **Blend until silky:** Using an immersion blender, puree the soup until completely smooth and velvety. (Alternatively, carefully transfer to a countertop blender in batches, filling only halfway and covering with a kitchen towel.) Return to pot if needed.

5. **Adjust and rest:** Taste and adjust seasonings. Let the soup rest off heat for 5 minutes—this allows the flavors to deepen and marry.

6. **Make sage brown butter:** In a small skillet, melt butter over medium heat. Add sage leaves and cook until butter turns golden brown and nutty-smelling, about 3-4 minutes. Watch carefully—it can burn quickly.

7. **Serve:** Ladle soup into bowls. Drizzle each serving with sage brown butter and scatter with roasted pumpkin seeds and a fresh sage leaf.

Diane's Tip: "The secret my great-grandmother taught us: never rush the onions. Let them cook slow and sweet—that's where the soup's foundation comes from. And always taste before serving. Every pumpkin is different, every batch needs its own adjustment. Cooking is listening, not just following."

MILLIE HART'S GRANDMOTHER'S LEMON SCONES

THE RECIPE WORTH FIGHTING FOR

Makes 8 scones

"Some recipes are more than just food—they're family history, love made tangible, memories you can taste. This one was stolen, but it can never truly be taken from us. It lives in every person who tasted these scones and felt like they'd come home." —Millie Hart

Ingredients:

- 2 cups all-purpose flour
- ⅓ cup granulated sugar
- 1 tablespoon baking powder
- ½ teaspoon salt
- Zest of 2 large lemons
- 6 tablespoons cold unsalted butter, cut into small cubes
- ½ cup heavy cream (plus extra for brushing)
- 1 large egg
- 2 tablespoons fresh lemon juice
- 1 teaspoon vanilla extract

For the Signature Glaze:

- 1 cup powdered sugar

- 3 tablespoons fresh lemon juice
- 1 tablespoon heavy cream
- Pinch of salt

Instructions:

1. Preheat oven to 425°F. Line a baking sheet with parchment paper.

2. The secret first step: Place your mixing bowl in the freezer for 10 minutes before starting. Cold tools make tender scones.

3. Mix dry ingredients: Whisk together flour, sugar, baking powder, salt, and lemon zest in your chilled bowl.

4. Cut in butter: Add cold butter cubes and use a pastry cutter or your fingertips to work the butter into the flour until the mixture resembles coarse crumbs with some pea-sized pieces remaining. Work quickly to keep everything cold.

5. Prepare wet ingredients: In a small bowl, whisk together cream, egg, lemon juice, and vanilla.

6. Combine: Make a well in the center of the dry ingredients and pour in the wet mixture. Stir gently with a fork just until the dough comes together. Don't overmix—some floury bits are fine.

7. Shape: Turn dough onto a lightly floured surface and gently pat into an 8-inch circle about ¾ inch thick. Cut into 8 wedges like a pie.

8. Bake: Place scones on prepared baking sheet, spacing them about 2 inches apart. Brush tops lightly with cream. Bake 12-15 minutes until golden brown and a toothpick inserted in the center comes out clean.

9. Make the glaze: While scones cool slightly, whisk together powdered sugar, lemon juice, cream, and salt until smooth. The glaze should be thick enough to coat the back of a spoon but still pourable.

10. Finish: Drizzle warm scones generously with glaze. Let set for 5 minutes before serving.

Millie's Note: "Grandmother always said the secret was cold butter and a light touch. Don't overwork the dough—tenderness comes from knowing when to stop. And serve them warm, always warm, with a proper cup of tea."

ALSO BY ELLA ANDREW

The Agatha Royale Mystery Series

- One Deadly Chapter
- One Deadly Batch
- One Deadly Needle
- One Deadly Safari
- One Deadly Premiere

The Ashford Creek Mysteries

Quick reads perfect for your lunch break or evening escape

- Death at the Teacup Inn
- Death at the Sweet Festival
- Death by Recipe
- Death at the Halloween Vigil
- Death at the Rosemary Cottage

Each Ashford Creek Mystery is a complete story you can enjoy in about 2 hours.

All books available on Amazon